ROBERT SILVERBERG

THE LONGEST WAY HOME

An Imprint of HarperCollins*Publishers*

This is a work of fiction. Names, characters, places, and incidents are products of the author's imagination or are used fictitiously and are not to be construed as real. Any resemblance to actual events, locales, organizations, or persons, living or dead, is entirely coincidental.

EOS
An Imprint of HarperCollins*Publishers*
10 East 53rd Street
New York, New York 10022-5299

Copyright © 2002 by Agberg, Ltd.
Excerpt from *Roma Eterna* copyright © 2003 by Agberg, Ltd.
ISBN: 0-380-81487-0
www.eosbooks.com

First Eos paperback printing: March 2003
First Eos hardcover printing: July 2002

Eos Trademark Reg. U.S. Pat. Off. and in Other Countries, Marca Registrada, Hecho en U.S.A.
HarperCollins ® is a trademark of HarperCollins Publishers Inc.

Printed in the U.S.A.

10 9 8 7 6 5 4 3 2 1

For Mark and Janet

All fixed, fast-frozen relations, with their train of ancient and venerable prejudices and opinions, are swept away. . . . All that is solid melts into air, all that is holy is profaned, and man is at last compelled to face with sober senses his real conditions of life, and his relations with his kind.

THE LONGEST
WAY HOME

one ——————————————————————

THE FIRST EXPLOSIONS SEEMED VERY FAR AWAY: A string of distant, muffled bangs, booms, and thuds that might have been nothing more than thunder on the horizon. Joseph, more asleep than not in his comfortable bed in the guest quarters of Getfen House, stirred, drifted a little way up toward wakefulness, cocked half an ear, listened a moment without really listening. Yes, he thought: thunder. His only concern was that thunder might betoken rain, and rain would spoil tomorrow's hunt. But this was supposed to be the middle of the dry season up here in High Manza, was it not? So how could it rain tomorrow?

It was not going to rain, and therefore Joseph knew that what he thought he had heard could not be the sound of thunder—could not, in fact, be anything at all. It is just a dream, he told himself. Tomorrow will be bright and beautiful, and I will ride out into the game preserve with my cousins of High Manza and we will have a glorious time.

He slipped easily back to sleep. An active fifteen-year-old boy is able to dissolve into slumber without effort at the end of day.

But then came more sounds, sharper ones, insistent hard-edged pops and cracks, demanding and getting his attention. He sat up, blinking, rubbing his eyes with his knuckles. Through the darkness beyond his window came a bright flash of light that did not in any way have the sharpness or linearity of lightning. It was more like a blossom unfolding, creamy yellow at the center, purplish at the edges. Joseph was still blinking at it in surprise when the next burst of sound erupted, this one in several phases, a low rolling roar followed by a sudden emphatic boom followed by a long, dying rumble, a slow subsiding. He went to the window, crouching by the sill and peering out.

Tongues of red flame were rising across the way, over by Getfen House's main wing. Flickering shadows climbing the great gray stone wall of the façade told him that the building must be ablaze. That was incredible, that Getfen House could be on fire. He saw figures running to and fro, cutting across the smooth, serene expanse of the central lawn with utter disregard for the delicacy of the close-cropped turf. He heard shouting and the sound, unmistakable and undeniable now, of gunfire. He saw other fires blazing toward the perimeter of the estate, four, five, maybe six of them. A new one flared up as he watched. The outbuildings over on the western side seemed to be on fire, and the rows of haystacks toward the east, and perhaps the field-hand quarters near the road that led to the river.

It was a bewildering, incomprehensible scene. Getfen House was under attack, evidently. But by whom, and why?

He watched, fascinated, as though this were some chapter out of his history books come to life, a reenactment of the Conquest, perhaps, or even some scene from the turbulent, half-mythical past of the Mother World itself, where for thousands of years, so it was said, clashing empires had made the ancient streets of that distant planet run crimson with blood.

The study of history was oddly congenial to Joseph. There was a kind of poetry in it for him. He had always loved those flamboyant tales of far-off strife, the carefully preserved legends of the fabled kings and kingdoms of Old Earth. But they were just tales to him, gaudy legends, ingenious dramatic fictions. He did not seriously think that men like Agamemnon and Julius Caesar and Alexander the Great and Genghis Khan had ever existed. No doubt life on Old Earth in primitive times had been a harsh, bloody affair, though probably not quite as bloody as the myths that had survived from that remote era suggested; but everyone was quite sure that the qualities that had made such bloodshed possible had long since been bred out of the human race. Now, though, Joseph found himself peering out his window at actual warfare. He could not take his eyes away. It had not yet occurred to him that he might be in actual danger himself.

All was chaos down below. No moons were in the sky this night; the only illumination came from the flickering fires along the rim of the garden and up the side of the main wing of the house. Joseph struggled to make out patterns in the movements he saw. Bands of men were running up and down the garden paths, yelling, gesticulating furiously to each other. They appeared to be carrying weapons: rifles, mainly, but some of them just pitchforks or scythes. Now and again one of the riflemen would pause, drop to one knee, aim, fire into the darkness.

Some of the animals seemed to be loose now, too. Half a dozen of the big racing-bandars from the stable, long-limbed and elegantly slender, were capering wildly about, right in the center of the lawn, prancing and bucking as though driven mad by panic. Through their midst moved shorter, slower, bulkier shapes, stolid shadowy forms that most likely were the herd of dairy ganuilles, freed of their confinement. They were grazing placidly, unconcerned by the erupting madness all about them, on the rare shrubs and flowers of the garden. The house-dogs, too, were out and yelping: Joseph saw one leap high toward the throat of one of the running men, who without breaking stride swept it away with a fierce stroke of his scythe.

Joseph, staring, continued to wonder what was happening here, and could not arrive at even the hint of an answer.

One Great House would not attack another. That was a given. The Masters of Homeworld were bound, all of them, by an unbreakable web-work of kinship. Never in the long centuries since the Conquest had any Master struck a blow against another, not for anger's sake, not for greed's.

Nor was it possible that the Indigenes, weary after thousands of years of the occupation of their world by settlers from Old Earth, had decided finally to take back their planet. They were innately unwarlike, were the Indigenes: trees would sing and frogs would write dictionaries sooner than the Indigenes would begin raising their hands in violence.

Joseph rejected just as swiftly the likelihood that some unknown band of spacefarers had landed in the night to seize the world from its present masters, even as Joseph's own race had seized it from the Folk so long ago. Such things might have happened two or three thousand years before, but the worlds of the Imperium were too tightly bound by sacred treaties now, and the movements of any sort of hostile force through the interstellar spaces would quickly be detected and halted.

His orderly mind could offer only one final hypothesis: that this was an uprising at long last of the Folk against the Masters of House Getfen. That was the least unlikely theory of the four, not at all impossible, merely improbable. This was a prosperous estate. What grievances could exist here? In any case the relationship of Folk to Masters everywhere was a settled thing; it benefited both groups; why would anyone want to destabilize a system that worked so well for everyone?

That he could not say. But flames were licking the side of Getfen House tonight, and barns were burning, and livestock was being set free, and angry men were running to and fro, shooting at people. The sounds of conflict did not cease: the sharp report of gunfire, the dull booming of explosive weapons, the sudden ragged screams of victims whose identity he did not know.

He began to dress. Very likely the lives of his kinsmen here in Getfen House were in peril, and it was his duty to go to their aid. Even if this were indeed a rebellion of the Folk against the Getfens, he did not think that he himself would be at any risk. He was no Getfen, really, except by the most tenuous lines of blood. He belonged to House Keilloran. He was only a guest here, a visitor from Helikis, the southern continent, ten thousand miles away. Joseph did not even look much like a Getfen. He was taller and more slender than Getfen boys of his age, duskier of skin, as southerners tended to be, dark-eyed where Getfen eyes were bright blue, dark-haired where Getfens were golden. No one would attack him. There was no reason why they should.

Before he left his room and entered the chaos outside, though, Joseph felt impelled by habit and training to report the events of the night, at least as he understood them thus far, to his father at Keilloran House. By the yellow light of the next bomb-burst Joseph located his combinant where he had set it down at the side of his bed, thumbed its command button, and waited for the blue globe betokening contact to take form in the air before him.

The darkness remained unbroken. No blue globe formed.

Strange. Perhaps there was some little problem with the circuit. He nudged the "off" button and thumbed the initiator command again. In the eye of his mind he tracked the electrical impulse as it leaped skyward, connected with the satellite station overhead, and was instantly relayed southward. Normally it took no more than seconds for the combinant to make contact anywhere in the world. Not now, though.

"Father?" he said hopefully, into the darkness before his face. "Father, it's Joseph. I can't see your globe, but maybe we're in contact anyway. It's the middle of the night at Getfen House, and

I want to tell you that some sort of attack is going on, that there have been explosions, and rifle shots, and—"

He paused. He could hear a soft knocking at the door.

"Master Joseph?" A woman's voice, low, hoarse. "Are you awake, Master Joseph? Please. Please, open."

A servant, it must be. She was speaking the language of the Folk. He let her wait. Staring into the space where the blue globe should have been, he said, "Father, can you hear me? Can you give me any sort of return signal?"

"Master Joseph—please—there's very little time. This is Thustin. I will take you to safety."

Thustin. The name meant nothing to him. She must belong to the Getfens. He wondered why none of his own people had come to him yet. Was this some sort of trap?

But she would not go away, and his combinant did not seem to be working. Mystery upon mystery upon mystery. Cautiously he opened the door a crack.

She stared up at him, almost worshipfully.

"Master Joseph," she said. "Oh, sir—"

Thustin, he remembered now, was his chambermaid—a short, blocky woman who wore the usual servant garb, a loose linen shirt over a half-length tunic of brown leather. To Joseph she seemed old, fifty or so, perhaps sixty. With the women of the Folk it was hard to tell ages. She was thick through from front to back and side to side as Folk often were, practically cubical in shape. Ordinarily she was a quiet, steady sort of woman, who usually came and went without attracting his notice, but she was animated now by distress. Her heavy-jowled face was sallow with shock, and her eyes had taken on an unnerving fluttering motion, as if they were rolling about free in their sockets. Her lips, thin and pale, were trembling. She was carrying a servant's gray cloak over one arm, and thrust it toward him, urgently signalling to him to put it on.

"What's happening?" Joseph asked, speaking Folkish.

"Jakkirod and his men are killing everyone. They'll kill you too, if you don't come with me. Now!"

Jakkirod was the estate foreman, a big hearty red-haired man—tenth generation in Getfen service, according to Gryilin Master Getfen, Joseph's second cousin, who ruled here. A pillar of the house staff, Jakkirod was, said Gryilin Master Getfen. Joseph had seen Jakkirod only a few days before, lifting an enormous log that had somehow fallen across the mouth of a well, tossing it aside as if it were a straw. Jakkirod had looked at Joseph and smiled, an easy, self-satisfied smile, and winked. That had been strange, that wink.

Though he was bubbling over with questions, Joseph found his little hip-purse and began automatically to stuff it with the things he knew he ought not to leave behind in his room. The combinant, of course, and the reader on which his textbooks were stored, and his utility case, which was full of all manner of miniature devices for wayfarers that he had rarely bothered to inspect but which might very well come in handy now, wherever he might be going. That took care of the basics. He tried to think of other possessions that might be important to take along, but, though he still felt relatively calm and clear-headed, he had no idea where he might be heading from here, or for how long, or what he would really need, and Thustin's skittery impatience made it hard for him to think in any useful way. She was tugging at his sleeve, now.

"Why are you here?" he asked, abruptly. "Where are my own servants? Balbu—Anceph—Rollin—?"

"Dead," she said, a husky voice, barely audible. "You will see them lying downstairs. I tell you, they are killing everyone."

Belief was still slow to penetrate him. "The Master Getfen and his sons? And his daughter too?"

"Dead. Everyone dead."

That stunned him, that the Getfens might be dead. Such a thing was almost unthinkable, that Folk would slay members of one of the Great Houses. Such a thing had never happened in all the years since the Conquest. But was it true? Had she seen the actual corpses? No doubt something bad was happening here, but surely it was only a wild rumor that the Getfens were dead. Let that be so, he thought, and and muttered a prayer under his breath.

But when he asked her for some sort of confirmation, Thustin only snorted. "Death is everywhere tonight," she told him. "They have not reached this building yet, but they will in just a little while. Will you come, Master Joseph? Because if you do not, you will die, and I will die with you."

He was obstinate. "Have all the Folk of House Getfen rebelled, then? Are you one of the rebels too, Thustin? And are you trying to lead me to my death?"

"I am too old for rebellions, Master Joseph. I serve the Getfens, and I serve their kin. Your lives are sacred to me." There was another explosion outside; from the corner of his eye Joseph saw a frightful burst of blue-white flame spurting up rooftop-high. A volley of cheers resounded from without. No screams, only cheers. They are blowing the whole place up, he thought. And Thustin, standing like a block of meat before him, had silently begun to weep. By the furious flaring light of the newest fire he saw the shining silvery trails of moisture running down her grayish, furrowed cheeks, and he knew that she had not come to him on any mission of treachery.

Joseph slipped the cloak on, pulled the hood

up over his head, and followed her from the room.

The brick building that served as the guest quarters of Getfen House was in fact the original mansion of the Getfens, a thousand or fifteen hundred years old, probably quite grand in its day but long since dwarfed by the present stone-walled mansion-house that dominated the north and east sides of the quadrangle surrounding the estate's sprawling central greensward. Joseph's room was on the third floor. A great ornate staircase done in medieval mode, with steps of pink granite and a balustrade of black wood bedecked every foot or two with ornamental knurls and sprigs and bosses, led to the great hall at ground level. But on the second landing Thustin guided him through a small door that opened onto the grand staircase and drew him down a set of unglamorous back stairs that he knew nothing about, descending two more flights to a part of the building that lay somewhere below ground level. It was musty and dank here. They were in a sort of tunnel. There were no lights anywhere, but Thustin seemed to know her way.

"We must go outside for a moment now," she said. "There will be risk. Say nothing if we are stopped."

At the end of the tunnel was a little stone staircase that took them back up to the surface level. They emerged into a grassy side courtyard that lay between the rear face of the main building and the guest quarters.

The cool night air was harsh with the smells of burning things. Bodies were strewn about like discarded toys. It was necessary to step over them. Joseph could barely bring himself to look into their faces, fearing that he would see his cousin Wykkin lying here, or Domian, or, what would be much worse, their beautiful sister Kesti, who had been so flirtatious with him only yesterday, or perhaps even Master Gryilin himself, the lord of House Getfen. But these were all Folk bodies lying here, servants of the House. Joseph supposed that they had been deemed guilty of excessive loyalty to the Masters; or perhaps they had been slain simply as part of some general settling of old domestic scores once Jakkirod had let loose the forces of rebellion.

Through a gate that stood open at the corner of the courtyard Joseph saw the bodies of his own servants lying outside in a welter of blood: Balbus, his tutor, and Anceph, who had shown him how to hunt, and the bluff, hearty coachman, Rollin. It was impossible for Joseph to question the fact that they were dead. He was too well bred to weep for them, and too wary to cry out in roars of anger and outrage, but he was shaken by the sight of those three bodies as he had never before been shaken by anything in his life, and only his awareness of himself as a Master, descended from a long line of Masters, permitted him to keep his emotions under control. Masters must never weep before servants; Masters must never weep at all, if they could help it. Balbus had taught him that life is ultimately tragic for everyone, even for Masters, and that was altogether natural and normal and universal, and must never be decried. Joseph had nodded then as though he understood with every fiber of his being, and at the moment he thought that he had; but now Balbus was lying right over there in a heap with his throat slit, having committed no worse a sin than being tutor of natural philosophy to a young Master, and it was not all that easy for Joseph to accept such a thing with proper philosophical equanimity.

Thustin took him on a diagonal path across the courtyard, heading for a place where there was a double-sided wooden door, set flush with the ground, just at the edge of Getfen House's foundation. She lifted the right-hand side of the door and brusquely beckoned to Joseph to descend. A passageway opened before him, and yet another stairway. He could see candlelight flickering somewhere ahead. The sound of new explosions came to him from behind, a sound made blurred and woolly by all these levels of the building that lay between them and him.

Halting at the first landing, Joseph allowed Thustin to overtake him and lead him onward. Narrow, dimly lit tunnels spread in every direction, a baffling maze. This was the basement of the main house, he assumed, an antique musty world beneath the world, the world of the Getfen servants, a place of the Folk. Unerringly Thustin moved along from one passage to another until at last they reached a chilly candlelit chamber, low-roofed but long, where fifteen or twenty of the Getfen house-Folk sat huddled together around a bare wooden table. They all had a dazed, terrified look. Most were women, and most of those were of Thustin's age. There were a few very old men, and one youngish one propped up on crutches, and some children. Joseph saw no one who might have been capable of taking part in the rebellion. These were noncombatants, cooks and laundry-maids and aged bodyservants and footmen, all of them frightened refugees from the bloody tumult going on upstairs.

Joseph's presence among them upset them instantly. Half a dozen of them surrounded Thustin, muttering harshly and gesticulating. It was hard for Joseph to make out what they were saying, for, although like all Masters he was fluent in Folkish as well as the Master tongue and the Indigene language also, the northern dialect these people used was unfamiliar to him and when they spoke rapidly and more than one was speaking at once, as they were doing now, he quickly lost the thread of their words. But their general meaning seemed clear enough. They were angry with Thustin for having brought a Master into their hiding place, even a strange Master who was not of House Getfen, because the rebels might come looking for him down here and, if they did, they would very likely put them all to death for having given him refuge.

"He is not going to stay among you," Thustin answered them, when they were quiet enough to allow her a reply. "I will be taking him outside as soon as I collect some food and wine for our journey."

"Outside?" someone asked. "Have you lost your mind, Thustin?"

"His life is sacred. Doubly so, for he is not only a Master but a guest of this House. He must be escorted to safety."

"Let his own servants escort him, then," said another, sullenly. "Why should you risk yourself in this, can you tell me that?"

"His own people are dead," Thustin said, and offered no other explanation of her decision. Her voice had become deep, almost mannish. She stood squarely before the others, a blocky, defiant figure. "Give me that pack," she told one woman, who sat with a cloth-sided carryall on the table before her. Thustin dumped its contents out: clothes, mainly, and some tawdry beaded necklaces. "Who has bread? Meat? And who has wine? Give it to me." They were helpless before the sudden authority of this short plump woman. She had found a strength that perhaps even she had not known she possessed. Thustin went around the room, taking what she wanted from them, and gestured to Joseph. "Come, Master Joseph. There is little time to waste."

"Where are we going, then?"

"Into Getfen Park, and from there to the open woods, where I think you will be safe. And then you must begin making your journey home."

"My journey home?" he said blankly. "My home is ten thousand miles from here!"

He meant it to sound as though it was as far away as one of the moons. But the number obviously meant nothing to her. She merely shrugged and made a second impatient gesture. "They will kill you if they find you here. They are like wolves, now that they have been set loose. I would not have your death on my soul. Come, boy! Come now!"

Still Joseph halted. "I must tell my father what is happening here. They will send people to rescue me and save House Getfen from destruction." And he drew the combinant from his purse and thumbed its command button again, waiting for the blue globe to appear and his father's austere, thin-lipped face to glow forth within it, but once again there was no response.

Thustin clamped her lips together and shook her head in annoyance. "Put your machine away, boy. There is no strength in it anymore. Surely the first thing they did was to blow up the relay stations." He noticed that she had begun calling him *boy*, suddenly, instead of the reverential "Master Joseph." And what was that about blowing up relay stations? He had never so much as considered the possibility that the communications lines that spanned the world were vulnerable. You touched your button, your signal went up into space and came down somewhere else on Homeworld, and you saw the face of the person with whom you wanted to speak. It was that simple. You took it for granted that the image would always be there as soon as you summoned it. It had never occurred to him that under certain circumstances it might not be. Was it really that simple to disrupt the combinant circuit? Could a few Folkish malcontents actually cut him off from contact with his family with a couple of bombs?

But this was no moment for pondering whys and wherefores. He was all alone, half a world way from his home, and he was plainly in danger; this old woman, for whatever reason, was planning to guide him to a safer place than he was in right now; any further delay would be foolish.

She put the heavy pack between her shoulders, turned, plodded down toward the far end of the long room. Joseph followed her. They went through a rear exit, down more drafty passageways, doubled back as though she had taken a false turn, and eventually reached yet another staircase that went switching up and up until it brought them to a broad landing culminating in a massive iron-bound doorway that stood slightly ajar. Thustin nudged it open a little farther and peeped into whatever lay beyond. Almost at once she pulled her head swiftly backward, like a sand-baron pulling its head into its shell, but after a moment she looked again, and signalled to him without looking back. They tiptoed through, entering a stone-paved hallway that must surely be some part of the main house. There was smoke in the air here, an acrid reek that made Joseph's eyes sting, but the structure itself was intact: Getfen House was so big that whole wings of it could be on fire and other sections could go untouched.

Hurriedly Thustin took him down the hallway, through an arched door, up half a flight of stairs—he had given up all hope of making sense of the route—and then, very suddenly, they were out of the building and in the forest that lay behind it.

It was not a truly wild forest. The trees, straight and tall, were arrayed in careful rows, with wide avenues between them. These trees had been planted, long ago, to form an ornamental transition to the real woods beyond. This was Getfen Park, the hunting preserve of House Getfen, where later today Joseph and his cousins Wykkin and Dorian were to have gone hunting. It was still the middle of the dark moonless night, but by the red light from the buildings burning behind him Joseph saw the tall trees at his sides meeting in neat overhead bowers with the bright hard dots of stars peeping between them, and then the dark mysterious wall of the real woods not far beyond.

"Quickly, quickly," Thustin murmured. "If there's anyone standing sentinel on the roof up there, he'll be able to see us." And hardly had she said that but there were two quick cracks of gunfire behind them, and—was it an illusion?—two red streaks of flame zipping through the air next to him. They began to run. There was a third shot, and a fourth, and at the fourth one Thustin made a little thick-throated sound and stumbled and nearly fell, halting and dropping to one knee instead for a moment before picking herself up and moving along. Joseph ran alongside her, forcing himself to match her slow pace although his legs were much longer than hers.

"Are you all right?" he asked. "Were you hit?"

"It only grazed me," she said. "Run, boy! Run!"

She did not seem really to know which way to go out here, and she seemed under increasing strain besides, her breathing growing increasingly harsh and ragged and her stride becoming erratic. He began to think that she had in fact been wounded. In any case Joseph was beginning to see that he should have been the one to carry that pack, but it had not occurred to him to offer, since a Master did not carry packs in the presence of a servant, and she probably would not have permitted it anyway. Nor would she permit it now. But no further shots came after them, and soon they were deep in the wilder part of the game preserve, where no one was likely to come upon them at this hour.

He could hear the sound of gurgling water ahead, no doubt coming from one of the many small streams that ran through the park. They reached it moments later. Thustin unslung her pack, grunting in relief, and dropped down on both knees beside the water. Joseph watched in surprise as she pulled her shirt up from under her tunic and cast it aside, baring the whole upper part of her body. Her breasts were heavy, low-slung, big-nippled. He had very rarely seen breasts before. And even by starlight alone he was able to make out the bloody track that ran along the thick flesh of her left shoulder from its summit to a point well down her chest.

"You *were* hit," he said. "Let me see."

"What can you see, here in the dark?"

"Let me see," Joseph said, and knelt beside her, gingerly touching two fingertips to her shoulder and probing the wounded area as lightly as he could. There seemed to be a lot of blood. It ran down freely over his hand. There is Folkish blood on me, he thought. It was an odd sort of thought. He put his fingers to his lips and tasted it, sweet and salty at the same time. "Am I hurting you?" Joseph asked. Her only response was an indistinct one, and he pressed a little more closely. "We need to clean this," he said, and he fumbled around until he found her discarded shirt in the darkness, and dipped the edge of it in the stream

and dabbed it carefully about on both sides of the
wound, mopping away the blood. But he could
feel new blood welling up almost at once. The
wound will have to be bound, he thought, and allowed to clot, and then, at first light, he would
take a good look at it and see what he might try
to do next, and—

"We are facing south," she said. "You will cross
the stream and keep going through the park, until
you reach the woods. Beyond the woods there is
a village of Indigenes. You speak their language,
do you?"

"Of course. But what about—"

"They will help you, I think. Tell them that you
are a stranger, a person from far away who wants
only to get home. Say that there has been some
trouble at Getfen House, where you were a guest.
Say no more than that. They are gentle people.
They will be kind to you. They will not care
whether you are Master or Folk. They will lead
you to the nearest house of Masters south of here.
Its name is Ludbrek House."

"Ludbrek House. And how far is that?"

"I could not say. I have never in all my life left
the domain of House Getfen. The Ludbreks are
kinsmen of Master Getfen, though. Heaven grant
that they are safe. If you tell them you are a Master, they will help you reach your own home."

"Yes. That they surely will." He knew nothing
of these Ludbreks, but all Masters were kinsmen,
and he was altogether certain that no one would

refuse aid to the wandering eldest son of Martin Master Keilloran of House Keilloran. It went without saying. Even here in far-off High Manza, ten thousand miles to the north, any Master would have heard of Martin Master Keilloran of House Keilloran and would do for his son that which was appropriate. By his dark hair and dark eyes they would recognize him as a southerner, and by his demeanor they would know that he was of Master blood.

"Until you come to Ludbrek House, tell no one you encounter that you are a Master yourself—few here will be able to guess it, because you look nothing like the Masters we know, but best to keep the truth to yourself anyway—and as you travel stay clear of Folk as much as you can, for this uprising of Jakkirod's may reach well beyond these woods already. That was his plan, you know, to spread the rebellion far and wide, to overthrow the Masters entirely, at least in Manza. —Go, now. Soon it will be dawn and you would not want the forest wardens to find you here."

"You want me to leave you?"

"What else can you do, Master Joseph? I am useless to you now, and worse than useless. If I go with you, I'll only slow you down, and very likely I'll bleed to death in a few days even if we are not caught, and my body will be a burden to you. I will go back to Getfen House and tell them that I was hurt in the darkness and confusion, and they will bind my wound, and if no one who saw us together says anything, Jakkirod will let me live. But you must go. If you are found here in the morning, you will die. It is the plan to kill all the Masters, as I have just told you. To undo the Conquest, to purge the world of you and your kind. It is a terrible thing. I did not think they were serious when they began speaking of it. — Go, now, boy! *Go!*"

He hesitated. It seemed like an abomination to abandon her here, bleeding and probably half in shock, while he made his way on his own. He wanted to minister to her wound. He knew a little about doctoring; medicine was one of his father's areas of knowledge, a pastime of his, so to speak, and Joseph had often watched him treating the Folk who belonged to House Keilloran. But she was right: if she went with him she would not only hinder his escape but almost certainly would die from loss of blood in another day or two, but if she turned back now and slipped quietly into Getfen House by darkness she would probably be able to get help. And in any case Getfen House was her home. The land beyond the woods was as strange to her as it was going to be to him.

So he leaned forward and, with a spontaneity that astounded him and brought a gasp of shock and perhaps even dismay from her, he kissed her on her cheek, and squeezed her hand, and then he got to his feet and slipped the pack over his back and stepped lightly over the little brook, heading south, setting out alone on his long journey home.

He realized that he was, very likely, somewhat in a state of shock himself. Bombs had gone off, Getfen House was burning, his cousins and his servants had been butchered as they slept, he himself had escaped only by grace of a servingwoman's sense of obligation, and now, only an hour or two later, he was alone in a strange forest in the middle of the night, a continent and a half away from House Keilloran: how could he possibly have absorbed all of that so soon? He knew that he had inherited his father's lucidity of mind, that he was capable of quick and clear thinking and handled himself well in challenging situations, a true and fitting heir to the responsibilities of his House. But just how clearly am I thinking right now? he wondered. His first impulse, when the explosions had awakened him, had been to run to the defense of his Getfen cousins. He would be dead by now if he had done that. Even after he had realized the futility of that initial reaction, some part of him had wanted to believe that he could somehow move unharmed through the midst of the insurrection, because the target of the rebels was House Getfen, and he was a stranger, a mere distant kinsman, a member of a House that held sway thousands of miles from here, with whom Jakkirod and his men could have no possible quarrel. He did not even *look* like a Getfen. At least to some degree he had felt, while the bombs were going off and the bullets were flying through the air and even afterward, that he could simply sit tight amongst the carnage and wait for rescuers to come and take him away, and the rebels would just let him be. But that too was idiocy, Joseph saw. In the eyes of these rebels all Masters must be the enemy, be they Getfens or Ludbreks or the unknown Keillorans and Van Rhyns and Martylls of the Southland. This was a war, Homeworld's first since the Conquest itself, and the district where he was now was enemy territory, land that was apparently under the control of the foes of his people.

How far would he have to go before he reached friendly territory again?

He could not even guess. This might be an isolated uprising, confined just to the Getfen lands, or it might have been a carefully coordinated onslaught that took in the entire continent of Manza, or even Manza and Helikis both. For all he knew he was the only Master still left alive anywhere on Homeworld this night, though that was a thought too terrible and monstrous to embrace for more than a moment. He could not believe that the Folk of House Keilloran would ever rise against his father, or, for that matter, that any of the Folk of any House of Helikis would ever strike a blow against any Master. But doubtless Gryilin Master Getfen and his sons Wykkin and Dorian had felt the same way about their own Folk, and Gryilin and Wykkin and Dorian were dead now, and—this was a new thought, and an appalling one—the lovely Mistress Kesti of the long golden hair must be dead as well, perhaps after suffering great indignities. How many other Masters had died this night, he wondered, up and down the length and breadth of Homeworld?

As Joseph walked on and on, following his nose southward like a sleepwalker, he turned his thoughts now to the realities of the task ahead of him.

He was fifteen, tall for his age, a stalwart boy, but a boy nonetheless. Servants of his House had cared for him every day of his life. There had always been food, a clean bed, a fresh set of clothes. Now he was alone, weaponless, on foot, trudging through the darkness of a mysterious region of a continent he knew next to nothing about. He wanted to believe that there would be friendly Indigenes just beyond these woods who would convey him obligingly to Ludbrek House, where he would be greeted like a long-lost brother, taken in and bathed and fed and sheltered, and after a time sent on his way by private flier to his home in Helikis. But what if the Ludbreks, too, were dead? What if all Masters were, everywhere in the continent of Manza?

That thought would not leave him, that the Folk of the north, striking in coordinated fashion all in a single night, had killed every member of every Great House of Manza.

And if they had? If there was no one anywhere to help him along in his journey?

Was he, he asked himself, supposed to *walk* from here to the Isthmus, five or six thousand miles, providing for himself the whole way? How long might it take to walk five thousand miles? At twenty miles a day, day in and day out—was such a pace possible, he wondered?—it would take, what, two hundred fifty days. And then he would have five thousand miles more to go, from the Isthmus to Keilloran. At home they would long ago have given him up for dead, by the time he could cover so great a distance. His father would have mourned for him, and his sisters and his brothers. They would have draped the yellow bunting over the gate of Keilloran House, they would have read the words for the dead, they would have put up a stone for him in the family burial-ground. As well they should, because how was he to survive such a journey, anyway? Clever as he was, quick and strong as he was, he was in no way fitted for month after month of foraging in the wilderness that was the heart of this raw, half-settled continent.

These, Joseph told himself, were useless thoughts. He forced them from his mind.

He kept up a steady pace, hour after hour. The forest was dense and the ground uneven and the night very dark, and at times the going was difficult, but he forged ahead notwithstanding, dropping ultimately into a kind of automatic robotic

stride, a mindless machinelike forward movement that made a kind of virtue out of his growing fatigue. His progress was punctuated by
some uneasy moments, mysterious rustlings and
chitterings in the underbrush, and a couple of
times he heard the sound of some large animal
crashing around nearby. From the multitude of
things in his utility case Joseph selected a cutting-
tool, small but powerful, and sliced a slender
stem from a sturdy many-branched shrub, and
used the utility's blade to whittle it into a stick to
carry as he walked. That provided some little
measure of reassurance. In a little while the first
pale light of dawn came through the treetops,
and, very tired now, he halted under a great red-
boled tree and went rummaging through the
pack that Thustin had assembled for him to see
what sort of provisions she had managed to collect from the assembled Folk in that underground
chamber.

It was Folkish food, rough simple stuff. But
that was only to be expected. A long lopsided loaf
of hard grayish bread, a piece of cold meat, pretty
gray also, some lumpy biscuits, a flask of dark
wine. She had particularly asked for wine. Why
was that? Did the Folk think of wine as a basic
beverage of life? Joseph tasted it: dark and sour, it
was, a sharp edge on it, nothing whatever like the
velvety wine of his father's table. But after his
first wince he became aware of the welcome
warmth of it on the way down. The air here in

early morning was cold. Gusts of ghostly fog wandered through the forest. He took another sip and contemplated a third. But then he put the stopper back in and went to work on the bread and meat.

Soon he moved along. He wanted nothing more than to curl up under a bush and close his eyes—he had had only an hour or two of sleep and at his age he needed a good deal more than that, and the strain and shock of the night's events were exacting their toll—but it was a wise idea, Joseph knew, to put as much distance as he could between himself and what might be taking place back at Getfen House.

His notion of where he was right now was hazy. In the three weeks he had spent at Getfen House his cousins had taken him riding several times in the park, and he was aware that the game preserve itself, stocked with interesting beasts and patrolled against poachers by wardens of the House, shaded almost imperceptibly into the untrammeled woods beyond. But whether he was still in the park or had entered the woods by now was something that he had no way of telling.

One thing that he feared was that in the darkness he had unknowingly looped around and headed back toward the house. But that did not seem to be the case. Now that the sun had risen, he saw that it stood to his left, so he must surely be heading south. Even in this northern continent, where everything seemed upside down to him, the sun still rose in the east. A glance at the compass that he found in his utility case confirmed that. And the wind, blowing from his rear, brought him occasional whiffs of bitter smoke that he assumed came from the fire at Getfen House.

There came a thinning of the forest, which led Joseph to think that he might be leaving the woods and approaching the village of Indigenes that Thustin had said lay on the far side.

She had said nothing about a highway, though. But there was one, smack in his path, and he came upon it so suddenly, moving as he was now in such a rhythmic mechanical way, that he nearly went stumbling out onto the broad grassy verge that bordered it before he realized what he was looking at, which was a four-lane road, broad and perfectly straight, emerging out of the east and vanishing toward the westward horizon, a wide strip of black concrete that separated the woods out of which he had come from a further section of forest just in front of him like a line drawn by a ruler.

For a moment, only a moment, Joseph believed that the road was devoid of traffic and he could safely dart across and lose himself among the trees on the other side. But very quickly he came to understand his error. This present silence and emptiness betokened only a fortuitous momentary gap in the activity on this highway. He heard a rumbling off to his left that quickly grew into a tremendous pulsing boom, and then saw the snouts of the first vehicles of an immense convoy coming toward him, a line of big trucks, some of them gray-green, some black, flanked by armed outriders on motorcycles. Joseph pulled back into the woods just in time to avoid being seen.

There, stretched out flat on his belly between two bushes, he watched the convoy go by: big trucks first, then lighter ones, vans, canvas-covered farm wagons, vehicles of all sorts, all of them pounding away with ferocious vehemence toward some destination in the west. Instantly a burst of hopeful conviction grew in him that this must be a punitive force sent by one of the local Great Houses to put down the uprising that had broken out on the Getfen lands, but then he realized that the motorcycle outriders, though they were helmeted and carried rifles, did not wear the uniforms of any formal peacekeeping-force but rather were clad in a hodgepodge of Folkish dress, jerkins, doublets, overalls, tunics, the clothing of a peasantry that had abruptly been transformed into an improvised militia.

A shiver ran through him from nape of neck to base of spine. He understood completely now that what had happened at Getfen House was no mere outburst of wrath directed at one particular family of Masters by one particular band of disgruntled Folk. This was true war, total war, carefully planned and elaborately equipped, the Folk of High Manza against the Masters of High

Manza, perhaps spreading over many provinces, perhaps over the entire northern continent. The first blows had been struck during the night by Jakkirod and his like, swingers of scythes and wielders of pitchforks, but armed troops were on the way to follow up on the initial strike.

Joseph lay mesmerized, horror-stricken. He could not take his eyes from the passing force. As the procession was nearing its end one of the outriders happened to turn and look toward the margin of the road just as he went past Joseph's position, and Joseph was convinced that the man had seen him, had stared directly into his eyes, had given him a cold, searching look, baleful and malevolent, bright with hatred, as he sped by. Perhaps not. Perhaps it was only his imagination at work. Still, the thought struck him that the rider might halt and dismount and come in pursuit of him, and he wondered whether he should risk getting to his feet and scrambling back into the forest.

But no, no, the man rode on and did not reappear, and a few moments later one final truck, open-bodied and packed front to back with Folkish troops standing shoulder to shoulder, went rolling by, and the road was empty again. An eerie silence descended, broken only by the strident ticking chirps of a chorus of peg-beetles clinging in congested orange clumps to the twigs of the brush at the edge of the woods.

Joseph waited two or three minutes. Then he

crept out onto the grassy margin. He looked to his left, saw no more vehicles coming, looked to his right and found that the last of the convoy was only a swiftly diminishing gray dot in the distance. He raced across and lost himself as fast as he could in the woods on the south side of the road.

As midday approached there was still no sign of the promised Indigene village, or any other sort of habitation, and he knew he had to pause here and get some rest. The cold fogs of dawn had given way to mild morning warmth and then to the dry heat of a summer noon. It seemed to Joseph that this march had lasted for days, already, though it could not have been much more than twelve hours since he and Thustin had fled the chaotic scene at Getfen House. There were limits even to the resilience of youth, evidently. The forest here was choked with underbrush and every step was a battle. He was strong and healthy and agile, but he was a Master, after all, a child of privilege, not at all used to this kind of scrambling through rough, scruffy woodlands. Hot as the day now was, he was shivering with weariness. There was a throbbing sensation along his left leg from calf to thigh, and a sharper pain farther down, as though he might have turned his ankle along the way without even noticing. His eyelids felt rough and raw from lack of sleep, his clothes were stained and torn in a couple of places, his throat was dry, his stomach was calling out impatiently for some kind of meal. He settled down in a dip between two clumps of angular, ungainly little trees and made a kind of lunch out of the rest of the bread, as much of the meat as he could force himself to nibble, and half of what was left of his wine.

Another try at contacting House Keilloran got him nowhere. The combinant seemed utterly dead.

The most important thing now seemed to be to halt for a little while and let his strength rebuild itself. He was starting to be too tired to think clearly, and that could be a lethal handicap. The sobering sight of that convoy told him that at any given moment he might find himself unexpectedly amidst enemies, and only the swiftness of his reaction time would save him. It was only a matter of luck that he had not sauntered out onto that highway just as those Folkish troops passed by, and very likely they would have shot him on sight if they had noticed him standing there. Therefore stopping for rest now was not only desirable but necessary. It was probably better to sleep by day and walk by night, anyway. He was less likely to be seen under cover of darkness.

That meant, of course, leaving himself open to discovery while he slept. The idea of simply settling down in bright daylight, unconcealed, stretched out asleep beneath some tree where he could be come upon unawares by any passing farmer or poacher or, perhaps, sentry, seemed far

too risky to him. He would have liked to find a
cave of some sort and crawl into it for a few
hours. But there were no caves in sight and he
had neither the will nor the means, just now, to
dig a hole for himself. And so in the end he
scooped together a mattress of dry leaves and
ripped some boughs from the nearby bushes and
flung them together in what he hoped was a
natural-looking way to form a coverlet, and bur-
rowed down under them and closed his eyes.

Hard and bumpy as the ground was beneath
his leaves, he fell asleep easily and dreamed that
he was strolling in the gardens of Keilloran
House, some part of the garden that he must
never have seen before, where strange thick-
bellied tree-ferns grew, striking ferns with feath-
ery pinkish-green fronds that terminated in
globular structures very much like eyeballs. His
father was with him, that splendid princely man,
handsome and tall, and also one of Joseph's
younger brothers—he could not be sure which
one, Rickard or Eitan, they kept wavering from
one to the other—and one of his sisters also, who
by her height and her flowing cascade of jet hair
he knew to be Cailin, closest of all the family to
him in age. To his surprise his mother was
strolling just ahead of them, the beautiful, stately
Mistress Wireille, although in fact she had been
dead these three years past. As they all proceeded
up the soft pathway of crumbled redshaft bark
that ran through the middle of the fern garden,

various Folk attached to the House, chamberlains and other high officials, came forth and bowed deeply to them, far more formally and subserviently than his father would ever have tolerated in reality, and as each of the household people went by, some member of the family would hold out a hand to be kissed, not only the Master and Mistress, but the children too, all but Joseph, who found himself snatching back his hand every time it was sought. He did not know why, but he would not allow it, even though it appeared to be a perfectly natural kind of obeisance within the context of the scene. To his surprise his father was angry at his refusal to be greeted in this way, and said something harsh to him, and glared. Even while he dreamed Joseph knew that there was something wrong with that, for it had never been his father's way to speak so harshly to him.

Then the dream faded and was followed by others, more discordant and fragmentary than that one, a jumble of disturbing images and pointless conversations and journeys down long passageways, and then, suddenly, many hours later, he awoke and was bewildered to find himself lying in a shelter made of leafy boughs with the dark starry vault of the night above him, close and heavy. It was a moment before he remembered where he was, and why. He had slept past sundown and on into evening.

The long afternoon's sleep seemed to have

cleared Joseph's mind of many of its fears and doubts. He felt ready to move along, to do whatever might be needful to reach his distant home, to walk all the way to Helikis if that was what he had to do. No harm would come to him, of that he was certain—not because he was a Master of the highest rank, which would count for nothing in this hostile wilderness, but because he was quick-witted and resourceful and well fitted by nature and training to deal with whatever challenges might await him.

Though night had arrived, he said the morning prayers. That was permissible, wasn't it? He had just awakened, after all. For him, with day and night now reversed, it was the beginning of a new day. Then he found a pond nearby, stripped and washed himself thoroughly in the cold water, trying to scrub away the stiffness that the long hours lying on the ground had caused, and washed his clothing as well.

While Joseph waited for his clothes to dry he tried yet again to make combinant contact with his father, and once more failed. He had no doubt now that the rebels had managed to damage the worldwide communications system and that he was not going to be able to get any message through to the people of House Keilloran or anyone else. I might just as well throw the combinant away, he thought, although he could not bring himself to do it.

Then he gathered some stubby twigs from the

forest floor, arranged them in three small cairns, and offered the words that were due the souls of Balbus, Anceph, and Rollin. That was his responsibility: he had not been able to give their bodies a proper burial but he must at least do what had to be done to send their souls on their way. They were of Master stock, after all, subordinate in rank but still in a certain sense his kin. And, since they had been good servants, loyal and true to him, the task now fell to him to look after their wandering spirits. He should have done it before going to sleep, he knew, but he had been too tired, too confused, to think of it then. As Joseph finished the third of the three sets of prayers, the ones for Balbus, he was swept for a moment by a powerful sense of loneliness and loss, for Balbus had been a dear man and a wise teacher and Joseph had expected him to go on guiding him until he had passed the threshold of adulthood. One did not look primarily to one's father for guidance of that sort; one looked to one's tutor. Now Balbus was gone, and Joseph was alone not merely in this forest but, in a manner of speaking, in the world as well. It was not quite the same as losing one's father, or one's mother, for that matter, but it was a stunning blow all the same.

The moment passed quickly, though. Balbus had equipped him to deal with losses of all sorts, even the loss of Balbus himself. He stood for a time above the three cairns, remembering little things about Balbus and Anceph and Rollin, a turn of phrase or a way of grinning or how they moved when coming into a room, until he had fixed them forever in his mind as he had known them alive, and not as he had seen them lying bloodied in that courtyard.

Afterward Joseph finished the last of the meat and wine, tucking the round-bellied flask back in his pack to use as a vessel for carrying water thereafter, and set out into the night, checking his compass often to make certain that he was continuing on a southward path in the darkness. He picked his way warily through this dark loamy-smelling wilderness of uneven ground, watching out for straggling roots and sudden declivities, listening for the hissing or clacking of some watchful hostile beast, and prodding with his stick at the thicker patches of soft, rotting leaves before venturing out on them. The leg that he seemed to have injured unawares had stiffened while he slept, and gave him increasing trouble: he feared reinjuring it with a careless step. Sometimes he saw glowing yellow eyes studying him from a branch high overhead, or contemplating him from the safety of a lofty boulder, and he stared boldly back to show that he was unafraid. He wondered, though, whether he *should* be afraid. He had no notion of what sort of creatures these might be.

Around midnight he heard the sounds of another highway ahead of him, and soon he saw the lights of moving traffic, once more crossing the route he must follow but this time passing from west to east rather than east to west. That seemed odd, so much traffic this late at night: he decided it must be another of the rebels' military convoys, and he approached the break in the forest with extreme caution, not wanting to blunder forth into view and attract some passing rebel's attention.

But when he was close enough to see the road Joseph discovered that its traffic was no grim purposeful convoy of roaring trucks, but a slow, muddled procession of humble peasant conveyances, farm tractors, open carts drawn by animals, flatbed wagons, pushcarts, wheelbarrows. Aboard them, or in some cases pulling or pushing them, was a desperate-looking raggle-taggle horde of Folkish refugees, people who had piled their household belongings and their domestic animals and anything else they could take with them into this collection of improvised vehicles and were, plainly, fleeing as hurriedly as they could from some horrifying catastrophe that was happening in the west. Perhaps that catastrophe was the work of the very convoy Joseph had encountered the day before. As Thustin had already demonstrated, not all the Folk of Getfen House were in sympathy with the rebellion, and Joseph began now to suspect that at some of the Great Houses there could be as many Folkish victims of the uprising as there were Masters—Folk striking out at other Folk. So what was going on, then, might be mere anarchy, rather than a clear-cut revolt of the underclass against its lords. And then a third possibility occurred to him: that the Masters in the west had already put the rebellion down, and were exacting a dread vengeance upon the Folk of their region, and these people were trying to escape their fury. He did not know which possibility he found more frightening.

Joseph waited close to an hour for the refugees to finish going past. Then, when the last few stragglers had disappeared and the road was empty, he sprinted across, heedless of the protests of his aching leg, and plunged into the heavy tangle of brush on the other side.

The hour was growing late and he was starting to think about finding a safe nest in which to spend the upcoming day when he realized that someone or something was following him.

He was aware of it, first, as a seemingly random crashing or crunching in the underbrush to his rear. That was, he supposed, some animal or perhaps several, moving about on their nightly rounds. Since it was reasonable to expect the forest to be full of wild creatures, and since none of them had presented any threat to him so far, he did not feel any great alarm.

But then, when he halted at a swift little brook to refill his flask with fresh water, he noticed that the crashing sounds had ceased; and when he resumed his march, the sounds were resumed also. After ten minutes he stopped again, and the sounds stopped. He started, and immediately the sounds began again. A foraging animal would not behave that way. But these were not the sounds that any human who might be pursuing him would make, either, for no serious attempt at concealment was being made. Something— something *big*, Joseph began to think, and probably not very bright—was crashing blithely through the underbrush behind him, tramping along in his wake, matching him step for step, halting when he halted, starting up again when he started.

He had nothing that could serve very well as a weapon: just his flimsy walking-stick, and the little cutting-tools in his utility case, which only a fool would try to use in hand-to-hand combat. But perhaps he would not need any weapon. The rhythmic pattern of the footsteps behind him— crash *crash*, crash *crash*, crash *crash*—made it seem more likely that his follower was a two-legged creature than some low-slung brutish beast of the forest. If there was any truth whatever to Thustin's tale of there being an Indigene village down this way, he might well have entered its territory by now, and this might be a scout from that village, skulking along behind him to see what this human interloper might be up to.

Joseph turned and stared back into the darkness of the forest through which he had just come. He was fairly sure that he could hear the sound of breathing nearby: slow, heavy breathing.

"Who's there?" Joseph asked, saying it in the Indigene tongue.

Silence.

"I call for an answer," Joseph said crisply, still using Indigene. He spoke with the unmistakable tone of a Master. Perhaps that was a mistake, he thought, but there was no helping it now. An Indigene would not care whether he was Master or Folk, anyway.

But still no answer came. He could still hear the sound of hoarse breathing, though. No question about that, now. "I know you're there," said Joseph. "I call on you to identify yourself to me." Only a Master would have spoken that way, and so, when the silence continued, he said it again in Master-speech, to underscore his rank. Then, for good measure, he repeated the words in Folkish. Silence. Silence. He might just as well have called out to the creature in the language of Old Earth, he realized. Joseph had studied that language under Balbus's tutelage and after a fashion could actually speak a little of it.

Then he remembered that there was a pocket torch in his utility case. He groped around for it, drew it out, and switched it on, putting it on widest beam.

A looming massive noctambulo stood before him, no more than twenty feet away, blinking and gaping in the light.

"So you're what's been following me," Joseph said. He spoke in Indigene. He knew that in his home district that was a language noctambulos were capable of understanding. "Well, hello, there." One did not fear noctambulos, at least not those of Helikis. They were huge and potentially could do great damage as they blundered about, but they were innately harmless. "What is it you want with me, will you tell me?"

The noctambulo simply stared at him, slowly opening and closing its long rubbery beak in the silly way that noctambulos had. The creature was gigantic, eight feet tall, maybe nine, with a narrow spindling head, thick huddled shoulders, enormously long arms that culminated in vast paddle-shaped outward-turned hands. Its close-set red eyes, glistening like polished garnets in the diffuse light of Joseph's torch, were saucer-sized. Its body was covered with broad, leathery pinkish-yellow scales. The noctambulos of Helikis were a darker color, almost blue. A regional difference, Joseph thought. Perhaps this was even a different species, though obviously closely related.

"Well?" Joseph said. "Will you speak to me? My name is Joseph Master Keilloran," he said. "Who are you?" And, into the continuing silence: "I know you can understand me. Speak to me. I won't harm you. See? I have no weapons."

"The light—" said the noctambulo. "In my eyes—" Its voice sounded rusty. It was the clanking sound of a machine that had not been used for many years.

"Is that it," Joseph said. "How's this, then?" He lowered the beam, turning it at an angle so he could continue to see the noctambulo without blinding it. The great shambling being flapped its loose-jointed wrists in what might have been a gesture of gratitude.

The noctambulos of Helikis were stupid creatures, just barely across the threshold of intelligence, and there was no reason to think that those of Manza were any cleverer. But they had to be treated as something more than mere animals. They were capable of speaking Indigene, however poorly and inarticulately, and they had some sort of language of their own besides. And they had definite self-awareness, undeniable consciousnesses. Two apiece, indeed, for noctambulos, as their name implied, were creatures that prowled by night, but also remained active during their daytime sleep periods, and, insofar as Joseph understood it, had secondary identities and personalities that came into operation by day while the primary identity that inhabited their brains was sleeping. How much communication existed between the day and night identities of each noctambulo was something that no one had been clearly able to determine.

Intelligence had developed differently on Homeworld than it had on Earth: instead of one dominant species that had subjugated all others, Homeworld had several sorts of native races that qualified as intelligent, each of which had a language and the ability to form abstract concepts and even art of a kind, and the members of which had distinct individual identities. The race known as Indigenes, though they were more nearly humanoid in appearance than any of the others and were undoubtedly the most intelligent, had never shown any impulse toward dominance whatsoever, so that they could not really be regarded as the species that had ruled this world before the first humans came. No one had ruled this world, which had made it much easier for the firstcomers, the humans now known as the Folk, to take possession of it. And, since the Folk had been lulled to placidity after having lived here so long without any hint of challenge from the native life-forms, that had perhaps made it such an easy matter for the second wave of humans, the conquering Masters, to reduce them to a subordinate position.

Since the noctambulo did not seem to want to explain why it had been following Joseph through the woods, perhaps did not even know itself, Joseph let the point pass. He told the creature, speaking slowly and carefully in Indigene, that he was a solitary traveler searching for a nearby village of Indigenes where he hoped to take refuge from trouble among his own people.

The noctambulo replied—thickly, almost incoherently—that it would do what it could to help.

There was something dreamlike about conducting a conversation with a noctambulo, but

Joseph was glad enough for company of any sort after the unaccustomed solitude of his sojourn in the forest. He could not remember when he had last been alone for so long: there had always been one of his servants around, or his brothers or his sisters.

They went on their way, the noctambulo in the lead. Joseph had no idea why the creature had been following him through the forest. Probably, he thought, he would never find out. Perhaps it had had no reason at all, simply had fallen in behind the wayfarer in a foolish automatic way. It made little difference.

Before long Joseph felt hunger coming over him. With the provisions that Thustin had given him gone, all that he had left was the water in his flask. Finishing the last of the meat a few hours before, he had not paused to consider what he would do for meals thereafter on his journey, for he had never had to think about such a thing before. But he thought about it now. In the tales he had read about lone wandering castaways, they had always lived on roots and berries in the forest, or killed small animals with well-aimed rocks. Joseph had no way of knowing how to distinguish the edible roots or berries from the poisonous ones, though, and there did not seem to be any fruit on the trees and shrubs around here anyway at this time of year. As for killing wild animals by throwing rocks at them, that seemed to be something that was possible only in boys' storybooks.

He had to eat something, though. He wondered what he was going to do. From minute to minute the pangs increased in intensity. He had always had a hearty appetite. And in the short while since his escape from Getfen House he had called mightily on his body's reserves of strength.

It did not occur to him to discuss the problem with the noctambulo. After a couple of hours, however, they came to another small brook, and, since these little forest streams were becoming less common as they proceeded southward, Joseph thought it would be wise to fill his flask once again, even though it was less than half empty. He did so, and knelt also for a deep drink directly from the brook. Afterward he stayed in his crouching position for a few moments, enjoying the simple pleasure of resting here like this. The thought came to him of the clean warm bed in the guest quarters of Getfen House where he had been lying half asleep when the first sounds of the rebellion reached his ears, and of his own comfortable little apartment at home, his bed with its coverlet of purple and gold, his lopsided old chair, his well-stocked bookcase, his tile-bordered washbasin, the robust breakfast that was brought to his door by a servant every morning. All those things seemed like the stuff of dreams to him now. If only this were the dream,

Joseph thought, and they were the reality into which he would at any moment awaken.

Finally he looked up and noticed that the noctambulo had moved a short distance upstream from him and was grubbing about intently in the mud of the shore with its great scooplike hands, prodding and poking in it, dredging up large handfuls of mud that it turned over and over, inspecting them with almost comically deep attention. Joseph perceived that the noctambulo was pulling small many-legged creatures, crustaceans of some sort, from nests eight or nine inches down in the mud. It had found perhaps a dozen of them already, and, as Joseph watched, it scooped up a couple more, deftly giving them a quick pinch apiece to crack their necks and laying them carefully down beside the others.

This went on until it had caught about twenty. It divided the little animals into two approximately equal groups and shoved one of the piles toward Joseph, and said something in its thick-tongued, barely intelligible way that Joseph realized, after some thought, had been, "We eat now."

He was touched by the creature's kindness in sharing its meal unasked with him. But he wondered how he was going to eat these things. Covertly he glanced across at the noctambulo, who had hunkered down at the edge of the stream and was taking up the little mud-crawlers one by one, carefully folding the edges of one big hand over them and squeezing in such a way as to split the horny shell and bring bright scarlet meat popping into view. It sucked each tender morsel free, tossed the now empty shell over its shoulder into the brook, and went on to the next.

Joseph shuddered and fought back a spasm of nausea. The thought of eating such a thing—raw, no less—disgusted him. It would be like eating insects.

But it was clear to him that his choice lay between eating and starving. He knew what he would have said and done if his steward had brought him a tray of these crawlers one morning at Keilloran House. But this was not Keilloran House. Gingerly he picked up one of the mud-crawlers and tried to crack it open with his hand as he had seen the noctambulo do. The chitinous shell, though, was harder than he had expected. Even when he pushed inward with both hands he could not cause it to split.

The noctambulo watched benignly, perhaps pityingly. But it did not offer to help. It went methodically on with its own meal.

Joseph drew his knife from his utility case and by punching down vigorously was able to cut a slit about an inch long into the crawler's shell. That gave him enough of a start so that he now could, by pressing from both ends with all his strength, extend the crack far enough to make the red flesh show.

He stared down at it, quailing at the idea of actually putting this stuff in his mouth. Then, as a sudden wild burst of hunger overwhelmed him and obliterated all inhibition, he quickly lifted it and clamped his lips over the cracked shell and sucked the meat out, gulping it hurriedly down as if he could somehow avoid tasting it that way.

He could not avoid tasting it. The flavor was musky and pungent, as pungent as anything he had ever tasted, a harsh spiky taste that cut right into his palate. It seemed to him that the crawler flesh had the taste of mud in it too, or of the clay that lay below the mud in the bed of the brook. He gagged on it. A powerful shudder ran through him and his stomach seemed to rise and leap about. But after a couple of hasty gulps of water the worst of the sensations quickly subsided, leaving a reasonably tolerable aftertaste, and he realized that that first mouthful of strange meat had somehow taken the hard edge from his hunger. Joseph cracked open a second crawler and ate it less timidly, and a third, and a fourth, until it began to seem almost unremarkable to be eating such things. He still hated the initial muddy taste, nor was there any sort of pleasure for him in the aftertaste, but this was, at least, a way of easing the gripings of hunger. When he had eaten six of the crawlers he decided that he had had enough and pushed the rest of the heap back toward the noctambulo, who gathered them up without comment and set about devouring them.

A dozen or so mud-crawlers could not have

been much of a meal for an entity the size of the noctambulo. Indeed, as the two of them went onward through the night, the big creature continued to gather food. It went about the task with considerable skill, too. Joseph watched with unforced admiration as the noctambulo unerringly sniffed out an underground burrow, laid it bare with a few quick scoops of its great paddle-shaped hands, and pounced with phenomenal speed on the frantic inhabitants, a colony of small long-nosed mammals with bright yellow eyes, perhaps of the same sort that Joseph had seen staring down at him the night before. It caught four, killing them efficiently, and laid them out in a row on the ground, once again dividing them in two groups and nudging one pair toward Joseph.

Joseph stared at them, perplexed. The noctambulo had its face deep in the abdomen of one of the little beasts and was already happily gnawing away.

That was something Joseph could not or at least would not do. He could flay them and butcher them, he supposed, but he drew the line, at least this early in his journey, at eating the raw and bloody meat of mammals. Grimly he peeled the skin from the limbs of one of the long-nosed animals and then the other, and hacked away at the lean pink flesh along the fragile-looking bones until he had sliced off a fair-sized pile of meat. For the first time he deployed the firestarter from his utility case, using it to kindle a little blaze from twigs and dry leaves, and dangled one strip of meat after another into it from skewers until they were more or less cooked, or at any rate charred on the outside, though disagreeably moist within. Joseph ate them joylessly but without any great difficulty. The meat had little flavor; the effect was certainly that of eating meat, however stringy and drab in texture, but it made scarcely any impact on the tongue. Still, there would be some nourishment here, or so he hoped.

The noctambulo by this time had finished its meat and had excavated some thick crooked white tubers as a second course. These too it divided with Joseph, who began to push a skewer through one of them so he could hold it over the fire.

"No," said the noctambulo. "No fire. Do like this." And bit off a beakful from one without troubling even to brush the crust of soil from its sides. "Is good. You eat."

Joseph fastidiously cleaned the dirt from the tuber as well as he could and took a wary bite. To his surprise the taste was superb. The tuber's soft pulp was fragrant and fruity, and it detonated a complex mixture of responses in his mouth, all of them pleasing—a sugary sweetness, with an interesting winy tartness just behind it, and then a warm, starchy glow. It seemed a perfect antidote to the nastiness of the mud-crawler flesh and the insipidity of the meat of the burrowers. In great delight Joseph finished one tuber and then a second, and was reaching for a third when the noctambulo intervened. "Is too much," it said. "Take with. You eat later." The saucer eyes seemed to be giving him a sternly protective look. It was almost like having Balbus back in a bizarrely altered form.

Soon it would be morning. Joseph began to feel a little sleepy. He had adapted swiftly to this new regime of marching by night and sleeping by day. But the food, and particularly the tubers, had given him a fresh access of strength. He marched on steadily behind the noctambulo through a region that seemed much hillier and rockier than the terrain they had just traversed, and not quite as thickly vegetated, until, as the full blaze of daylight descended on the forest, the noctambulo halted suddenly and said, looking down at him from its great height, "Sleep now."

It was referring to itself, evidently, not to Joseph. And he watched sleep come over it. The noctambulo remained standing, but between one moment and the next *something* had changed. The noctambulo had little ability, so far as Joseph could detect, to register alterations in facial expression, and yet the glint in its huge eyes seemed somehow harder now, and it held its beak tightly closed instead of drooping ajar as it usually did, and the tapering head appeared to be tilted now at an odd quizzical angle.

After a moment Joseph remembered: daytime

brought a consciousness shift for noctambulos. The nighttime self had gone to sleep and the daytime personality was operating the huge body. In the hours just ahead, Joseph realized, he would essentially be dealing with a different noctambulo.

"My name is Joseph Master Keilloran," he felt obliged to announce to it. "I am a traveler who has come here from a far-off place. Your night-self has been guiding me through the forest to the nearest village of Indigenes."

The noctambulo made no response: did not, in fact, seem to comprehend anything Joseph had said, did not react in any way. Very likely it had no recollection of anything its other self had been doing in the night just past. It might not even have a very good understanding of the Indigene language. Or perhaps it was searching through the memories of the nighttime self to discover why it found itself in the company of this unfamiliar being.

"It is nearly my sleeping-time now," Joseph continued. "I must stop here and rest. Do you understand me?"

No immediate answer was forthcoming. The noctambulo continued to stare.

Then it said, brusquely, dispassionately, "You come," and strode off through the forest.

Unwilling to lose his guide, Joseph followed, though he would rather have been searching for a sheltered place in which to spend the daylight hours. The noctambulo did not look back, nor did it accommodate its pace to Joseph's. It might not be guiding Joseph at all any longer, Joseph realized. For an hour or more he forced himself onward, keeping pace with the noctambulo with difficulty, and then he knew he must stop and rest, even if that meant that the daytime noctambulo would go on without him and disappear while he slept. When another stream appeared, the first he had seen in a long while, Joseph halted and drank and made camp for himself beneath a bower of slender trees joined overhead by a dense tangle of aerial vines. The noctambulo did not halt. Joseph watched it vanish into the distance on the far side of the stream.

There was nothing he could do about that. He ate one of his remaining tubers, made another fruitless attempt to use his combinant, offered up the appropriate prayers for bedtime, and settled down for sleep. The ground was rougher and rockier than it looked and it was not easy to find a comfortable position, and the leg that had given him trouble on and off during the march was throbbing again from ankle to knee, and for hours, it seemed, he could not get to sleep despite his weariness. But somewhere along the way it must have happened, for a dream came to him in which he and his sister Cailin had been bathing in a mountain lake and he had gone ashore first and mischievously taken her clothes away with him; and then he opened his eyes and saw that night had begun to fall, and that the noctambulo was standing above him, patiently watching.

Was this *his* noctambulo, or the unfriendly daytime self, or a different noctambulo altogether? He could not tell.

But evidently it was his, for the ungainly creature not only had come back to him but had solicitously set out an array of food beside the stream-bank: a little heap of mud-crawlers, and two dead animals the size of small dogs with red fur marked with silvery stripes and short, powerful-looking limbs, and, what was rather more alluring, a goodly stack of the delicious white tubers. Joseph said morning prayers and washed in the stream and went about the task of building a fire. He was beginning to settle into the rhythm of this forest life, he saw.

"Are we very far from the Indigene village now?" he asked the noctambulo, when they had resumed their journey.

The noctambulo offered no response. Perhaps it had not understood. Joseph asked again, again to no avail. He realized that the noctambulo had never actually said it knew where the Indigene village was, or even that such a village existed anywhere in this region, but only that it would do what it could to help Joseph. How much faith, he wondered, should he place in Thustin's statement that an Indigene village lay just beyond the forest? Thustin had also said that she herself had never gone beyond the boundaries of the domain of House Getfen. And in any case the village, if indeed there was one, might be off in some other direction entirely from the one Joseph and the noctambulo had taken.

But he had no choice, he knew, except to continue along this path and hope for the best. Three more days passed in this way. He felt himself growing tougher, harder, leaner all the time. The noctambulo provided food for them both, forest food, little gray scuttering animals that it caught with amazing agility, bright-plumaged birds that it snatched astonishingly out of mid-air as they fluttered by, odd gnarled roots and tubers, the occasional batch of mud-crawlers. Joseph began to grow inured to the strangeness and frequent unpleasantness of what was given him to eat. He accepted whatever came his way. So long as it did not actually make him ill, he thought, he would regard it as useful nutriment. He knew that he must replenish his vitality daily, using any means at hand, or he would never survive the rigors of this march.

He began to grow a beard. It was only about a year since Joseph had first begun shaving, and he had never liked doing it. It was no longer the custom for Masters to be bearded, not since his grandfather's time, but that hardly mattered to him under the present circumstances. The beard came in soft and furry and sparse at first, but soon it became bristly, like a man's beard. He did not think of himself as a man, not yet. But he suspected darkly that he might well become one before this journey had reached its end.

The nature of the forest was changing again. There was no longer any regularity to the forest floor: it was riven everywhere by ravines and gullies and upthrust hillocks of rock, so that Joseph and the noctambulo were forever climbing up one little slope and down another. Sometimes Joseph found himself panting from the effort. The trees were different too, much larger than the ones in the woods behind them, and set much farther apart. From their multitude of branches sprouted a myriad of tiny gleaming needles of a metallic blue-green color, which they shed copiously with every good gust of wind. Thus a constant rainfall of needles came drifting through the air, tumbling down to form a thick layer of fine, treacherously slippery duff under foot.

Early one morning, just after the noctambulo had made the shift from the night-self to the day-self, Joseph stumbled over a concealed rock in a patch of that duff and began to topple. In an effort to regain his balance he took three wild lurching steps forward, but on the third of them he placed his left foot unknowingly on the smooth, flat upper surface of yet another hidden rock, slipped, felt the already weakened ankle giving way. He flung his arms out in a desperate attempt to stabilize himself, but it was no use: he skidded, pivoted, twisted in mid-air, landed heavily on his right elbow with his left leg bent sharply backward and crumpled up beneath his body.

The pain was incredible. He had never felt anything like it.

The first jolt came from his elbow, but that was obliterated an instant later by the uproar emanating from his leg. For the next few moments all he could do was lie there, half dazed, and let it go rippling up and down his entire left side. It felt as though streams of molten metal were running along his leg through tracks in his flesh. Then the effects went radiating out to all parts of his body. There was a stabbing sensation in his chest; his heart pounded terrifyingly; his vision grew blurred; he felt a strange tingling in his toes and fingers. Even his jaw began to ache. Simply drawing breath seemed to require conscious effort. The whole upper part of his body was trembling uncontrollably.

Gradually the initial shock abated. He caught his breath; he damped down the trembling. With great care Joseph levered himself upward, pushing against the ground with his hand, delicately raising his left hip so that he could unfold the twisted leg that now was trapped beneath his right thigh.

To his relief he was able to straighten it without enormous complications, though doing it was a slow and agonizing business. Gingerly he probed it with his fingertips. He had not broken any bones, so far as he was able to tell. But he knew that he had wrenched his knee very badly as he fell, and certainly there had been some sort of damage: torn ligaments, he supposed, or ruptured cartilage, or maybe the knee had been dislocated. Was that possible, he wondered—to dislocate your knee? It was hips or shoulders that you dislocated, not knees, right? He had watched his father once resetting the dislocated shoulder of a man of House Keilloran who had fallen from a hay-cart. Joseph thought that he understood the process; but if he had dislocated one of his own joints, how could he ever manage to reset it himself? Surely the noctambulo would be of no help.

In fact, he realized, the noctambulo was nowhere to be seen. He called out to it, but only the echo of his own voice returned to him. Of course: at the time of the accident it was the day-self, with whom Joseph had not established anything more than the most perfunctory relationship, that had been accompanying him. Uncaring or unaware, the big creature had simply gone shuffling onward through the woods when Joseph fell.

Joseph lay still for a long while, assessing the likelihood that he would be able to get to his feet unaided. He was growing used to the pain, the way he had grown used to the taste of mud-crawlers. The first horrendous anguish had faded and there was only a steady hot throb. But when he tried to rise, even the smallest movement sent startling tremors through the injured leg.

Well, it was about time for sleep, anyway. Perhaps by the time he awoke the pain would have diminished, or the noctambulo would have returned, or both.

He closed his eyes and tried not to think about the fiery bulletins coming from his injured leg. Eventually he dropped into a fitful, uncertain sleep.

When he woke night had come and the noctambulo was back, having once again brought food. Joseph beckoned to him. "I have hurt myself," he said. "Hold out your hand to me." He had to say it two or three more times, but at length the noctambulo understood, and stooped down to extend one great dangling arm. Joseph clutched the noctambulo's wrist and pulled himself upward. He had just reached an upright position when the noctambulo, as though deciding its services were no longer needed, began to move away. Joseph swayed and tottered, but stayed on his feet, though he dared not put any but the lightest pressure on the left leg. His walking-stick lay nearby; he hobbled over to it and gathered it gratefully into his hand.

When they resumed their march after eating Joseph discovered that he was able to walk, after a fashion, although his knee was beginning to swell now and the pain, though it continued to lessen, was still considerable. He thought he might be becoming feverish, too. He limped along behind the noctambulo, wishing the gigantic thing would simply pick him up and carry him on its shoulder. But it did not occur to the noctambulo to do any such thing—it seemed entirely unaware that Joseph was operating under any handicap—and Joseph would not ask it. So he went limping on, sometimes falling far behind his huge companion and having to struggle in order to keep it in view. Several times he lost sight of it completely and managed to proceed only by following the noctambulo's trail through the duff. Then at last the duff gave out and Joseph, alone again, could not guess which way to go.

He halted and waited. He barely had the strength to go any farther just now, anyway. Either the noctambulo would come back or it would not, but either way Joseph needed to pause here until he felt ready to go on.

Then after a time he saw the noctambulo reappearing up ahead, haloed in the double shadow of the light from the two moons that were in the sky this night, great bright ruddy Sanivark high overhead with the littlest one, white-faced Mebriel, in its wake. There was a phosphorescent orange lichen here too, long flat sheets of it clinging to the limbs of the nearby trees like shrouds, casting a ghostly purple glow.

"Not stop here," the creature said, making a loose, swinging gesture with its arms. "Village over there."

Village? By this time Joseph had given up all hope of the village's existence.

The noctambulo turned again and went off in the direction from which it had just come. After a dozen steps or so it turned and plainly signalled to Joseph to follow along. Though he was at the edge of exhaustion, Joseph forced himself to go on. They descended a sloping plateau where the only vegetation was low sprawling shrubbery, as though they really had reached the far side of the forest at last, and then Joseph saw, clearly limned in the moonlight, row upon row of slender conical structures of familiar shape set close together in the field just before him, each one right up against the next, and he knew beyond doubt that he had finally come to the Indigene village that he had sought so long.

two _____

A WAVE OF DIZZINESS CAME OVER HIM IN THAT SAME moment. Joseph could not tell whether it was born of relief or fatigue, or both. He knew that he had just about reached the end of his endurance. The pain in his leg was excruciating. He gripped his staff with both hands, leaned forward, fought to remain standing. After that everything took on a kind of red hallucinatory nimbus and he became uncertain of events for a while. Misty figures floated in the air before him, and at times he thought he heard his father's voice, or his sister's. When things were somewhat clear again he realized that he was lying atop a pile of furs within one of the Indigene houses, with a little ring of Indigenes sitting facing him in a circle, staring at him solemnly and with what appeared to be a show of deep interest.

"This will help your trouble," a voice said, and one of the Indigenes handed him a cluster of green, succulent stems. One of their healing herbs, Joseph assumed. According to his father, the Indigenes had an extensive pharmacopoeia of herbal remedies, and many of them were said to be great merit. Joseph took the stems without hesitation. They were full of a juice that stung his lips and tongue, but not in any unpleasant way. Almost at once, so it seemed, he felt his fever lessening and the turmoil in his damaged leg beginning to abate a little.

He had been inside an Indigene house only once before. There was a settlement of Indigenes just at the border of the Keilloran lands, and his father had taken him to visit them when he was ten. The strange claustrophobic architecture, the thick, rough-surfaced mud-and-wattle walls tapering to a narrow point high overhead, the elaborate crosshatched planking of the floors, the slitlike windows that admitted only enough light to create a shadowy gloom, had made a deep impression on him. It was all much the same here, down to the odd sickroom sweetness, something like the odor of boiled milk, of the stagnant air.

Indigenes were found everywhere on Homeworld, though their aggregate population was not large, and apparently never had been, even in the years before the arrival of the first human settlers. They lived in small scattered villages in the forested regions that were not utilized by humans and also at the periphery of the settled regions, and no friction existed between them and the humans who had come to occupy their planet. There was scarcely any interaction between humans and Indigenes at all. They were gentle creatures who kept apart from humans as much as possible, coming and going as they pleased but generally staying on the lands that were universally considered to be theirs. Quietly they went about their Indigenous business, whatever that might be, without ever betraying the slightest sign of resentment or dismay that their world had been invaded not once but twice by strangers from the stars—first the easy-going villagers known as the Folk today and then, much later, the turbulent, more intense people whom the Folk had come to accept under the name and authority of Masters. Whether the Indigenes saw the Masters as masters too was something that Joseph did not know. Perhaps no one did. Balbus had hinted that they had a philosophy of deep indifference to all outside power. But he had never elaborated on that, and now Balbus was dead.

Joseph was aware that some Masters of scholarly leanings took a special interest in these people. His father was among that group. He collected their artifacts, their mysterious little sculptures and somber ceramic vessels, and supposedly, so said Balbus, he had made a study at one time of those profound philosophical beliefs of theirs. Joseph had no idea what those beliefs might be. His father had never discussed them with him in detail, any more than Balbus had. It was his impression that his father's interest in Indigenes was in no way reciprocated by the Indigenes themselves: on that one visit to the village near House Keilloran they had seemed as indifferent to his presence and Joseph's among them as the day-noctambulo had been when they were in the forest together. When Joseph's father made inquiries about certain Indigene artifacts that he had hoped to acquire they replied in subdued monotones, saying as little as necessary and never volunteering anything that was not a direct response to something Joseph's father had asked.

But perhaps they had felt intimidated by the presence among them of the powerful Martin Master Keilloran of House Keilloran, or else the Indigenes of the north were of another sort of temperament from those of Helikis. Joseph sensed no indifference here. These people had offered him a medicine for his leg, unasked. Their intent stares seemed to be the sign of real curiosity about him. Though he could not say why, Joseph did not feel in the slightest way like an intruder here. It was more like being a guest.

He returned their stares with curiosity of his own. They were strangely handsome people, though distinctly alien of form, with long, tubular heads that were flattened fore and aft, fleshy throats that pouted out in flamboyant extension

in moments of excitement. Their eyes were little
slits protected by bony arches that seemed almost
like goggles, with peeps of scarlet showing
through, the same vivid color as the eyes of noctambulos. Those red eyes were a clue: perhaps
these races had been cousins somewhere far back
on the evolutionary track, Joseph thought. And
they walked upright, as noctambulos did. But the
Indigenes were much smaller and slighter than
noctambulos in build, closer to humans in general dimension. They had narrow ropy limbs that
looked as though they had no muscular strength
at all, though they could muster startling tensile
force when needed: Joseph had seen Indigenes
lift bundles of faggots that would break the back
of a sturdy Folker. Their skins were a dull bronze,
waxy-looking, with unsettling orange highlights
glowing through. Their feet were splayed, long-
toed. Their double-jointed seven-fingered hands
were similarly rangy and pliant. Males and fe-
males looked identical to human eyes, although,
Joseph supposed, not to other Indigenes.

The Indigenes sitting by his bedside, who were
eight or nine in number, interrogated him, wanting to know who he was, where he was going. No
one of them seemed to be in a position of leadership. Nor was there any special order in the way
they questioned him. One would ask, and they
would listen to his reply, and then another elsewhere in the group would ask something else.

The dialect they spoke was somewhat different

from the version of Indigene that Joseph knew, but he had no particular difficulty understanding it or in shaping his own responses so that the pronunciation was closer to what seemed to be the norm here. He had studied the Indigene language since early childhood. It was something that all Masters were expected to learn, as a matter of courtesy toward the original inhabitants of the planet. You grew up speaking Folkish too—that was only common sense, in a world where nine humans out of ten were of the Folk—and of course the Masters had a language of their own, the language of the Great Houses. So every Master was trilingual. It had been Balbus's idea that Joseph study the language of Old Earth, also: an extra little scholarly fillip. It was ancestral to Master, and, so said Balbus, the more deeply versed you were in the ancient language, the better command you would have of the modern one. Joseph had not yet had time to discover whether that was so.

He thought it would be obvious to these Indigenes that he was a Master, but he made a point of telling them anyway. It produced no discernible reaction. He explained that he was the eldest son of Martin Master Keilloran of House Keilloran, who was one of the great men of the southern continent. That too seemed to leave them unmoved. "I was sent north to spend the summer with my kinsmen at House Getfen," he said. "It is our custom for the eldest son of every

Great House to visit some distant House for a time just before he comes of age."

"There has been trouble at Getfen House," one of the Indigenes said gravely.

"Great trouble, yes. It was only by luck that I escaped." Joseph could not bring himself to ask for details of the events at Getfen House. "I need to return to my home now. I ask your assistance in conveying me to the nearest Great House. The people there will be able to help me get home." He was careful to use the supplicatory tense: he was not really asking, he was simply suggesting. Indigenes did not make direct requests of each other except under the most unusual of circumstances, let alone give each other orders: they merely indicated the existence of a need and awaited a confirmation that the need would be met. Whenever a human, even a Master, had reason to make a request of an Indigene, the same grammatical nicety was observed, not just because it was simple politeness to do so but because the Indigene ordinarily would not respond to, and perhaps would not even comprehend, anything that was couched in the mode reserved for a direct order. "Will you do that?" he asked. "I understand the closest Great House is House Ludbrek."

"That is correct, Master Joseph."

"Then that is where I must go."

"We will take you there," said another of the Indigenes. "But first you must rest and heal."

"Yes. Yes. I understand that."

They brought him food, a thick dark porridge and some stewed shredded meat that tasted like illimani and a cluster of small, juicy red berries: simple country stuff but a great improvement over raw mud-crawlers and half-cooked roots. Joseph's father had a serious interest in fine food and wine, but Joseph himself, who had been growing swiftly over the past year and a half, had up until now generally been more concerned with the quantity of the food he ate than with its quality.

So he fell with great avidity upon the tray of Indigene food, but was surprised to find he could not eat very much of it despite the intensity of his appetite. The fever was returning, he realized. His head had begun to ache, his skin felt hot and dry to his own touch, his throat was constricted. He asked for and received a few more of the green succulent stems, which provided the same short-term relief as before, and then the Indigenes left him and he settled back on his bed of furs to get some sleep. The furs had a sour, tangy, insistent odor that he did not like, nor did he care for the unpleasant milky sweetness of the air itself in here, but despite those distractions he fell quickly into a deep, welcome sleep.

When he opened his eyes again daylight was coming through the slits in the walls. It had been late at night when he arrived here, practically morning; he wondered whether he had slept through an entire day and a night, and this was the second morning. Probably so. And just as well, he thought, considering the fragmentary nature of the sleep he had had in the forest.

For the first time since his arrival he thought of the noctambulo who had been his guide in the wilderness. He asked the Indigenes about it, but the only answer he got was a gesture of crossed arms, the Indigene equivalent of a shrug. The Indigenes knew nothing of the noctambulo. Perhaps they had not even noticed its presence, and it had simply wandered off after delivering him. Joseph realized that from first to last he had understood nothing of the noctambulo's purposes and motives, if it had any. It had tracked him, it had fed him, it had brought him here, and now it was gone, and he never would know anything more.

The fever did not seem to be much of a problem this morning. It was easier for him to eat than before. Afterward he asked one of the Indigenes to help him rise. The Indigene extended one loose-jointed ropy arm and drew him to his feet, raising him in one smooth motion as though Joseph had no weight at all.

He leaned on his walking-stick and inspected himself. His left leg was purple and black with bruises and terribly swollen from mid-thigh to ankle. Even his toes seemed puffy. The leg looked grotesque, ghastly, a limb that belonged to a creature of another species entirely. Little arrows of pain traversed its length. Simply *looking* at the leg made it hurt.

Cautiously Joseph tried putting some weight on his foot, the merest bit of experimental pressure. That was a mistake. He touched just the tips of his toes to the floor and winced as an immediate stern warning came rocketing up toward his brain: *Stop! Don't!* All right, he told himself. A bad idea. He would have to wait a little longer. How long would healing take, though? Three days? A week? A month? He had to get on his way. They would be worried sick about him at home. Surely word had reached Helikis by now of the uprising in the north. The interruption in combinant communication alone would be indication enough that something was wrong.

He was confident that once he reached Ludbrek House he would be able to send some sort of message to his family, even if the Ludbreks could not arrange transportation to Helikis for him right away, because of the present troubles. But first he had to get to Ludbrek House. Joseph could not guess how far from here that might be. The Great Houses of Helikis were set at considerable distances from one another, and probably that was true up here, too. Still, it should be no more than three days' journey, or four by wagon. Unless these Indigenes had more interest in the machines of the Masters than those of the Southland did, they would not have cars or trucks of any sort, but they should, at least, have wagons, drawn by teams of bandars or more likely, he supposed, yaramirs, that could get them there. He would inquire about that later in the day. But also he had to recover to a point where he would be able to withstand the rigors of the journey.

Joseph hunted through the utility case to see if it contained medicines of any sort, something to control fever, or to reduce inflammation. There did not seem to be. An odd omission, he thought. He did find a couple of small devices that perhaps were medical instruments: one that looked as if it could be used for stitching up minor wounds, and another that apparently provided a way of testing water for bacterial contamination. Neither of those, though, would do him any good at present.

He asked for and got more of the succulent herb. That eased things a little. Then, when it occurred to him that bandaging his leg might speed the process of healing, he suggested to one of the Indigenes who seemed to be in virtually constant attendance on him that it would be helpful if the Indigene were to bring him a bolt or two of the light cottony fabric out of which they fashioned their own clothing.

"I will do that," the Indigene replied.

But there was a problem. The leg was so stiff and swollen that he could not flex it. There was no way Joseph could reach down as far as his ankle to do the wrapping himself.

"What is your name?" he said to the Indigene

who had brought the cloth. It was time to start making an attempt to look upon these people as individuals.

"I am Ulvas."

"Ulvas, I need your help in this," Joseph said. As always, he employed the supplicatory tense. It was becoming quite natural for him to frame his sentences that way, which Joseph took as a sign that he was not just translating his thoughts from the Master tongue to Indigene, but actually thinking in the language of the Indigenes.

"I will help you," Ulvas replied, the customary response to almost any supplication. But the Indigene gave Joseph a look of unmistakable perplexity. "Is it that you wish to do something with the cloth? Then it is needful that you tell me what is it is that you wish me to do."

"To bind my leg," Joseph said, gesturing. "From here to here."

The Indigene did not seem to have any very clear concept of what binding Joseph's leg would involve. On its first attempt it merely draped a useless loose shroud of cloth around his ankle. Carefully, using the most courteous mode of instruction he could find, Joseph explained that that was not what he had in mind. Other Indigenes gathered in the room. They murmured to one another. Ulvas turned away from Joseph and consulted them. A lengthy discussion ensued, all of it too softly and swiftly spoken for Joseph to be able to follow. Then the Indigene began again, turning to Joseph for approval at every step of the way. This time it wound the cloth more tightly, beginning with the arch of Joseph's foot, going around the ankle, up along his calf. Whenever Ulvas allowed the binding to slacken, Joseph offered mild correction.

The whole group of Indigenes crowded around, staring with unusual wide-eyed intensity. Joseph had had little experience in deciphering the facial expressions of Indigenes, but it seemed quite apparent that they were watching as though something extraordinary were under way.

From time to time during the process Joseph gasped as the tightening bandage, in the course of bringing things back into alignment, struck a lode of pain in the battered limb. But he knew that he was doing the right thing in having his leg bandaged like this. Immobilize the damned leg: that way, at least, he would not constantly be putting stress on the torn or twisted parts whenever he made the slightest movement, and it would begin to heal. Already he could feel the bandage's beneficial effects. The thick binding gripped and held his leg firmly, though not so firmly, he hoped, as to cut off circulation, just tightly enough to constrain it into the proper position.

When the wrapping had reached as far as his knee, Joseph released the Indigene from its task and finished the job himself, winding the bandage upward and upward until it terminated at the fleshiest part of his thigh. He fastened it there to keep it from unraveling and looked up in satisfaction. "That should do it, I think," he said.

The entire group of Indigenes was still staring at him in the same wonderstruck way.

He wondered what could arouse such curiosity in them. Was it the fact that his body was bare from the waist down? Very likely that was it. Joseph smiled. These people would never have had reason to see a naked human before. This was something quite new to them. Having no external genitalia of their own, they must be fascinated by those strange organs dangling between his legs. That had to be the explanation, he thought. It was hard to imagine that they would get so worked up over a simple thing like the bandaging of a leg.

But he was wrong. It *was* the bandage, not the unfamiliarities of his anatomy, that was the focus of their attention.

He found that out a few hours later, after he had spent some time hobbling about his room with the aid of his stick, and had had a midday meal of stewed vegetables and braised illimani meat brought to him. He was experimenting with the still useless combinant once again, his first attempt with it in days, when there came a sound of reed-flute music from the corridor, the breathy, toneless music that had some special significance for the Indigenes, and then an Indigene of obvious grandeur and rank entered the room, a personage who very likely was the chieftain of the village, or perhaps the high priest, if they had such things as high priests. It was clad not in simple cotton robes but in a brightly painted leather cape and a knee-length leather skirt much bedecked with strings of seashells, and it carried itself with unusual dignity and majesty. Signalling to the musicians to be still, it looked toward Joseph and said, "I am the Ardardin. I give the visiting Master good greeting and grant him the favor of our village."

Ardardin was not a word in Joseph's vocabulary, but he took it to be a title among these people. The Ardardin asked Joseph briefly about the uprising at Getfen House and his own flight through the forest. Then, indicating Joseph's bandaged leg, it said, "Will that wrapping cause your injuries to heal more quickly?"

"So I expect, yes."

"The matagava of the Masters is a powerful thing."

Matagava, Joseph knew, was a word that meant something like "magic," "supernatural power," "spiritual force." But he suspected that in this context it had other meanings too: "scientific skill," "technical prowess." The Indigenes were known to have great respect for such abilities in that area as the humans who lived on their world manifested—their technology, their engineering achievements, their capacity to fly through the air from continent to continent and through space from world to world. They did not seem to covet such powers themselves, not in the slightest, but they clearly admired them. And now he was being hailed as a person of great matagava himself. Why, though, should a simple thing like bandaging an injured leg qualify as a display of matagava? Joseph wanted to protest that the Ardardin did him too much honor. But he was fearful of giving offense, and said nothing.

"Can you walk a short distance?" the Ardardin asked. "There is something I would like to show you nearby, if you will come."

Since he had already discovered that a certain amount of walking was, though difficult, not impossible for him, Joseph said that he would. He used his stick as a crutch, so that he would not have to touch his sore foot to the ground. Two Indigenes, the one named Ulvas and another one, walked close beside him so that they could steady him if he began to fall.

The Ardardin led Joseph along a spiral corridor that opened unexpectedly into fresh air, and thence to a second building behind the one where he had been staying. Within its gloomy central hall were three Indigenes lying on fur mats. Joseph could see at first glance that all three were sick, that this must be an infirmary of some sort.

"Will you examine them?" the Ardardin asked.

The request took Joseph by surprise. *Examine* them? Had they somehow decided that he must be a skilled physician, simply because he had been able to manage something as elementary as bandaging a sprained knee?

But he could hardly refuse the request. He looked down at the trio of Indigenes. One, he saw, had a nasty ulcerated wound in its thigh, seemingly not deep but badly infected. Its forehead was bright with the glow of a high fever. Another had apparently broken its arm: no bone was showing, but the way the arm was bent argued for a fracture. There was nothing outwardly wrong with the third Indigene, but it held both its hands pressed tight against its abdomen, making what had to be an indication of severe pain.

The Ardardin stared at Joseph in an unambiguously expectant way. Its fleshy throat-pouch was pouting in and out at great speed. Joseph felt mounting uneasiness.

It began to occur to him that the medical techniques of the Indigenes might go no farther than the use of simple herbal remedies. Anything more complicated than the brewing of potions might be beyond them. Closing a wound, say, or setting a broken bone. Getting a pregnant woman through a difficult childbirth. And any kind of surgery, certainly. You needed very great matagava to perform such feats, greater matagava than had been granted to these people.

And the human Masters had that kind of matagava, yes. With the greatest of ease they could perform feats that to the Indigenes must seem like miracles.

Joseph knew that if his father were here right now, he would deal swiftly enough with the problems of these three—do something about the infected thigh, set the broken arm, arrive at an explanation of the third one's pain and cope with its cause. At home he had many times seen Martin, in the course of his circuits around the estate, handle cases far more challenging than these seemed to be. His father's matagava was a powerful thing, yes: or, to put it another way, it was his father's responsibility to look after the lives and welfare of all those who lived on the lands of House Keilloran and he accepted that responsibility fully, and so he had taken the trouble to learn at least certain basic techniques of medicine in order that he could meet an emergency in the fields.

But Joseph was not the lord of House Keilloran, and he had had no formal medical training. He was only a boy of fifteen, who might one day inherit his father's title and his father's responsibilities, and he was a long way just now from being prepared to undertake any sort of adult tasks. Did the Ardardin not realize how young he was? Probably not. Indigenes might be no better able to distinguish an adolescent human from an adult one than humans were when it came to distinguishing a male Indigene from a female one. The Ardardin perceived him as a human, that was all, and very likely as a full-grown one. His height and the new beard he had grown would help in fostering that belief. And humans had great matagava; this Joseph Master Keilloran who had come among them was a human; therefore—

"Will you do it?" the Ardardin said, using not just the supplicatory tense but a form that Joseph thought might be known to grammarians as the intensive supplicatory. The Indigene—the chieftain, the high priest—was *begging* him.

He could not bear to disappoint them. He hated doing anything under false pretenses, and he did not want to arouse any false hopes, either. But he could not resist an abject plea, either. These people had willingly taken him in, and they had cared for him these two days past, and they had promised to transport him to Ludbrek House when he was strong enough to leave their village. Now they wanted something from him in return. And he did have at least some common-sense notions of first aid. There was no way he could refuse this request.

"Can you raise them up a little higher?" he asked. "I'm not able to bend, because of my leg."

The Ardardin gestured, and several Indigenes piled up a tall stack of furs and placed the one with the wound in its thigh on top. Bending forward a little, Joseph inspected the cut. It was three or four inches long, perhaps half an inch wide, fairly shallow. There was swelling all around, and reddening of the bronze-colored skin. Hesitantly Joseph placed his fingertips against the ragged edges of the opening. The texture of the alien skin was smooth, unyielding, almost slippery, oddly unreal. A small sighing sound came from the Indigene at Joseph's touch, but nothing more. That did not sound like an indicator of severe pain. Gently Joseph drew the sides of the wound apart and peered in.

He saw pus, plenty of it. But the wound was filthy, besides, covered with a myriad of black spots, the dirt of whatever object had caused it. Joseph doubted that it had ever been cleaned. Did these people not even have enough sense to wash a gash like this out?

"I need a bowl of hot water," Joseph said. "And clean cloth of the kind I used for bandaging my leg."

This was like being an actor in a play, he thought. He was playing the role of The Doctor.

But that was no actor lying on the pile of furs before him, and that wound was no artifact of stage makeup. He felt a little queasy as he swabbed it clean. The Indigene stirred, moaned a little, made a small shuddering movement.

"The juice that you gave me, to make my fever go down: give some of that to him too."

"To her," someone behind him corrected.

"To her," said Joseph, searching for and not finding any indication that his patient was female. Doubtless the Indigenes did have two sexes, because there were both male and female pronouns in their language, but all of them, male and female both, had the same kind of narrow transverse slit at the base of the abdomen, and whatever sort of transformation came over that slit during the sexual process, what organs of intromission or reception might emerge at that time, was not anything that the Indigenes had ever thought necessary to explain to any human.

He cleaned the wound of as much superficial dirt as he could, and expressed a good deal of pus, and laved the opening several times with warm water. The queasiness he had felt at first while handling the wound quickly vanished. He grew very calm, almost detached: after a while all that mattered to him was the task itself, the process of undoing the damage that neglect and infection had caused. Not only was he able to steel himself against whatever incidental pain he might be causing the patient in the course of the work, but he realized a little while further on that he was concentrating so profoundly on the enterprise that he had begun to forget to notice the pain of his own injury.

He wished he had some kind of antiseptic ointment to apply, but his command of the Indigene language did not extend as far as any word for antisepsis, and when he asked if their herbal remedies included anything for reducing the inflammation of an open wound, they did not seem to understand what he was saying. No antisepsis, then. He hoped that the Indigene's natural healing processes were up to the task of fighting off such infection as had already taken hold.

When he had done all that he could to clean the wound Joseph instructed Ulvas in the art of bandaging it to hold it closed. He did not want to experiment with using the device from his utility case that seemed to be designed for stitching wounds, partly because he was not certain that that was what it was for, and partly because he doubted that he had cleaned the wound sufficiently to make stitching it up at this point a wise thing to do. Later, he thought, he would ask Ulvas to bring him a chunk of raw meat and he would practice using the device to close an incision, and then, perhaps, he could wash the wound out a second time and close it. But he dared not attempt to use the instrument now, not with everyone watching.

Dealing with the broken arm was a more straightforward business. The field-hands of House Keilloran broke limbs all the time, and it was a routine thing for them to be brought to his father for repairs. Joseph had watched the process often enough. A compound fracture would have been beyond him, but this looked like nothing more than a simple break. What you did, he knew, was manipulate the limb to make the fractured bone drop back into its proper alignment, and bind it up to keep the broken ends from moving around, and do what was necessary to reduce inflammation. Time would take care of the rest. At least, that was how it worked with Folkish fractures. But there was no reason to think that In-

digene bones were very different in basic physi-
ology.

Joseph wanted to be gentle as he went about
the work. But what he discovered very quickly
was that in working on an unanaesthetized patient the key lay in getting the job over with as
fast as possible, rather than moving with tiny cir-
cumspect steps in an attempt to avoid inflicting
pain. That would only draw things out and make
it worse. You had to take hold, pull, push, hope
for the best. The patient—this one was male, they
told him—made one sharp grunting sound as
Joseph, acting out an imitation of the things he
had seen his father do, grasped his limply dangling forearm with one hand and the upper part
of his arm with the other and exerted sudden
swift inward pressure. After the grunt came a
gasp, and then a sigh, and then a kind of exhala-
tion that seemed to be entirely one of relief.

There, Joseph thought, with a hot burst of satisfaction. He had done it. Matagava, indeed!
"Bind the arm the way you bound my leg," he
told Ulvas, no supplication this time, simple instruction, and moved to the next patient.

But the third case was a baffling one. What was
he supposed to do about a swollen abdomen? He
had no way of making a rational diagnosis. Perhaps there was a tumor in there, perhaps it was
an intestinal blockage, or perhaps—this patient
was another female—the problem was a compli-
cation of pregnancy. But, though he had blithely

enough talked himself into going through with this medical masquerade, Joseph's audacity did not begin to extend to a willingness to perform a surgical exploration of the patient's interior. He had no notion of how to go about such a thing, for one—the thought of trying to make an incision in living flesh brought terrifying images to his mind—nor would there be any purpose in it, anyway, for he had no inkling of internal Indigene anatomy, would not be able to tell one organ from another, let alone detect any abnormality. So he did nothing more than solemnly pass his hands up and down over the patient's taut skin with a kind of stagy solemnity, feeling the strangeness again, that cool dry inorganic unreality, lightly pressing here and there, as though seeking by touch alone some understanding of the malady within. He thought he should at least seem to be making an attempt of some kind at performing an examination, however empty and foolish he knew it to be, and since he did not dare do anything real this would have to suffice. He was, at any rate, unable to feel anything unusual within the abdominal cavity by these palpations, no convulsive heavings of troubled organs, no sign of some massive cancerous growth. But then, thinking he should do something more and obeying a sudden stab of inspiration, Joseph found himself making broad sweeping gestures in the air above the Indigene and intoning a nonsensical little rhythmic chant, as primitive witch-doctors were known to do in old adventure stories that he had read. It was sheer play-acting, and a surge of contempt for his own childishness went sweeping through him even as he did it, but for the moment he was unable to resist his own silly impulse.

Only for a moment. Then he could no longer go on with the game.

Joseph looked away, embarrassed. "For this one I am unable to do anything further," he told the Ardardin. "And you must allow me to lie down now. I am not well myself, and very tired."

"Yes. Of course. But we thank you deeply, Master Joseph."

He felt bitter shame for the fraud he had just perpetrated. Not just the preposterous business at the end, but the entire cruel charade. What would his father say, he wondered? A boy of fifteen, posing as a doctor? Piously laying claim to skills he did not in any way possess? The proper thing to do, he knew, would have been to say, "I'm sorry, I'm just a boy, the truth is that I have no right to be doing this." But they had wanted so badly for him to heal these three people with the shining omnipotent human matagava that they knew he must have within him. The very grammar of the Ardardin's request had revealed the intensity of their desire. And he had done no real harm, had he? Surely it was better to wash and bind a gash like that than to leave it open to fester. He felt confident that he had actually set that broken arm properly, too. He could not for-

give himself, though, for that last bit of disgrace-
ful chicanery.

His leg was hurting again, too. They had left a
beaker of the succulent-juice by his bedside. He
took enough of it to ease the pain and slipped off
into a fitful sleep.

When he awoke the next day he found that
they had set out inviting-looking bowls of fruit at
his side and had put festive bundles of flowers all
around his chamber, long-tubed reddish blos-
soms that had a peppery aroma. It all looked cel-
ebratory. They had not brought him flowers
before. Several Indigenes were kneeling beside
him, waiting for him to open his eyes. Joseph was
beginning to recognize the distinct features of different individuals, now. He saw Ulvas nearby,
and another who had told him yesterday that its
name was Cuithal, and a third whom he did not
know. Then the Ardardin entered, bearing an additional armload of flowers: plainly an offering. It
laid them at Joseph's feet and made an intricate
gesture that seemed certainly, alien though it was,
to be one of honor and respect.

The Ardardin earnestly inquired after the state
of Joseph's health. It seemed to Joseph that his leg
was giving him less discomfort this morning, and
he said so. To this the Ardardin replied that his
three patients were greatly improved also, and
were waiting just outside in the hallway to ex-
press their thanks.

So this will go on and on, Joseph thought,

abashed. But he could hardly refuse to see them. They came in one by one, each bearing little gifts to add to those already filling Joseph's room: more flowers, more fruit, smooth-sided ceramic vessels that his father would gladly have owned, brightly colored weavings. Their eyes were gleaming with gratitude, awe, perhaps even love. The one who had had the infected wound in her thigh looked plainly less feverish. The one with the broken arm—it had been very nicely bound by Ulvas, Joseph saw—seemed absolutely cheerful. Joseph was relieved and considerably gratified to see that his amateur ministrations had not only done no harm but seemed actually to have been beneficial.

But the great surprise was the third patient, the one with the swollen abdomen, over whom Joseph had made those shameful witch-doctor conjurations. She appeared to be in a state of transcendental well-being, wholly aglow with radiant emanations of health. Throwing herself at Joseph's feet, she burst forth with a gushing, barely coherent expression of thankfulness that was almost impossible for him to follow in any detailed way, but was clear enough in general meaning.

Joseph hardly knew how to react. The code of honor by which he had been raised left no room for taking credit for something you had not done. Certainly it would be even worse to accept credit for something achieved accidentally, something you had brought about in the most cynical and flippant manner.

Yet he could not deny that this woman had risen from her bed of pain just hours after he had made those foolish conjurations above her body. A purely coincidental recovery, he thought. Or else his idiotic mumblings had engendered in her such a powerful wave of faith in his great matagava that she had expelled the demon of torment from her body on her own. What could he say? "No, you are mistaken to thank me, I did nothing of any value for you, this is all an illusion?" He did not have the heart to say any such things. There was the risk of shattering her fragile recovery by doing so, if indeed faith alone had healed her. Nor did he want to reject ungraciously the gratitude of these people for what they thought he had done for them. He remained aware that he was still dependent on them himself. If a little inward embarrassment was the price of getting himself from here to Ludbrek House, so be it. Let them think he had worked miracles, then. Perhaps he had. In any event let them feel obligated to him, because he needed help from them. Even the honor of a Master must sometimes be subordinated to the needs of sheer survival, eh, Balbus? Eh?

Besides—no question about this part of it— there was real satisfaction in doing something useful for others, no matter how muddledly he had accomplished it. The one thing that had been dinned into him from childhood, as the heir to House Keilloran, is that Masters did not simply rule, they also served. The two concepts were inextricably intertwined. You had the good luck to be born a Master instead of one of the Folk, yes, and that meant you lived a privileged life of comfort and power. But it was not merely a life of casual taking, of living cheerfully at one's ease at the expense of hardworking humbler people. Only a fool would think that that was what a Master's life was like. A Master lived daily in a sense of duty and obligation to all those around him.

Thus far Joseph had not had much opportunity to discharge those duties and obligations. At this stage of his life he was expected mainly to observe and learn. He would not be given any actual administrative tasks at the House until his sixteenth birthday. For now his job was only to prepare himself for his ultimate responsibilities. And there always were servants on all sides of him to take care of the things that ordinary people had to do for themselves, making things easy for him while he was doing his observing and learning.

He felt a little guilty about that. He was quite aware that up till now, up till the moment of his flight into the woods with Getfen House ablaze behind him, his life had been one of much privilege and little responsibility. He was not a doer yet, only someone for whom things were done.

There had been no real tests for him, neither of his abilities nor of his innate character.

Was he, then, truly a good person? That remained open to question. Since he had never been tested, he had no way of knowing. He had done things he should not have done. He had rebelled sometimes, at least inwardly, against his father's absolute authority. He had been guilty of little blasphemies and minor acts of wickedness. He had been needlessly harsh with his younger brothers, enjoying the power that his age and strength gave him over them, and he knew that that was wrong. He had gone through a phase of wanting to torment his sometimes irritating sister Cailin, mocking her little frailties of logic and hiding or even destroying her cherished things, and had felt real pleasure mingled with the guilt of that. All these things, he knew, were things that most boys did and would outgrow, and he could not really condemn himself for doing them, but even so they left him with some uncertainty about whether he had been living on the path of virtue, as by definition a good person must do. He understood how to *imitate* being a good person, yes, how to do the kind of things that good persons did, but how sincere was it, really, to do that? Was it not the case that good people did good things through natural innate virtue, rather than consciously working up some flurry of good-deed-doing on special demand?

Well, there had been special demand just now,

and, responding to it, he had wantonly allowed himself to pose as a doctor, which, considering that he had no real medical knowledge, could only be considered a bad thing, or at least morally questionable. But he had managed, all the same, to heal or at least improve the condition of three suffering people, and that was beyond doubt a good thing. What did that say about his own goodness, that he had achieved something virtuous by morally questionable means? He still did not know. But at least, for this murky reason or that one, this shabby motive or that, he had accomplished something that was undeniably good. He tried to cling to that awareness. Perhaps there were no innately good people, only people who made it their conscious task, for whatever reason, to do things that would be deemed good. Time alone would give him the answer to that. But still Joseph found himself hoping that he would discover, as he entered adulthood, that in fact he was fundamentally good, not simply pretending to goodness, and that everything he did would be for the best, not just for himself but for others.

Having done indisputably good deeds here in this village, the one thing Joseph feared more than anything else now was that they would not want to let such a powerful healer out of their grasp. But that was not how the minds of these people worked, evidently. In another few days his own healing had progressed to the point where he was able to walk with only a slight limp. Removing the bandage, he saw that the swelling was greatly reduced and the discoloration of his flesh was beginning to fade. Shortly Ulvas came to him and said they had a wagon ready to take him, now, to Ludbrek House.

It was a simple vehicle of the kind they used for hauling farm produce from place to place: big wooden wheels set on a wooden axle, an open cabin in back, a seat up front for the driver, a team of squat broad-shouldered yaramirs tethered to the shafts. The planked floor of the cabin in which Joseph rode had borne a cargo of vegetables not long before, and the scent of dark moist soil was still on the wood, and subtle smells of rotting leaves and stems. Two Indigenes whose names Joseph did not know sat up front to guide the team; another two, Ulvas and Cuithal, who seemed to have been appointed his special attendants, sat with him in back. They had given him a pile of furs to sit on, but the cart was not built for pleasure-riding and he felt every movement of the creaking irregular wheels against the ancient uneven road below.

This was no longer forest country, here, the ruggedly beautiful north country that was, or had been, the domain of House Getfen. This was farmland. Perhaps it was shared by Indigenes of several villages who came out from their settlements to work it. Most of it was perfectly flat, though it was broken in places by rolling meadows and fields, and Joseph could see low hills in the distance that were covered with stiff, close-set ranks of slender trees with purplish leaves.

His geography textbook might tell him something about the part of the country that he was entering. But since leaving Getfen House he had not so much as glanced at the little hand-held reader on which all his textbooks were stored, and he could not bring himself to take it out now. He was supposed to study every day, of course, even while he was up there in High Manza on holiday among his Getfen cousins: his science, his mathematics, his philosophy, his studies in languages and literature, and most particularly his history and geography lessons, designed to prepare him for his eventual role as a Master among Masters. The geography book described Homeworld from pole to pole, including things that he had never expected to experience at the close range he was seeing them now. The history of Homeworld was mainly the history of its great families and the regime that they had imposed on the Folk who had come here before them, although his lessons told him also of the first Homeworld, the ancient one called Earth, from which all humans had come once upon a time, and whose own history must never be forgotten, shadowy and remote though it was to its descendants here, because there were sorry aspects of that history that those descendants must take care never to recapitulate. And then there were all the other subjects that he knew he should be reading, even without Balbus here to direct him. *Especially* without Balbus here to direct him.

His energies had been focused on sheer survival during the days that had just gone by, though, and while he was wandering in the forest it seemed almost comically incongruous to sit huddled under some shelter of boughs reading about the distant past or the niceties of philosophy when at any moment some band of rebellious Folk might come upon him and put an end to his life. And then, later, when he was safe at the Indigene village, any thought of resuming his studies immediately brought to Joseph's mind the image of his tutor Balbus lying sprawled on his back in the courtyard of Getfen House with his throat cut, and it became too painful for him to proceed. Now, jolting and bumping along through this Manza farm country, reading seemed impossible for other reasons. Joseph simply wanted to reach Ludbrek House as quickly as possible and return at long last to the company of his own people.

But Ludbrek House, when they came to it after a three-day journey, stood devastated atop its hilltop ridge. What was left of it was no more than a desolate scar across the green land. The burned roofless walls of the estate house stood out above cold dark heaps of rubble. Its mighty structural members were laid bare, charred and blackened timbers, spars, joists, beams, like the great skeleton of some giant prehistoric beast rising in a haunting fragmentary way from the matrix that enclosed it. There was the bitter ugly smell of smoke everywhere, old smoke, dead smoke, the smoke of fierce fires that had cooled many days ago.

The rest of the huge estate, so far as Joseph was able to see from where he stood, was in equally sorry condition. House Ludbrek, like House Getfen and House Keilloran, like any of the Great Houses of Homeworld, was the center of an immense sphere of productive activity. Radiating outward from the manor-house and its fields and gardens and parks were zone after zone of agricultural and industrial compounds, the farms and the homes of the farmers over here, the factories over there, the mills and millponds, the barns, the stables, the workers' quarters and the commercial sectors that served them, and everything else that went to make up the virtually self-sufficient economic unit that was a Great House. It seemed to Joseph from where he stood looking out over the Ludbrek lands from his vantage point atop this hill that all of that had been given over to ruination. It was a sickening sight. The landscape was a nightmarish scene of wholesale destruction, long stretches of burned buildings, trucks and carts overturned, machinery smashed, farm animals slain, roads cut, dams broken, fields flooded. An oppressive stillness prevailed. Nothing moved; no sound could be heard.

Through him as he scanned the devastation from east to west and then from west to east again, gradually coming to terms with the reality of it, ran a storm of emotion: shock, horror, fear, sadness, and then, moments later, disgust and anger, a burst of fury at the stupidity of it all. There was no way at that moment for Joseph to step away from his own identity as a Master: and, as a Master, he raged at the idiotic wastefulness of the thing that had been done here.

What had these people believed they were accomplishing when they put not only Ludbrek House but House Ludbrek itself to the torch? Did they imagine they were striking a blow for freedom? Liberating themselves finally, after thousands of years of slavery, from the cruel grasp of the tyrannical overlords who had dropped down out of the stars to thrust their rule on them?

Well, yes, Joseph thought, that was surely what they believed they were doing. But what the Folk here had actually achieved was to destroy their own livelihoods: to wipe out in one brief orgy of blood and flame the fruits of centuries of careful planning and building. How would they support themselves now that the factories and mills were gone? Would they go back to tilling the soil as their ancestors had done before the first Masters arrived? If that was too much for them, they could simply scrabble in the woods for mud-crawlers and roots, as he himself had done not long before. Or would they just wander from province to province, begging their food from those who had not been so foolish as to torch their estates, or possibly just taking it from them? They had not given any thought to any of that. They had wanted only to overthrow their Masters, no doubt, but then when that was done they had been unable to halt their own juggernaut of destructiveness, and they had allowed it to go mindlessly on and on and on beyond that until they had completely broken, surely beyond any hope of repair, the very system that sustained their lives.

His four Indigenes stood to one side, silently watching him. Their slitted eyes and thin expressionless lips gave Joseph no clue to what they might be thinking. Perhaps they were thinking nothing at all: he had asked them to take him to this place, and they had done so, and here they were, and what one group of humans seemed to have done to the property of the other group of humans was no affair of theirs. They were waiting, he assumed, to find out what he wished them to do for him now, since it was plain that he would find nothing of any use to him here.

What *did* he want them to do for him now? What *could* they do for him now?

He moistened his lips and said, "What is the name of the next Great House to the south? How far is it from here?"

They made no reply. None of them reacted to

Joseph's question in any way. It was almost as though they had not understood his words.

"Ulvas? Cuithal?" He shot a direct glance at them this time, a Master's glance, and put a slight sharpness in his tone this time. For whatever that might be worth, a Master speaking to Indigenes, for whom his status as a Master very likely had no very important significance. Especially now, here, amid these ruins. But probably not under any other circumstances, either. Whatever respect for him they might have was founded on his deeds as a healer, not on the rank he might hold among humans.

This time, though, he got an answer, though not a satisfying one. It was Ulvas who spoke. "Master Joseph, we are not able to say."

"And why is that?"

"Because we do not know." This time the response came from Cuithal. "We know House Getfen to the north of us, beyond the forest. We know House Ludbrek to the south of us. Other than those two, we know nothing about the Great Houses. There has never been need for us to know."

That seemed plausible enough. Joseph could not claim any real skill in interpreting the shades of meaning in an Indigene's tone of voice, but there was no reason to think they would lie to him about a matter of mere fact, or, indeed, about anything whatever. And it might well be that if he got back into the wagon and asked them to take him on toward the south until they came to the domain of another Great House, they would do so.

The next House, though, might be hundreds of miles away. And might well turn out to be in the same sorry shape as this one. Joseph could not ask these Indigenes, however devoted to him they might be, to travel on and on and on with him indefinitely, taking him some unstipulated distance beyond from their own village in the pursuit of so dubious a quest. But the only other alternative, short of his continuing on alone through this wrecked and probably dangerous province, was to return to the village of the Indigenes, and what use was there in that? He had to keep on moving southward. He did not want to end his days serving as tribal witch-doctor to a village of Indigenes somewhere in High Manza.

They stood perfectly still, waiting for him to speak. But he did not know what to tell them. Suddenly he could not bear their silent stares. Perhaps he would do better going a short distance off to collect his thoughts. Their proximity was distracting. "Stay here," Joseph said, after a long uncomfortable moment. "I want to look around a bit."

"You do not want us to accompany you, Master Joseph?"

"No. Not now. Just stay here until I come back."

He turned away from them. The burned-out

manor-house lay about a hundred yards in front of him. He walked slowly toward it. It was a frightful thing to see. Was this what Getfen House looked like this morning? Keilloran House, even? It was painful just to draw a breath here. That bleak, stale, sour stink of extinct combustion, of ashes turned cold but still imbued with the sharp chemical odor of fast oxidation, jabbed at his nostrils with palpable force. Joseph imagined it coating his lungs with dark specks. He went past the gaping façade and found himself in the ash-choked ruins of a grand vestibule, with a series of even grander rooms opening before him, though they were only the jagged crusts of rooms now. He stood at the lip of a vast crater that might once have been a ballroom or a festival-hall. There was no way to proceed here, for the floor was mostly gone, and where it still remained the fallen timbers of the roof jutted upward before him, blocking the way. He had to move carefully, on account of his injured leg. Going around to the left, Joseph entered what might have been a servants' station, leading to a low-roofed room that from the looks of it had probably been a way-kitchen for the re-heating of dishes brought up from the main kitchens below. A hallway behind that took him to rooms of a grander nature, where blackened stone sculptures stood in alcoves and tattered tapestries dangled from the walls.

The splendor and richness of Ludbrek House was evident in every inch of the place, even now.

This chamber might have been a music room; this, a library; this long hall, a gallery of paintings. The destruction had been so monstrously thorough that very little was left of any of that. But also the very monstrosity of it numbed Joseph's mind to what he was seeing. One could not continue endlessly to react in shock to this. The capacity to react soon was exhausted. One could only, after a while, absorb it in a state of calm acceptance and even with a certain cool fascination, the sort of reaction one might have while visiting the excavated ruins of some city that had been buried by a flood of volcanic lava five thousand years before.

By one route and another, bypassing places where there had been serious structural collapses, Joseph came out at last on a broad flagstone terrace that looked down into the main garden of the estate. The garden had been laid out in a broad bowl-shaped depression that sloped gradually away toward a wooded zone beyond, and, to Joseph's surprise, it bore scarcely any trace of damage. The velvety lawns were green and unmarked. The avenues of shrubbery were intact. The marble fountains that flanked the long string of reflecting pools still were spouting, and the pools themselves gleamed like newly polished mirrors in the midday light. The winding pathways of crushed white stone were as neat as if gardeners had come out this very morning to tidy them. Perhaps, he thought, surprised at himself for being able to summon even an atom of playfulness amidst these terrible surroundings, it was the estate's gardeners who had organized the uprising here, and they had taken care to have the attack bypass the grounds to which they had devoted so much of their energy. But more probably it had simply been more effective to break into the manor-house from the opposite side.

He stood for a time clutching the cool marble rail of the terrace, looking out into the immaculate garden and trying to focus on the problems that now confronted him. But no answers came. He had come up north to Getfen House for what was supposed to be a happy coming-of-age trip, a southern boy learning new ways far from home, making new friends, subtly forging alliances that would stand him in good stead in his adult life ahead. It had all gone so well. The Getfens had gathered him in as though he were one of their own. Joseph had even quietly fallen in love, although he had kept all that very much to himself, with his beautiful gentle golden-haired cousin Kesti. Now Kesti and all the Getfens were dead; and here he was at Ludbrek House, where he had hoped he would find an exit from the tumult that had engulfed this land, and everything was ruined here too, and no exit was in sight. Truly a coming-of-age trip, Joseph thought. But not in any way that he had imagined it would be.

And then as he stood there pondering these things he thought he heard a sound down toward his left, a creaking board, perhaps, a thump or two, as if someone were moving around in one of the lower levels of the shattered building. Another thump. Another.

Joseph stiffened. Those unexpected creaks and thumps rose up over the icy deathly silence that prevailed here as conspicuously as though what he was hearing was the pounding of drums.

"Who is it?" he called instantly. "Who's there?" And regretted that at once. He realized that he had unthinkingly spoken in Master: an addlepated mistake, possibly a fatal one if that happened to be a rebel sentry who was marching around down there.

Quickly all was silent again.

Not a sentry, no. A straggler, he thought. A survivor. Perhaps even a fugitive like himself. It had to be. There were no rebels left here, or he would have caught sight of them by this time. They had done their work and they had moved on. If they were still here they would be openly patrolling the grounds, not skulking around in the cellars like that, and they would not recoil into instant wary silence at the sound of a human voice, either. A Master's voice at that. Rebels would be up here in a moment to see who was speaking.

So who was it, then? Joseph wondered if that could be one of the Ludbreks down there, someone who had managed to survive the massacre of his House and had been hiding here ever since.

Was that too wild a thing to consider? He had to know.

Checking it out alone and unarmed, though, was a crazy thing to do. Moving faster than was really good for his injured leg, he doubled back toward the front of the gutted house, following his own trail in the ashes. As he emerged from the vestibule he beckoned to the Indigenes, who were waiting where he had left them and did not seem to have moved at all in his absence. They were unarmed also, of course, and inherently peaceful people as well, but they had great physical strength and he was sure they would protect him if any kind of trouble should manifest itself.

"There's someone alive here, hidden away below the building," Joseph told them. "I heard the sounds he was making. Come help me find him."

They followed unquestioningly. He led them back through the dark immensities of the ruined house and out onto the terrace, and jabbed a pointing finger downward. "There," Joseph said. "Under the terrace."

A curving stone staircase linked the terrace to the garden. Joseph descended, with the Indigenes close behind. There was a whole warren of subterranean chambers beneath the terrace, he saw, that opened out onto the garden. Perhaps these rooms had been used for the storage of tables and utensils for the lawn parties that the Masters of

Ludbrek House had enjoyed in days gone by. They were mostly empty now. Joseph stared in.

"Over there, Master Joseph," Ulvas said.

The Indigene's eyesight was better adapted to darkness than his. Joseph saw nothing. But as he moved cautiously inward he heard a sound—a little shuffling sound, perhaps—and then a cough, and then a quavering voice was addressing him in a muddled mixture of Folkish and Master, imploring him to be merciful with a poor old man, begging him to show compassion: "I have committed no crimes. I have done nothing wrong, I promise you that. Do not hurt me, please. Please. Do not hurt me."

"Come out where I can see you," Joseph said, in Master.

Out of the musty darkness came a stooped slow-moving figure, an old man indeed, sixty or perhaps even seventy years old, dressed in rags, with coarse matted hair that had cobwebs in it, and great smudges of dirt on his face. Plainly he was of the Folk. He had the thick shoulders and deep chest of the Folk, and the broad wide-nostrilled nose, and the heavy jaw. He must have been very strong, once. A field-serf, Joseph supposed. His frame was still powerful. But now he looked haggard and feeble, his face grayish beneath all the dirt, his cheeks hanging in loose folds as though he had eaten nothing in days, dark shadows below his haunted red-streaked eyes. Blinking, trembling, terrified-looking, he advanced with uncertain wavering steps toward Joseph, halted a few feet away, sank slowly to his knees before him.

"Spare me!" he cried, looking down at Joseph's feet. "I am guilty of nothing! Nothing!"

"You are in no danger, old man. Look up at me. Yes, that's right. —I tell you, no harm will come to you."

"You are truly a Master?" the man asked, as though fearing that Joseph were some sort of apparition.

"Truly I am."

"You do not look like other Masters I have seen. But yet you speak their language. You have the bearing of a Master. Of which House are you, Master?"

"House Keilloran."

"House Keilloran," the old man repeated. He had obviously never heard the name before.

"It is in Helikis," said Joseph, still speaking in Master. "That is in the south." Then, this time using Folkish, he said: "Who are you, and what are you doing here?"

"I am Waerna of Ludbrek. This is my home."

"This is nobody's home now."

"Not now, no. Not any more. But I have never known any other. My home is here, Master. When the others left, I stayed behind, for where would I go? What would I do?" A distraught look came into the bloodshot brown eyes. "They killed all the Masters, do you know that, Master? I saw it happen. It was in the night. Master Vennek was the first to die, and then Master Huist, Master Seebod, Master Graene, and all the wives, and the children also. All of them. And even their dogs. The wives and children had to watch while they killed the men, and then they were killed too. It was Vaniye who did it. I heard him say, 'Kill them all, leave no Master alive.' Vaniye who was practically like a son to Master Vennek. They killed everyone with knives, and then they burned the bodies, and they burned the house also. And then they went away, but I stayed, for where would I go? This is my place. My wife is long dead. My daughter as well. I have no one. I could not leave. I am of Ludbrek House."

"Indeed you are all that remains of Ludbrek House," said Joseph, barely able to contain the sadness he felt.

The old man's teeth were chattering. He huddled miserably into himself and a great convulsive quiver went rippling through him. He must be right at the edge of starvation, Joseph thought. He asked the Indigenes to fetch some food for him. One of the two drivers went back to the wagon and returned with smoked meat, dried berries, a little flask of the milky-colored Indigene wine. Waerna contemplated the food with interest but also with a certain show of hesitation. Joseph thought it might be because Indigene food was unfamiliar to him, but that was not it at all: it was only that he had not eaten anything in so long that his stomach was rebelling at the mere idea of food. The old man nibbled at the fruit and took a tentative sip of the wine. After that it was easier, and he ate steadily, though not greedily, one bite after another until everything before him was gone.

Some color was returning to his cheeks, now. He seemed already to be regaining his strength. He looked up at Joseph and said, almost tearfully, "You are very kind, Master. I have never known Masters to be anything but kind. When they killed the Masters here, I felt as though they were ripping my own heart out of my body." And then, in a different tone, a new thought suddenly occurring: "But why are you here, Master? This is no place for you to visit. It is not safe for you, here."

"I am only passing through these parts. Traveling south, to my home in Helikis."

"But how will you do that? If they find you, they will kill you. They are killing Masters everywhere."

"Everywhere?" said Joseph, thinking of Keilloran.

"Everywhere. It was the plan, and now they have done it. The Masters of House Ludbrek and those of House Getfen and those of House Siembri for certain, and I heard House Fyelk also, and House Odum, and House Garn. It was the plan to rise up against all the Great Houses of Manza, and burn the buildings, and kill all the Masters.

As I saw done here. And they have done it, this I know. Dead, dead, everyone dead in all the Houses, or nearly so. Roads have been closed. Rebel patrols search for those who escaped the slaughter." Waerna was trembling again. He seemed on the verge of tears.

Joseph felt a sudden terrifying flood of despair himself. He had not left room in his spirit for this disappointment. Having from the beginning of his flight into the woods expected to find succor at Ludbrek House, an end to his solitary travail and the beginning of his return to his home and family, and discovering instead nothing but ashes and ruination and this shattered old man, he found himself struggling to maintain equilibrium in his soul. It was not easy. A vision rose before him of a chain of charred and desolate manor-houses stretching all the way south to the Isthmus, triumphant Folkish rebels controlling the roads everywhere, the last few surviving Masters hunted down one by one and given over to death.

He looked toward Ulvas and said, speaking in Indigene, "He tells me that all the Houses everywhere in Manza have been destroyed."

"Perhaps that is not so, Master Joseph," said the Indigene gently.

"But what if it is? What am I to do, if it is?" Joseph's voice sounded weirdly shrill in his own ears. For the moment he felt as helpless and forlorn as old Waerna. This was new to him, this weakness, this fear. He had not known that he was capable of such feelings. But of course he had never been tested in this way. "How will I manage? Where will I go?"

As soon as the shameful words had escaped his lips, Joseph wanted passionately to call them back. It was the first time since the night of the massacre at Getfen House that he had allowed any show of uncertainty over the ultimate success of his journey to break through into the open. "You must never deceive yourself about the difficulties you face," Balbus had often told him, "but neither should you let yourself be taken prisoner by fear." Joseph had known from the start that it would be no easy thing to find his way alone across this unfamiliar continent to safety, but he had been taught to meet each day's challenges as they arose, and so he had. Whenever doubts had begun to come drifting up out of the depths of his mind he had been able to shove them back. This time, confronted with the harsh reality of the gutted Ludbrek House, he had allowed them to master him, if only for a moment. But, he told himself sternly, he should never have let such thoughts take form in his mind in the first place, let alone voice them before Indigenes and a man of the Folk.

The moment passed. His outburst drew no response from the Indigenes. Perhaps they took his anguished questions as rhetorical ones, or else they simply had no answers for them.

Quickly Joseph felt his usual calmness and self-assurance return. All this, he thought, is part of my education, even when I let myself give way to the weakness that is within me. Everyone has some area of weakness within him somewhere. You must not let it rule you, that is all. What is happening here is that I am learning who I am.

But he understood now that he had to abandon hope, at least for the time being, of continuing onward to the south. Maybe Waerna was correct that all the Great Houses of Manza had fallen, maybe not; but either way he could not ask Ulvas and his companions to risk their lives transporting him any farther, nor did it seem to make much sense to set out from here by himself. Aside from all the other problems he might face as he made his way through the rebel-held territory to the south, his leg was not well enough healed yet for him to attempt the journey on his own. The only rational choice that was open to him was to go back to the Indigene village and use that as his base while trying to work out his next move.

He offered to take Waerna along with him. But the old man would not be removed from this place. Ludbrek House, or what was left of it, was his home. He had been born here, he said, and he would die here. There could be no life for him anywhere else.

Probably that was so, Joseph thought. He tried to imagine Waerna living among the rebels who had killed the Masters of this House, those Mas-

ters whom Waerna had so loved, and brought destruction to their properties, to the upkeep of
which Waerna had dedicated his whole life. No,
he thought, no, Waerna had done the right thing
in separating himself from those people. He was
Folk to the core, a loyal member of a system that
did not seem to exist anymore. Thustin had been
like that too. There was no place for the Waernas
and the Thustins in the strange new world that
the rebels were creating here in Manza.

Joseph gave Waerna as much food as Ulvas
thought they could spare, and embraced him
with such warmth and tenderness that the old
man looked up at him in disbelief. Then he set out
on his way back north. He would not let himself
dwell on the fact that every rotation of the
wagon-wheels was taking him farther from his
home. Probably it had been folly all along to
imagine that his journey from Getfen House to
Keilloran would be a simple straight-line affair
down the heart of Manza to Helikis.

The weather was starting to change, he saw, as
he headed back to the village: a coolish wind was
blowing out of the south, a sign that the rainy season was on its way.

Joseph wished he knew more of what to expect
of the weather of High Manza, now that there
was a real possibility that he might still be here as
winter arrived. How cold would it get? Would it
snow? He had never seen snow, only pictures of
it, and he was not particularly eager to make its

acquaintance just now. Well, he would find out, he supposed.

The Ardardin did not seem greatly surprised to see Joseph returning to the village. Surprise did not appear to be a characteristic that played a very important role in the emotional makeup of the Indigenes, or else Joseph simply did not know how they normally expressed it. But the matter-of-fact greeting that Joseph received from the Ardardin led him to think that the tribal leader might well have expected from the beginning to be seeing him again before long. He wondered just how much the Ardardin actually knew about the reach and success of the Folkish uprising.

The Ardardin did not ask him for details of his expedition to Ludbrek House. Nor did Joseph volunteer any, other than to say that he had found no one at Ludbrek House who could give him any assistance. He did not feel like being more specific with the Indigene chieftain. For the moment it was all too painful to speak about. Ulvas and the others who had accompanied him would surely provide the Ardardin with details of the destruction.

Once he was established again in the room that had been his before, Joseph tried once more to make contact via combinant with Keilloran. He had no more hope of success than before, but the sight of devastated Ludbrek had kindled a fierce desire in him to discover what, if anything, had been taking place on the other continent and to let his family know that he had not perished in the uprising that had broken out in Manza.

This time the device produced a strange sputtering sound and a dim pink glow. Neither of these was in any way a normal effect. But at least the combinant was producing something, now, whereas it had done nothing whatever since the night of the burning of Getfen House. Perhaps some part of the system was working again.

He said, "I am Joseph Master Keilloran, and I am calling my father, Martin Master Keilloran of House Keilloran in Helikis." If the combinant was working properly, that statement alone would suffice to connect him instantly. He stared urgently into the pink glow, wishing that he were seeing the familiar blue of a functioning combinant instead. "Father, can you hear me? This is Joseph. I am somewhere in High Manza, Father, a hundred miles or so south of Getfen House."

He paused, hoping for a reply.

Nothing. Nothing.

"They have killed everyone in Getfen House, and in other Houses too. I have been to Ludbrek House, which is south of the Getfen lands, and everything is in ruins there. An old serf told me that all the Ludbreks are dead. —Do you hear me, Father?"

Useless pink glow. Sputtering hissing sound.

"I want to tell you, Father, that I am all right. I hurt my leg in the forest but it's healing nicely now, and the Indigenes are looking after me. I'm staying in the first Indigene village due south of the Getfens. When my leg is better, I'm going to start out for home again, and I hope to see you very soon. Please try to reply to me. Please keep trying every day."

The thought came to him then that what he had just said could have been very rash, that perhaps the combinant system of Manza was in rebel hands, in which case they might have intercepted his call and possibly could trace it to this very village. In that case he could very well have doomed himself just now.

That was a chilling thought. It was becoming a bad habit of his, he saw, to speak without fully thinking through all consequences of his words. But, once again, there was no way he could unsay what he had just said. And maybe this enterprise of his, this immense trek across Manza, was doomed to end in failure sooner or later anyway, in which case what difference did it make that he might have just called the rebels down upon himself? At least there was a chance that the call would go through to Keilloran, that his words would reach his father and provide him with some comfort. The message might even set in motion the forces of rescue. It was a risk worth taking, he decided.

He undid his bandages and examined his leg. It still looked bad. The swelling had gone down, and the bruises had diminished considerably, the angry zones of purplish-black now a milder mottling of brownish-yellow. But when he sat on the edge of his bed of furs and swung the leg carefully back and forth, his knee made a disagreeable little clicking sound and hot billows of pain went shooting along his thigh. Perhaps there was no permanent damage but he was scarcely in shape for a long trek on his own yet.

Joseph asked for a basin of water and washed the leg thoroughly. Ulvas provided him with a fresh length of cloth so that he could bandage it again.

For the next few days they left him largely to his own devices. The faithful Ulvas brought him food regularly, but he had no other visitors. Now and then village children gathered in the hall outside the open door of his room and studied him intently, as though he were some museum exhibit or perhaps a sideshow freak. They never said a word. There was a flinty steadfast intensity to their little slitted eyes. When Joseph tried to speak with them, they turned and ran.

He resumed his studies, finally, after the long interruption, calling up his geography text and searching it for information about the climate and landscape of the continent of Manza, and then going into his history book to read once again the account of the Conquest. It was important to him now to understand why the Folk had suddenly turned with such violence against their overlords, after so many centuries of years of quiescent acceptance of Master rule.

But the textbook offered him no real guidance. All it contained was the traditional account, telling how the Folk had come to Homeworld in the early days of the colonization of the worlds of space and taken up a simple life of farming, which had degenerated after a couple of centuries into a bare subsistence existence because they were a dull, backward people who lacked the technical skills to exploit the soil and water of their adopted world properly. At least they were intelligent enough to understand that they needed help, though, and after a time they had invited people of the Master stock here to show them how to do things better, just a few Masters at first, but those had summoned others, and then, as the steadily increasing Masters began to explain to the Folk that there could be no real prosperity here unless the Folk allowed the Masters to take control of the means of production and put everything on a properly businesslike basis, a couple of hotheaded leaders appeared among the Folk and resistance broke out against Master influence, which led to the brief, bloody war known as the Conquest. That was the only instance in all of Homeworld's history, said the textbook, of friction between Folk and Masters. Once it was over the relationship between the two peoples settled into a stable and harmonious rhythm, each group understanding its place and playing its proper role in the life of the planet, and that was how things had remained for a very long time. Until, in fact, the outbreak of the current uprising.

Joseph understood why a truly dynamic, ambitious race would object to being conquered that way. He could not imagine the Masters, say, ever accepting the rule of invaders from space: they would fight on and on until all Homeworld was stained with blood, as it was said had happened in the time of the empires of Old Earth. But the Folk were in no way dynamic or ambitious. Before the Masters came, they had been slipping back into an almost prehistoric kind of life here. Under the rule of the Masters they were far more prosperous than they could ever have become on their own. And it was not as though they were slaves, after all. They had full rights and privileges. No one forced them to do anything. It was to their great benefit, as well as the Masters', for them to perform the tasks that were allotted them in the farms and factories. Master and Folk worked together for the common good: Joseph had heard his father say that a thousand times. He believed it. Every Master did. So far as Joseph knew, the Folk believed it too.

Because the system had always seemed to work so well, Joseph had never had any reason to look upon his own people as oppressors, or on the Folk as victims of aggression. Now, though, the system was not working at all. Joseph wished he could discuss the recent events in Manza with Balbus. Were the rebels mere brutal killers, or could there be some substance to their resentments? Joseph could see no justification, ever, for killing and burning, but from the rebels' point of view those things might well have seemed necessary. He did not know. He had lived too sheltered a life; he had never had occasion to question any of its basic assumptions. But now, suddenly, everything was called into question. *Everything.* He was too young and inexperienced to wrestle with these problems on his own. He needed someone older, someone with more perspective, with whom to discuss them. Someone like Balbus, yes. But Balbus was gone.

Unexpectedly Joseph found himself drifting, a few days later, into a series of conversations with the Ardardin that reminded him of his discussions with his late tutor. The Ardardin had taken to visiting him often in the afternoons. Now that Joseph had taken up residence in the village once more, his services as a healer were needed again, and the Ardardin would come to him and conduct him to the village infirmary, where some villager with a running sore, or a throbbing pain in his head, or a mysterious swelling on his thigh would be waiting for Joseph to cure him.

Joseph did not even try to struggle against his unwanted role as a healer now. It no longer embarrassed him to be engaging in such pretense. If that was the role they wanted him to play, why, he would play it as well as he could, and do it with a straight face. For one thing, his ministrations often seemed to bring about cures, even though he had only the most rudimentary of medical technique and no real notion of how to cope with most of the ailments that were presented to him. These Indigenes appeared to be a suggestible people. They had such faith in his skills that a mere laying on of hands, a mere murmuring of words, frequently did the job. He became accustomed to seeing such inexplicable things happen. That did not instill in him any belief in his own magical powers, only an awareness that faith could sometimes work miracles regardless of the cynicism of the miracle-worker. And his magical cures justified his presence among them in his own eyes. He was eating these people's food and taking up space in their village as he hobbled around waiting for his leg to heal. The least he could do for them was to give them succor for their ills, so long as they felt that such succor was within his power to give. What he had to watch out for was beginning to believe in the reality of his own powers.

Another thing that troubled him occasionally was the possibility that his medical services were becoming of such value to the villagers that they would keep him among them even after he was strong enough to get on his way. They had no reason to care whether he ever returned to his home or not, and every reason to want to maintain him in their midst forever.

That was not a problem he needed to deal with

now. Meanwhile he was making himself of use here; he was performing a worthwhile function, and that was no trivial thing. The whole purpose of this trip to the northern continent had been to prepare him for the tasks that someday would be his as Master of House Keilloran, and, though his father certainly had not ever imagined that ministering to the medical needs of a village of Indigenes would be part of that preparation, it was clear enough to Joseph that that was something entirely appropriate for a Master-in-the-making to undertake. He would not shirk his responsibilities here. Especially not for such an unworthy reason. The Indigenes would let him go, he was sure, when the time came.

The more doctoring he did, the more adventuresome he became about the things he would try that could be regarded by him as genuine medicine, and not just mere faith-healing. Joseph did not feel ready to perform any kind of major surgery, and did not ever think he would be; but, using the few simple tools he found in his utility case, he started stitching up minor wounds, now, and lancing infections, and pulling decayed teeth. One thing he feared was that they would ask him to deliver a child, a task for which he lacked even the most basic knowledge. But they never did. Whatever process it was by which these people brought their young in the world continued to be a mystery to him.

He began to learn something about Indigene

herbal medicine, also, and used it to supplement the kind of work he was already doing. It puzzled him that the Indigenes should have developed the use of such a wide range of drugs and potions without also having managed to invent even the simplest of mechanical medical techniques. They could not do surgery, they could not suture a wound, they could not set a fracture. But they had succeeded in finding natural medicines capable of reducing fever, of easing pain, of unblocking a jammed digestive tract, and much more of that sort. Their ignorance of the mechanical side of medicine, amounting almost to indifference, was one more example, Joseph thought, of their alien nature. They are simply not like us. Not just their bodies are different, but their minds.

His instructor in the use of Indigene herbs was a certain Thiyu, the village's master in this art. Joseph never found out whether Thiyu was male or female, but it was certain, at least, that Thiyu was *old*. You could see that in the faded tone of Thiyu's bronze skin, from which all the orange highlights had disappeared, and from the slack, puffy look of Thiyu's throat-pouch, which seemed to have lost the capacity to inflate. And Thiyu's voice was thin and frayed, like a delicate cord just at the verge of snapping in two.

In Thiyu's hut behind the infirmary were a hundred different identical-looking ceramic jars, all of them unmarked, each containing a different powder or juice that Thiyu had extracted from some native plant. How the Indigene knew what drug was contained in which jar was something Joseph never understood. He would describe to Thiyu the case he was currently working on, and Thiyu would go to the collection of jars and locate an appropriate medicine for him, and that was that.

Aware that knowledge of these drugs was valuable, Joseph made a point of asking Thiyu the name of each one used, and its properties, and a description of the plant from which it was derived. He carefully wrote all these things down. Bringing this information to his fellow Masters, if ever he returned to his own people again, would be part of the service that a Master must render to the world. Had any Master ever bothered, he wondered, to study Indigene medicine before?

He and Thiyu never spoke of anything but herbs and potions, and that only in the briefest possible terms. There was no conversation between them. Nor was there with any of the others, not even Ulvas. The Ardardin was the only Indigene in the village with whom Joseph had anything like a friendship. After Joseph had done his day's work in the infirmary the Ardardin often would accompany him back to his room, and gradually it fell into the habit of remaining for a while to talk with him.

The themes were wide-ranging, though always superficial. They would speak of Helikis, a place about which the Ardardin seemed to know almost nothing, or about the problems the Ardardin's people had had this summer with their crops, or the work Joseph was doing in the infirmary, or the improving condition of his leg, or the weather, or the sighting of some rarely seen wild animal in the vicinity of the village, but never about anything that had to do with Indigene-human relationships, or the civil war now going on between Masters and Folk. The Ardardin set the pace, and Joseph very swiftly saw which kinds of topics were appropriate and which were out of bounds.

The Ardardin seemed to enjoy these talks, to get definite pleasure from them, as though it had long been starved for intelligent company in this village before Joseph's arrival. Joseph was surprised to find that they were talking as equals, in a sense, sitting face to face and exchanging ideas and information on a one-to-one basis, although he was only a half-grown fugitive boy and the Ardardin was a person of stature and authority, the leader of the village. But maybe the Ardardin did not realize how young Joseph really was. Of course, Joseph was a Master, a person of rank among his own people, the heir to a great estate somewhere far away. But there was no reason why the Ardardin would be impressed by that. Was it that he was functioning as the tribal doctor? Maybe. More likely, though, the Ardardin was simply extending to him the courtesy that it felt one adult intelligent creature owed another.

There was, at any rate, a certain sense of equality for Joseph in their talks. He found it flattering. No one had ever spoken to Joseph in that way before. He took it as a high compliment.

Then the nature of his conversations with the Ardardin began to change. It was an almost imperceptible transformation. Joseph could not say how the change began, nor why the talks now became fixed on a single daily subject, which was the religious beliefs of the Indigenes and the light that those beliefs cast on the ultimate destiny of all the creatures of Homeworld. The result was a distinct alteration of the parity of the meetings. Now, once more, Joseph was back in the familiar role of the student listening to the master. Though the Ardardin seemed to be treating him as a scholar seeking information, not as a novice stumbling about in the darkness of his own ignorance, Joseph had no illusions about the modification of their relationship.

Perhaps it was a reference that the Ardardin made one afternoon to "the visible sky" and "the real sky" that had started it.

"But the visible sky *is* the real sky," said Joseph, mystified. "Is that not so?"

"Ah," said the Ardardin. "The sky that we see is a trivial simple thing. What has true meaning is the sky beyond it, the sky of the gods, the celestial sky."

Joseph had problems in following this. He was fluent enough in Indigene, but the abstract concepts that the Ardardin was dealing in now involved him in a lot of new terminology, ideas that he had never had to deal with before, and as the discussion unfolded he had to ask for frequent clarifications. Bit by bit he grasped the distinction that the Ardardin was making: the universe of visible phenomena on the one hand, and the much more significant universe of celestial forces, where the gods dwelled, on the other. It was the gods who dwelled in the *real* sky, the one that could not be seen by mortal eyes, but that generated the power by which the universe was held together.

That the Indigenes should have gods came as no surprise to Joseph. *All* peoples had gods of some sort. But he knew nothing whatever about theirs. No texts of Indigene mythology had ever come his way. In Keilloran there were Indigenes living all around; you constantly encountered them; and yet, Joseph saw now, they were so much taken for granted as part of the landscape that he had never paid any real attention to them, other than to learn the language, which was something that every Master was required to do. His father collected their artifacts, yes. But you could fill entire storehouses with pots and sculptures and weavings and still not know anything about a *people's* soul. And though Balbus had said that Martin had studied Indigene philosophy as well, he had never shared a syllable of his findings with his son.

Joseph strained to penetrate the mysteries that the Ardardin was expounding now, wondering whether these were the things that his father supposedly had studied. Perhaps not. Perhaps they had never been shared with a person of human blood before.

The world that surrounds us, the Ardardin said, its mountains and seas and rivers and forests, its cities and fields, its every tangible aspect, is the terrestrial counterpart of the celestial world in the sky. That world is the world of the gods, the *true* world, of which the world of living beings was a mere pallid imitation. Everything we see about us, said the Ardardin, represents the crude attempts of mortal beings to replicate the gods' own primordial act of creating their own world.

"Do you follow?" the Ardardin said.

"Not exactly," said Joseph.

The Ardardin did not appear troubled by that. It went on speaking of things that were completely new to Joseph, the sacred mountain at the center of the world where the visible world and the invisible one come together, the axis upon which all things spin, the place where mundane time and mythical time meet, which is the navel of the world. The distinction between the time-scheme of living things and the time-scheme of the gods, worldly time and godly time, was obviously very important to the Indigenes. The Ardardin made it seem as though the world of ordinary phenomena was a mere film, an overlay, a stencil, a shallow and trivial thing although linked by the most powerful bonds to the divine world where fundamental reality dwelled.

All this was fascinating in its way, though Joseph's mind did not ordinarily tend to go in these metaphysical directions. There was a certain strange beauty to it, the way a mathematical theorem has great beauty even if you could not see any way of putting it to practical use. After each conversation with the Ardardin he would dictate notes into his recorder, setting down all that he had been told while it was still fresh in his mind. By so doing he reinforced in his own mind the belief that he would somehow get out of Manza alive, that he would return to Helikis and share with others the remarkable fund of alien knowledge that he had brought back with him.

Even the most abstruse mathematical theorem, Joseph knew, represents one valid way of describing the universe, at least to those capable of comprehending it. But Joseph could not help looking upon what the Ardardin was telling him as a mere collection of fables, quaint primitive myths. One could admire them but on a fundamental level one could not believe them, certainly not in the way one believes that seven and six are thirteen, or that the square on the hypotenuse equals the sum of the squares on the other two sides. Those things were inherently, incontrovertibly true. The tales the Ardardin told were metaphors, ingenious inventions. They described nothing real. That did not make them any the less interesting, Joseph felt. But they had no relevance to him, so far as he could see, other than as curiosities of an alien civilization.

His talks with the Ardardin had gone on nearly a week before the Indigene abruptly stepped behind the legends and drew the astonished Joseph into the entirely unexpected realm of political reality.

"Your people call yourselves Masters," the Ardardin said. "Why is that? What is it that you are masters of?"

Joseph hesitated. "Why, the world," he replied. "This world, I mean. To use your terms, the *visible* world."

"Very good, yes. Masters of the visible world. Do you see, though, that to be masters of the visible world is a thing that has very little actual importance?"

"To us it does," said Joseph.

"To you, yes. But not to us, for the visible world itself is nothing, so what value is there in being masters of it? I mean no discourtesy here. I wish only to put before you something that I believe you should consider, which is that *your people do not hold possession of anything real*. You call yourself Masters, but in truth you are masters of nothing. Certainly not *our* masters; and from the way things seem, perhaps not even the masters of the people you call the Folk, any more. I cannot speak

of those people. But to us, Master Joseph, you
Masters have never had any significant existence
at all."

Joseph was lost. "Our cities—our roads—"

"Visible things. Temporary things. Not godly
things. Not truly real."

"What about the work I do in the infirmary?
People are sick. Their pain is real, would you not
say? I touch a sick person with my hands, and
that person gets better. Isn't that real? Is it only
some kind of illusion?"

"It is a secondary kind of reality," said the Ardardin. "We live in the true reality here. The reality of the gods."

Joseph's head was swimming. He remembered
Balbus telling him that there was something in
the Indigene religion that had allowed them to regard the presence of human settlers among them
as completely unimportant—as though Masters
and Folk had never come here in the first place.
They simply shrugged it off. It seemed clear that
the Ardardin was approaching that area of dis-
course now. But without Balbus, he was lost.
These abstractions were beyond him.

The Ardardin said, "I do not mean to minimize
the things you have done for us since your arrival
in our village. As for your people, it is true that
they seem to have the powers of gods. You fly between the stars like gods. You came down like
gods among us out of the heavens. You talk
across great distances, which seems magical to us.

You build cities and roads with the greatest of ease. You have ways of healing that are unknown to us. Yes, the things that you Masters have achieved on our world are great things indeed, in their way. You could have every reason to think of yourselves as gods. But even if you do—and I don't say that that is so—do you think that this is the first time that gods, or beings like gods, have come among us?"

Bewildered, Joseph said, "Other visitors from space, you mean?"

"From the heavens," said the Ardardin. "From the sky beyond the sky, the celestial sky, the true sky that is forever beyond our reach. In the early days of time they came down to us, minor gods, teaching-gods, the ones who showed us how to construct our houses and plant our crops and make tools and utensils."

"Yes. Culture-heroes, we call them."

"They did their work, and then they went away. They were only temporary gods, subordinate gods. The true gods of the celestial sky are the only enduring gods, and they do not allow us to see them. Whenever it is necessary to do so, the high gods send these subordinate gods to us to reveal godly ways to us. We do not confuse these gods with the real ones. What these lesser gods do is imitate the things the high gods do in the world that we are unable to see, and, where it is suitable, we learn those things themselves by imitating the lesser gods that imitate the greater ones. You who call yourselves Masters: you are just the latest of these emissaries from the high gods. Not the first. Not the last."

Joseph's eyes widened. "You see us as no more than a short-term phenomenon, then?"

"How can you be anything else? It is the way of the world. You will be here for a time and then you will pass from the scene, as other gods like you have done before you. For only the true gods are eternal. Do you begin to see, Master Joseph? Do you start to understand?"

"Yes. Yes, I think I do."

It was like a great door swinging open before him.

Now he comprehended the passivity of the Indigenes, their seeming indifference to the arrival of the Masters, and of the Folk before them. We do not matter to them, except insofar as we reflect the will of the gods. We are only shadows of the true reality, he thought. We are only transient reflections of the true gods. This is our little moment on this planet, and when it is over we will pass from the scene, and the Indigenes will remain, and the eternal gods in their heaven will remain as well.

Our time may be passing already, Joseph thought, seeing the blackened ruins of Ludbrek House rising before him in his mind. And he shivered.

"So the fact that we came down among you and took control of great sectors of your world and built our dams and our highways and all the rest is entirely unimportant to you," he said. "We don't matter to you in any way. Is that it?"

"You misunderstand, Master Joseph. Whatever the gods see fit to do is important to us. They have sent you to us for a purpose, though what that purpose is has not yet been made clear. You have done many good things, you have done some bad things, and it is up to us to discern the meaning of your presence on our world. Which we will do. We watch; we wait; we learn. And one day we will know why it was that you were sent to us."

"But we'll be gone by then."

"Surely so. Your cycle will have ended."

"Our cycle?"

"The world passes through a series of cycles. Each follows the last in a predetermined order. We are living now in a period of destruction, of disintegration. It will grow worse. We see the signs already. As the end of the cycle comes upon us, the year will be shortened, the month will diminish, and the day will contract. There will be darkness and fire; and then will come rebirth, a new dawn, the start of the new cycle."

This was more than indifference, Joseph realized.

This was a supremely confident dismissal of all the little petty pretensions of his people. Masters, indeed! To the Indigenes, Joseph saw, nothing mattered on this world except the Indigenes themselves, whose gods lay hidden in an invisible sky and comported themselves in altogether mysterious ways. The humans who had taken so much of this people's land were just one more passing nuisance, a kind of annoying natural phenomenon, comparable to a sandstorm, a flood, a shower of hail. We think we have been building a new civilization here, he thought. We try to behave kindly toward the Indigenes, but we look upon this planet as ours, now, no longer theirs: our Homeworld, we call it. Wrong. In the eyes of the Ardardin and his race we are a mere short-term phenomenon. We are instruments of their unknown gods, sent here to serve *their* needs, not our own.

Strange. Strange. Joseph wondered whether he would be able to explain any of this to his father, if ever he saw Keilloran House again.

He could not allow himself the luxury of these discursive conversations much longer, though. It was time to begin thinking seriously again of moving on toward the south. His leg was nearly back to normal. And, though it was pleasant enough to be living in this friendly village and engaging in fine philosophical discussions with its chieftain, he knew he must not let himself be deflected from his essential purpose, which was to get home.

The situation beyond the boundaries of the Ardardin's village was continuing to worsen, apparently. Indigenes from other villages passed through here often, bringing reports on the troubles outside. Joseph never had the opportunity to speak with these visitors himself, but from the Ardardin he learned that all Manza had by now turned into a war zone: a great many Houses of the Masters throughout the northern continent had been destroyed, roads were closed, rebel troops were on the march everywhere. It appeared also that in certain parts of the continent the Masters were counterattacking, although that was still unclear. Joseph got the impression that fighting was going on between different groups of Folk, too, some loyal to the Masters, others sworn to uphold the rebellion. And bands of refugees were straggling south in an attempt to reach the Isthmus of Helikis and the safety that lay beyond. These must be surviving Masters, Joseph thought. But the Ardardin could not say. It had not seen a need to go into such a degree of detail with its informants.

None of this chaos seemed to cause much of a problem for the Indigenes themselves. By now Joseph had come to see how completely their lives were bound up in their villages, and in the tenuous ties that linked one village to the next. So long as nobody's troops came swarming across their fields and their harvests went well, the struggles of Masters and Folk were matters of little import to them. His discussions with the Ardardin had made it clear to him why they had that attitude.

Commerce between the Indigene villages, therefore, still was proceeding as though nothing unusual were going on. The Ardardin proposed to turn that fact to Joseph's benefit. Other villages down the line would surely have need of Joseph's services as a healer. Now that he was capable of traveling, they would convey him to one of the nearby villages, where he could take care of whatever medical problems might need his attention there, and then those villagers would take him on to the next village, and so on and so on until he had reached a point from which he could cross over into the safety of Helikis.

Joseph, remembering his fears that the Ardardin's people might not allow him to leave at all, felt a burst of chagrin, and gratitude also for the Ardardin's kind willingness to help him along his way like this.

But it occurred to him that it might be just as wrong to imagine kindness here as it had been to fear enslavement earlier. It was a mistake, he realized, to ascribe conventional human feelings—altruism, selfishness, whatever—to Indigenes, indeed to interpret their motivations in any way analogous to human thinking. He had been guilty of that again and again in his dealings with the Ardardin and the villagers, but he knew by this time that it was something to avoid. They were alien beings. They had followed a wholly different evolutionary path for millions of years. They walk on their hind legs like us, he thought, and they have a language with nouns and verbs in it, and they know how to plant and harvest crops and fashion pottery, but that did not make them human in any essential way, and one had best take them on their own terms or else not try to take them at all.

He had another taste of that when it was time for him to go. He had imagined that there might be a fairly emotional farewell, but the silliness of that bit of self-deception quickly became evident. The Ardardin expressed no regret whatever at Joseph's departure and no hint that any sort of friendship had sprung up between the two of them: not a syllable of thanks for his work in the infirmary, none for their afternoon conversations. It simply stood looking on in silence while Joseph climbed into the wagon that would take him once again toward the south, and when the wagon pulled out of the village compound the Ardardin turned and went inside, and that was as much of a farewell as Joseph had.

They are not like us, Joseph thought. To them we are mere transient phenomena.

three _____

ONCE MORE HE RODE IN A WAGON DRAWN BY A TEAM of dull-eyed yaramirs, and once more Ulvas traveled with him, along with two other Indigenes whose names were Casqui and Paca. Joseph had no idea of the route he would be traveling now. There did not seem to be any word in Indigene for "map," and the Ardardin had not offered him much verbal information about the location of the next Indigene village.

The first part of the journey took him along the same slow, winding road, cobblestoned and narrow, that they had used in the trip to Ludbrek House. An old Indigene road, no doubt. *Very* old. Five thousand years? Ten thousand, even? It was suitable only for clumsy creaking wagons like this. In all the centuries and tens of centuries since this road had been built, probably nothing in it had been changed but for the replacement of a loose cobble every once in a while. It was just a quiet country road; the Indigenes had never seen any reason to transform it into a major highway.

It occurred to him that for the Indigenes time must seem to stand virtually still. They looked at everything under the auspices of eternity, the invisible sky, the hidden gods. Their gods were not much interested in change, and therefore neither were they. They made even a sleepy people like the Folk seem ferociously energetic. And the Folk themselves, he thought grimly, were not behaving all that sleepily these days.

As on his previous journey, a cool southern wind was blowing, stronger than it had been before and moist now, an unmistakable token of the coming rainy season that was still somewhere to the south of them but already sending its harbingers north. It never seemed to let up. Joseph turned sideways in the wagon to avoid its unending direct thrust.

The second day of plodding travel found them still moving along the road that led toward Ludbrek House. Joseph hoped they were not going to take him back there. He had no desire to see that sad ravaged place again. But that afternoon a second road appeared to their left, a road just as humble as the one they had been on, and the wagondriver Casqui swung the vehicle onto it with a couple of sharp syllables to the yaramirs.

Though their direction was easterly now rather than southerly, the countryside had not changed much. It was the same flat farmland as before, broken only by gently rolling meadows and, farther away, the purple humps of modest hills.

In late afternoon a big modern highway came into sight in the distance. It ran from north to south and thus lay squarely athwart their route. "Get under the furs," Ulvas told him. "Sometimes now they check the wagons that go by."

"Who does?" Joseph asked. "Masters, or Folk?"

Ulvas made the crossed-arms gesture, the Indigene shrug. "Whoever might be checking things that day. It does not matter, does it?"

The Indigene road, Joseph saw, ran right up to the great highway that the Masters had designed and the Folk had constructed. It halted at the edge of the highway and, he assumed, resumed on the other side. The broad smooth road was like a wall cutting across the land, marking a place where the native culture of this world and the culture of the Masters met. What had the Indigenes thought when these highways began sprouting on their land? Nothing at all, replied Joseph to his own question. Nothing at all. The highways meant nothing to them; the Masters meant nothing to them; this world itself meant nothing to them. This world was only a film lying over the invisible world that was true reality.

Trucks, big trucks newly repainted in drab

military-looking colors, were moving at a brisk pace in both directions on the highway. Rebel trucks, most likely. There were not enough Masters in this whole continent to staff a real army. The much more numerous Folk seemed to have conjured one up and equipped it with all the industrial and commercial vehicles in Manza, though. Just as he had on his first day in the Getfen forest, Joseph trembled at the thought that the rebels—the Folk, the supposedly obtuse and doltish Folk—had been able very quietly to plan this formidable insurrection and put it into operation while the vastly superior intellects of the dominant Masters had somehow failed to detect that anything unusual was going on. And he wondered for what grim purpose it was that this roaring convoy of trucks was heading across the land.

An overpass spanned the highway here to handle cross-traffic like this Indigene wagon. Joseph nestled down beneath the thick stack of sour-smelling furs in the back of the wagon, and Ulvas tucked them around him to hide him from view. He would not have thought a pile of furs could have so much weight. They pressed down hard against him, and the one nearest to his face was jammed against his mouth and nostrils so closely that he gagged at the stale leathery odor of its underside. Getting sufficient air to breathe was no simple trick, either. He wondered how long the highway crossing was going to take. Another minute or two and he would have no choice but to stick his head out for a gulp of air, and it would be unfortunate to find himself staring at a rebel crossing-guard when he did.

But the wagon quickly descended the sloping overpass, and on the far side, once it was toiling away on the cobblestones of the Indigene road again, Ulvas pulled the furs from him. None too soon it was, either. Joseph was just about at the point of nausea.

"How much longer to the village?" he asked.

"Soon. Soon."

That could mean anything: an hour, a day, a month. Twilight was coming on. He saw lights in the distance, and hoped they were the lights of the village; but then, in another few moments, he was dismayed to realize that what he was seeing were the lights of more trucks moving along yet another highway.

How could they have come to another highway so soon, though? This one was just as big as the last, and, like the last one, ran at right angles to their own route. In this thinly populated countryside there was no reason to build two such highways running on parallel courses such a short distance apart.

Nor had any such thing been done, Joseph realized moments later. The markings told him that this was the same highway as before, that the Indigene road must have gone wandering around this way and that and now was crossing the highway for a second time, in some other place. He could see from the deepening darkness to his right that they had returned to a southerly route. Once again Ulvas hastened to pull the stack of hides over him.

But this time there was a checkpoint of some sort at the approach to the overpass. The wagon came to a halt; Joseph heard muffled voices somewhere above him, discussing something in a language that sounded like a mixture of Folkish and Indigene, though through the pile of furs he could not make out more than an occasional individual word; and then came the unmistakable sound of booted feet very close by. They were inspecting the wagon, it seemed. Yes. Yes.

Why, he wondered, would anyone, rebel or Master, feel the need to search an Indigene wagon? Certainly anyone who had much knowledge of Indigenes would have little reason to think that the aloof, indifferent Indigenes would get so involved in human affairs as to be transporting anything that might be of interest to one set of combatants or the other.

Joseph lay absolutely motionless. He debated trying to hold his breath to keep from giving his presence away, and decided that that was a bad idea, that it would lead inevitably to the need to suck air into his lungs, which might reveal his presence under here, or else to make him cough, which certainly would. It seemed wiser to take very small, shallow breaths, just enough to keep himself supplied with oxygen. The horrible reek of the furs was another problem: he fought against the nausea, gagging. He bit down hard on his lip and tried not to notice the smell.

Someone was thumping around out there, poking this, checking that.

What if they pulled the hides off and found him lying there? How long would it take for them to identify him as a fugitive Master, and what was likely to happen to a Master, even one from the other continent, who fell into rebel hands?

But the thumping stopped. The voices faded. The wagon began to roll once more.

What seemed like ten years went by before Ulvas pulled the furs off him again. Night had fallen. Stars were glistening everywhere. Two moons were in the sky, the little ones, Mebriel and Keviel. He heard the sounds of the busy highway, growing faint now, somewhere behind him.

"What happened?" Joseph asked. "What did they want? Were they looking for refugees?"

"They were looking for wine," Ulvas told him. "They thought we might be carrying that as our cargo and they wanted some. The nights are becoming long this time of year and the soldiers at the checkpoints become bored."

"Wine," Joseph said. "Wine!" A flood of relief came over him and he broke into laughter.

The wagon continued onward until the highway sounds could no longer be heard. Then they halted and camped for the night, and one of the wagondrivers prepared a meal for them. Afterward Joseph tried to sleep, but he was too keyed up to manage it, and eventually he abandoned the attempt.

For hours he lay staring upward, studying the stars. It was a clear night, the constellations sharply delineated. He picked out the Hammer, the Whirlwind, the Mountain, the Axe. There was the Goddess plainly visible, her long flowing hair, her breasts, her broad dazzling hips, the bright triangle of stars that marked her loins. Joseph remembered the night his father first had showed her to him, the naked woman in the sky. It is something a man likes to show his son when his son reaches a certain age, his father had said. Joseph had been twelve, then. He had seen real naked women since then, once in a while, not often and usually not at very close range. They always were fascinating sights, although for him they could not begin to equal the voluptuousness of the starry goddess overhead, whose magnificent overflowing body spanned so many parsecs of the sky.

He wondered whether he would ever hold a woman in his arms, whether he would ever do with her the things that men did with women.

Certainly the opportunity for that had been there for him already if he had wanted it. None of the Folkish girls of the House would have dared refuse a young Master. But Joseph had not wanted to do it with a girl of the Folk. It would be too easy. There seemed something wrong about it, something cheap and brutal and cruel. Besides, it was said that all the Folkish girls began to make love when they were eleven or twelve, and thus he would be matching his innocence against some girl's vast experience, which might lead to embarrassment for him and perhaps even for her. As for girls of his own kind, no doubt there had been plenty of those around the estate too who would have been willing, certain flirtatious friends of his sister's, or Anceph's pretty daughter, or the long-legged red-haired one, Balbus's niece. And at Getfen House he knew he had entertained fantasies of embracing Kesti, although he knew the dangers that could come from an attempt by the son of the Master of one Great House to enter into a casual affair with the daughter of the Master of another.

He did not want a casual affair, anyway. He was not sure what he did want. Some sort of fastidiousness within him had held him back from doing anything with any girl. There would always be plenty of time for that, he had thought.

Now he could no longer be sure of any such thing. He might have died this very night, if the rebel officer searching the wagon for Indigene wine had found a hidden Master instead.

He lay looking straight up at the Goddess, and imagined himself reaching into the sky and putting his hands over her breasts. The thought brought a smile to his lips. And then the third

moon moved into view, big ruddy Sanivark, and
the Goddess could no longer be seen. Joseph
dozed then, and soon morning came, and they
made a quick breakfast of dried meat and berries
and moved along.

The landscape began to change. There were no
longer any farms here, just broad fields of
scrubby second-growth trees, and plateaus thick
with rank sedge and clumps of briar. The soil
looked bad, dry and pebbly, cut again and again
by deep ravines that displayed white and red stri-
ations, layers of sand, layers of clay.

Then the land began to improve again and on
the third day they came at last to the Indigene village that was their destination. It was laid out
much like the village where Joseph had been living before, tall conical buildings made from mud
that had been thickly but irregularly plastered
over a framework of interlaced laths and twigs, all
of them set cheek by jowl in tight curving rows
surrounding a central plaza that contained ceremonial buildings, with an agricultural zone forming a ring around the entire settlement. The layout
was so similar to that of the previous village that
Joseph half expected the Ardardin to come out
and greet him here. But in place of a single chieftain this village seemed to have a triumvirate of
rulers: at least, three dignified-looking older Indigenes, each of them clad in the same sort of
painted leather cape and seashell-decorated
leather skirt that the Ardardin had worn, pre-

sented themselves as Joseph was getting down from the wagon, and stood in aloof, somber silence, watching his arrival in a kind of bleak attentiveness, saying not a word.

The other villagers were considerably more demonstrative. Dozens of them, children and adults both, came running forward to swarm around Joseph. There was an endearing innocence to this unexpected enthusiasm. They pressed up close against him, narrow tubular heads butting at him like hammers, boldly bringing their faces within inches of his own, nose to nose. Their throat-pouches fluttered and swelled in flurries of spasmodic agitation. A few of the most courageous hesitantly put their hands for a moment or two to the dangling strips of his ragged clothing and lightly pulled at them, as though they found them amusing. As they encircled him they murmured excitedly to one another, but what they said was too indistinctly enunciated and too thickly colloquial for Joseph to be able to comprehend more than the occasional word.

One of them, carrying a little bag of woven cloth that contained a glossy black powder, solemnly poured some into the palm of its hand, dipped the tips of two long pliant fingers into it, and slowly and carefully rubbed a circle of the stuff onto each of Joseph's cheeks. Joseph tolerated this patiently. He noticed now that the faces of most of the others were similarly adorned with patterns done in the black pigment, not just circles but in some cases whorls, triangles, crosses.

Ulvas, meanwhile, had entered into a conversation with a villager of substantial size and presence who, from the looks of things, was an important minister in the government of the triumvirs, though it was not clad in any of the symbols of authority itself. Joseph could not hear what they were saying, but it began gradually to become clear to him that what was taking place was not so much a conversation as a negotiation; Ulvas was the seller, the big villager was the prospective purchaser, and the primary topic of the conversation was the price that would have to be paid.

As for the commodity being sold, that, Joseph swiftly realized, was himself.

He was not meant to be a party to the transaction. The entire interchange was being carried on in low tones and quickly exchanged phrases, most of them words that were unfamiliar to him and all of it so rapid and cryptic that Joseph had no hope of following it. A good deal of the process was purely gestural. After each set of offers and replies the villager would go across to the triumvirate and report the details. This led to further palaver among the four of them, after which a signal would be given by one of the ruling three, and humbler citizens of the village came forth bearing merchandise: furs, beaded necklaces, bowls containing dried seeds and berries. Ulvas appeared to dismiss each offer as insufficient. New negotiations ensued, leading to new discussions between the rulers and their minister, and even more goods would be brought out: molded balls of vegetable meal, a brown bundle of dried meat, the blanched skull of some horned beast of the forest.

Ulvas was holding out for a steep price, it seemed. At one point there appeared to be a total breakdown of the dealings, huffy turning of backs, foreheads touched with splayed fingers in the emphatic gesture that meant negation. But perhaps all that was a signal of a climax in the negotiations, not a collapse; for almost immediately afterward came apparently conciliatory postures, signs of agreement, a series of new gestures clearly indicating that a deal had been struck. That seemed to be the case. Ulvas, Casqui and Paca began loading the wagon with the things that stood stacked all about in the center of the plaza.

The big minister signalled to Joseph in an unmistakable way. He belonged to them, now.

And now he knew just how little altruism, if indeed there had been any at all, there was in the Ardardin's decision to pass him along to this neighboring village. The Ardardin had correctly seen that Joseph would be leaving its village as soon as he could; there was need of Joseph's medical services at other Indigene villages along the route south; no doubt it had seemed merely efficient, rather than in any way morally virtuous, to provide a wagon to take Joseph on his way and simultaneously to turn a nice profit by selling him to the next village in the chain instead of just bestowing him upon them.

Ulvas and Casqui and Paca departed without a word to him. But Joseph had already learned not to expect sentimental leavetakings from these people.

His new hosts—his *owners*, Joseph corrected himself—showed him to his dwelling-place, a room much smaller than the one he had had before, and even more musty and dimly lit, with only a couple of tatty-looking fur rugs for his bed. On the other hand they had set out a generous meal for him, two bowls of their milky wine, an assortment of berries, stewed meats, and cooked grain, and a tray of knobby greenish-purple fruits of a kind he had never seen before. They were sour and tangy, not unpleasant, although after eating a couple he observed that the thick red juice of them had left his tongue puckered and the entire interior of his mouth very dry. He let the rest of them go untouched.

This settlement, too, had a backlog of medical tasks awaiting his attention in an infirmary set a little way apart from the village core. There were the usual sprained limbs and minor infections, which Joseph dealt with in the ways that had by now become familiar to him. One case, though, was more complicated. There had been a hunting accident, it seemed—the only other explanation, which he found too implausible to consider, was that one Indigene had actually attacked another—and the patient, a young male, had a small projectile point embedded in the upper right side of his back. Apparently this had happened some time ago, for the wound, though infected, had partly healed. No attempt had been made to extract the point. Joseph wondered how deep it was. The patient was in obvious distress: weak, feverish, barely coherent when Joseph questioned him. Joseph held his hand lightly over the wound and felt an insistent pounding throb beneath, as of something in there that must be let out.

Very well, he thought. I will operate.

Joseph had come to accept his own medical masquerade so thoroughly that he felt no compunction about taking this project on. The man lying before him must already be in great discomfort, which would only increase if nothing were done, and finally the infection would spread to some vital zone and cost him his life. Joseph asked for and received the assistance of the village's master of herbal remedies, who at Joseph's direction administered a steep dose of the pain-deadening drug to Joseph's patient. He laid out his pitiful little collection of medical instruments, and cleansed the wound with a piece of cloth dipped in wine, which he hoped would have some antiseptic properties, and gently parted the healed section of the opening so that he could insert the tip of his knifeblade as a probe.

The patient did not seem to complain as Joseph ventured into the golden interior tissues. He wondered how deeply he dared to go; but the essential thing was to seem confident and composed, and that was surprisingly easy for him to achieve. Perhaps in these weeks among the Indigenes he had begun to acquire some form of their overriding indifference to the trivial realities of the visible world. Under the pressure of his blade blood had begun freely to flow, scarlet blood with emerald highlights. The blood is only an illusion, Joseph told himself. The knife I use is an illusion also. Whatever pain the patient may be feeling is illusory. The weapon-point that I'm seeking is another illusion.

His hand was steady. His conscience remained clear.

He touched something hard within. Was it the point, or was it a bone? He wiggled the knifeblade and thought he felt motion against its tip. A bone would not move, he thought. It must be the weapon-point. Coolly he widened the opening. A hint of something dark inside there, was it? He washed away the blood and took a close look. The point, yes. Deep in the meat of the Indigene's back.

Now came the hard part, for him, for his patient. He beckoned to two of the Indigene onlookers.

"Hold him down," Joseph said, using the grammatical mode of a direct command, not a supplication. He was the most important person in this room, right now. He did not need to beg for the assistance that was required. "You, put your hand here, and you, hold him over here. Don't let him move."

There was no kindly way to do this. He inserted the blade, listened for the little scraping sound as it made contact with the hidden point within, made a twisting motion with his wrist, brought the tip of the blade upward, involuntarily biting his lip as he did so. A great shudder went through the Indigene, who lay face down on the pile of rugs before him. The two villagers who were holding him did not waver.

"There it is," Joseph said, as the head of the point came into view.

He eased it farther upward, bringing it out of the Indigene's flesh with one smooth motion, and caught it for a moment in his hand, showing it around exultantly to his audience. Then he tossed it aside. Blood was flowing more heavily now than before. Covering the wound with his hand, he watched quizzically as it welled up between his fingers. He stanched, laved, stanched again. The flow began to slacken. Was it safe to close the incision at this point? He held the sides of the wound together, contemplated them, nodded thoughtfully, just as someone who really knew what he was doing might do.

"Hand that to me," Joseph said, indicating the little machine from his utility case that served to stitch wounds. He was still not entirely certain how to operate it, but he had enough of a rough idea to make the attempt worthwhile.

Three stitches seemed to do the job.

He prescribed rest for the patient, and the pain-killing drug, and then, an inspired thought, some wine also. The Indigenes were passing the extracted weapon-point from hand to hand around the room. They were staring at him with what certainly must be looks of awe. Joseph wondered, as he had before, whether this time he might not have played the role too well; he wanted these people to move him along to the next village along his route south, after all, not lay claim to him as a permanent village treasure. But once again he had misjudged the way their minds worked. They kept him only until he had had the opportunity to examine every sick person in the village; and then, two or three weeks later, when he had set things to rights as much as possible, they let him know that the time had come for him to be sent onward.

He was not going to miss this place. Joseph had made a point of introducing himself by name to the chief minister and the herbalist and several others, but they had absorbed the information with no evident show of interest, and during his entire stay in the village no one had ever called him by name. He had no relationship there similar to the one he had had with the Ardardin, or even with Ulvas. It was strangely depersonalizing. He felt as though he had no existence for these people other than as a pair of skilled hands. But he saw a reason for that: he had come to the first village as a refugee, and they had taken him in the way they would take in a guest. But here he had been purchased. He was considered mere property. At best a slave, perhaps.

The route to the next village took Joseph through a district of abandoned farms. There were no indications of any Great House in the vicinity; this seemed to be one of the regions, common also in Helikis, where the Masters were absentee landlords and the farms were operated in their name by bailiffs who were themselves of Folkish blood. But the Folk who farmed here must have been loyalists, for the destruction that had been worked was complete, the rebels striking against their own kind with the vindictiveness and vehemence that elsewhere they had reserved for the Masters. Joseph saw the same sort of ruination he had looked upon at Ludbrek House, a sorry wasteland of burned houses, wrecked carts, dead animals, drowned fields. Seven such farms lay along one fifteen-mile stretch of road, all of them shattered in the same fashion. There was no sign of life anywhere.

It rained for the first time that season on the day they passed the last of the dead farms. The three Indigenes who were transporting him took no notice whatever as it started. They said nothing, they made no attempt to cover themselves. But Joseph, riding unprotected in the back of the open wagon, was caught by surprise when the sky, which had been an iron gray for days, turned black and then silver and abruptly began pelting him with cold, hard, fierce rain. He was drenched almost before he knew what was happening. He managed to improvise a little shelter for himself out of some of the many fur mats that were lying about in the wagon and a few of the sticks that were there also, but it was a flimsy construction that did very little to keep the rain out, and he was soaked already anyway.

There was no letup in the rain all day, or on the one that followed. Joseph knew that rain in the eastern half of the northern continent was a highly seasonal thing, a dry season followed by a wet one, with the annual rains beginning in the south and working their way north to High Manza, but he had imagined the change from one to the other would be more gradual. This was like the tipping of a bucket over lands that had been parched for months, a vast bucket whose contents were infinite, inexhaustible. He had never felt so cold and wet in his life. He had not known that such discomfort was possible.

At first the rain disappeared into the ground as soon as it struck. But by the second day the land, which in these parts was coarse sandy gray stuff that had looked as if it had not felt rain for centuries, had been saturated by the downpour, was glutted by it, ceasing now to absorb it. Freshets and rivulets were beginning to make their way along the old dry watercourses that ran in multitudinous furrows across the sloping plains. Already little ponds were forming. Another few days of this, Joseph thought, and there would be lakes and rivers.

He wondered how the mud-and-wattle buildings that the Indigenes of this territory favored could stand up to such an onslaught. Rainfall like this ought to send them sluicing away. But they were hardly likely to build with such stuff if it came apart under the impact of the first rain, and indeed the village toward which they had been traveling, another one of conical towers crowded tightly together around a central plaza, was sloughing off the watery bombardment as easily as though its buildings were made of steel and concrete. They must add something to the mud to make it water-resistant, Joseph thought. The juice of one of their herbs, maybe. The entire science of these people appeared to be constructed out of a knowledge of the chemical properties of the plant life that grew about them. They had no physics, no astronomy, no technology, no real medicine other than the use of potions. But they could build houses out of twigs and mud that would stay intact in diabolical rainfall like this.

News of Joseph's healing powers had preceded him here. The villagers seemed prepared to pay a

heavy bounty for him, for they had filled one entire room of a building on the plaza with treas-
ures to offer: not just the usual fur mats and
beaded necklaces, but great branches of blue
coral from the eastern sea, and pouches of polished turquoise stones, and the vivid blue-and-
red feathers of birds of some tropic land far away,
and a great deal more. Even so, the negotiations
went on for an extraordinarily long time, and
they did not seem to be going smoothly. Though
they were conducted, as before, mostly with gestures, aided by quick spurts of conversation in
what seemed to be a commercial patois using
words unknown to Joseph, he could tell by the
tone of voice and the looks of unmistakable exas-
peration that no meeting of minds was occurring. Huddling soaked and miserable while his
soon-to-be former owners, Indigenes whose
names he had never learned, bargained with
these new Indigenes who sought possession of
him over the price of his services, Joseph thought
at one point that his current masters had found
even this enormous pile of goods inadequate. It
looked very much as though they were going to
break off the discussion and set out for some village other than this before he had even had a
chance to get dry.

Well, if they did, so be it, as long as the village
that they would be taking him to was one that
brought him closer to his home. But what if—it
was his old, constant fear—they simply hauled

him back to their own town and kept him as a permanent fixture there?

That did not happen. As abruptly as the dry season had given way to the rain, the contending hagglers reached an agreement and Joseph's transfer was consummated. Staggering under mats and necklaces and coral branches and all the rest, his sellers went off in the rain to their wagon and his buyers crowded round him for what was becoming the familiar tribal welcome.

These people wanted Joseph not only to heal their sick but to bring holy blessings to the food supplies that they had stored away during the harvest season. In a kind of weird pantomime they led him to their granaries and acted out a description of what it was they wanted him to do, until at last he said impatiently, "You can say it in words. I do understand your language, you know."

But that seemed to bewilder them. They continued to point and nod and jerk their heads at him.

"Can't you understand what I'm saying?" he asked.

Maybe they spoke some dialect here so different from the Indigene he had learned in Keilloran that they regarded him as speaking some foreign language. But he saw he was wrong: he heard them talking among themselves, and the words they were using were, in general, understandable enough. Finally he did succeed in getting them to address him directly. It was as though they did not *want* to speak with him. His using their language made them uncomfortable. This village must not have had much contact with Masters, or with Folk either, for that matter, and looked upon him as some sort of alien thing, which had come their way as a kind of gift of the gods but which was not to be regarded in any way as fit to hold converse with. It was another step in his depersonalization, Joseph thought. As he moved southward he was getting farther and farther from the sort of existence he had had in the village of the Ardardin. Back there he had not had any such sense of solitude, of lostness, of *thing*ness, as he was beginning to feel down here.

But it was important to bear in mind that he was getting closer to home all the time, though he knew that Keilloran and its House were still a tremendous distance away.

He had no objection to blessing their food supply, if that was what they wanted him to do. Joseph had long since ceased to care what sort of hocus-pocus he performed for the sake of earning his passage to the Southland. Just as at the beginning, in that time only a few months earlier when he was much more naive than he had since become, he had felt it was some obscure violation of his honor as a Master to pretend to know anything about medicine, and that had very quickly ceased to be an issue for him, so too now, if the folk here wanted him to play the role of a demigod, or of a demon, or of anything else that might suit their needs, he was quite willing to do it. Whatever got him homeward: that was his new motto.

And so he let himself be taken into their storage-houses, to their bins of grain and berries and their hanging sides of drying meat and their casks of wine and all the rest that they had laid down for their use in the coming winter, and he threw back his shoulders and raised his head toward the heavens and held up his hands with his fingers outspread, and he cried out anything that came into his mind. "Cailin, Rickard, and Eitan, bless this food! In the name of Kesti and Wykkin and Domian, may virtue enter this food! I call upon Balbus! I call upon Anceph! I call upon Rollin!" He called upon the great ones of Old Earth, too, Agamemnon and Caesar and Genghis Khan, Napoleon and Gilgamesh. What harm did it do? These bins of grain would be none the worse for it. And this village had paid a high price for him: he must try to make them feel they had had their money's worth.

I am becoming a terrible hypocrite, Joseph thought.

And then he thought, No, I am simply growing up.

He examined that little interchange with himself often during the long rainy days ahead, as he twisted dislocated joints back into place and soothed sprains and stitched cut flesh together and made important-looking holy passes in the air over the prostrate forms of Indigenes who were suffering from ailments that he could not diagnose. *I am simply growing up.* Throughout much of his adolescence he had wondered what it would be like to be grown up. He knew that he would change, of course. But how? What would he learn? What would he forget? How much of his present self would he remember, when he was a man like his father, carrying the responsibilities that men like his father carried? Would he become hard and cruel, like so many of the adults he had observed? Do foolish things? Make needless enemies?

Well, now he was growing up very fast, and growing up seemed to involve putting aside all the lofty Master ideals that his father had taught him by example and Balbus by direct precept, and simply doing whatever he had to do, day by day, in order to survive. Otherwise, he was not going to get to grow up at all. However much future he was going to have would depend to a great extent on how resourceful he showed himself to be on this strange, unexpected journey across unknown Manza.

It rained virtually every day, the whole time he was in this village. By the time they decided they had earned back the price they had paid for him and were ready to sell him to the next tribe down the road, rivers were leaping their banks and meadows had turned to marshes. But the rain did hold off on the day of his next transfer. Once again he rode in an open cart down a cobbled Indigene road.

The gray sky gave him little clue to the position of the sun, but he seemed to be going south: at least, he hoped so. Joseph had long ago lost track of how much time had passed since the wild night of his escape from Getfen House, nor did he have any notion of the distance he had covered in this series of jolting cart-rides from village to village. He hoped that he was out of High Manza by now and somewhere down in the central part of the continent, but the Indigenes neither would nor could give him any help in determining that, and the reference books he had with him afforded no useful information, other than to tell him that the central part of the continent was mountainous.

That was good news, because he did seem to be coming into higher country. He saw bare serrated hills off to the west, and what seemed like higher peaks behind them. The air was colder, too. Each day was a little chillier than the one preceding. Joseph had never experienced really cold weather before. In his region of the Southland a kind of eternal mild springtime prevailed, all the year round. He had managed to obtain new linen robes from one of the Indigene villages to replace the shredded and tattered clothes he had been wearing since the start of his journey, but Indigenes did not appear to be very sensitive to changes in temperature, and the fabric was light stuff, ill suited to a winter journey. Speaking in the grammar of a supplicant, he was able to get them to give him more, but, even wearing double and triple thicknesses, he found himself shivering most of the time.

He had grown very thin, also. He had always been active and athletic, and his build was naturally long-limbed and slender, but the privations of his trip and a diet made up mostly of meat and fruit had melted from him what little fat there was, and he was beginning to worry about the loss of muscle and bone. When he pinched his skin he felt nothing between his fingers but the skin itself. The various villages did not begrudge him food, but it did not appear to put any flesh on him. He had no access to mirrors here, but he could feel what was happening to his face, the cheeks becoming gaunt and drawn, the bones standing out sharply. He was gaunt all over, mere skin and bones. He knew he must look like a wild man. Though he attempted periodically to trim his hair, since Masters did not wear their hair long, he knew it must by now be an uncouth shaggy mane. His beard, which he also tried ineffectually to trim, had turned coarse and thick, a black pelt that covered most of his face to a point high up on his cheeks. No one would recognize him, he knew, if he were to be miraculously transported back to Keilloran House right now. They would run from him in fright, screaming.

The odd and disturbing thing was that as he grew thinner, his appetite, which had always been so voracious, seemed to be diminishing. He rarely felt hungry any more. Whatever they gave him to eat seemed to suffice. He had to force himself to swallow more than he really wanted, and sometimes, against all logic, he did not succeed. He had become light, very light, so light that he felt it would be no great task to kick himself free of the ground and go floating up into the sky, drifting like an untethered balloon above the clouds. That was an interesting fantasy, but it was also a bad sign that such thoughts were entering his mind. They were a sign of hallucinatory delusion, perhaps. He needed to keep his strength up, to build himself back toward whatever might be the minimum level he would need to carry him across the thousands of miles that stood between him and home.

Two more trades and he was in the foothills of what unquestionably must be the mountains of the region known as Middle Manza. It was still the rainy season, and there was a coating of snow on the distant peaks. The air was not only cooler but thinner here, so that his heart worked harder with every step he took and quickly began to pound, and he often had to pause to catch his breath as he moved about in a village. There were dizzy spells, too. One time Joseph thought he was going to faint. How much of his present weakness and lack of appetite was the result of the altitude and how much from loss of weight, he could not say.

When I come down out of these mountains, he promised himself, I will try to eat more and regain my strength. Whatever it is they give me to eat, I will eat all of it, and then I will ask them to let me have some more.

The world of Masters and Folk seemed very far away in these hilly parts. The kinds of farming that were practiced in the lowlands were difficult if not impossible in this harsh rocky terrain, and though occasional settlements had been attempted, it looked as though most of the region had been left untouched. There were no modern highways here, no dams, no cities, no Great Houses. Sometimes Joseph would catch sight of curling white plumes of smoke far away, rising from what he suspected were the chimneys of a Folkish village along the edge of some high slope. He had heard that in remote rural districts like these there had always been places where the Folk still lived apart from the modern world, lived as they had before the Conquest, simple farmers and hunters unaffected by the presence of Masters. They might occasionally have contact with outsiders but had never become part of the world's economic system. Joseph never was brought close enough to any of those smoke-plumes to determine whether his guess was correct, though. For the most part the foothill zone, where it was inhabited at all, was inhabited by Indigenes, dwelling as always in little widely separated villages.

He was shifted from one village to another every few weeks. Each shift brought him into higher territory: the air was no longer cool but cold, almost painfully so, and white cloaks of snow now could be seen not just on far-off peaks but along the summits of the hills overlooking the villages themselves. There seemed to be relatively less work for him to do here than in the lowlands, as if, perhaps, these mountain Indigenes were a hardier breed than their cousins below. The price that was being paid for him diminished as he was shuffled along through the mountains: a few handfuls of beads and some mangy mats were enough now to buy him. But his buyers did still seem to understand that he was a human being in transit, that they were supposed to keep him for only a little while and then pass him along to the next tribe to the south.

They rarely spoke to him, in these villages. The farther Joseph got from the Indigenes of the north, who had lived in the territory between House Getfen and House Ludbrek and were at least accustomed to having glancing contact with Masters, the less responsive the villagers became to him in general. It was inescapably clear that he was simply a commodity to them, an itinerant medicine-man, something to be traded from village to village according to the rhythms of the villagers' own needs. They did not perceive themselves as having any direct transaction with him. He barely seemed even to exist for them. Somehow he had lost human status in their eyes, whatever human status might actually mean to them. It had actually been interesting to live among the northern Indigenes, not just a fugitive but also an observer studying the folkways of this intelligent and appealing race, but that was over, now. He had passed into some new realm of being in which he was practically inanimate, a thing to be bought and sold like a stack of furs. It made for a stark, frighteningly lonely existence. More than once Joseph awoke to find himself in tears.

Most of their communication with him, always minimal at best, was carried out by means of gestures. More and more they gave him the impression that they did not expect him to understand their language, and even when he showed them that he did, that impression did not appear to be dispelled. His words barely registered on them, and they would go right back to using gestures the next time. But otherwise most of them treated him reasonably well, giving him plenty of food and decent lodgings. In one village, when they saw how badly he was taking the chill of the mountain air, they provided him with a mantle of dark furs to wrap around himself, and let him keep it when they sold him onward to the adjacent tribe a little while afterward.

The trouble was that he did not think he was

moving southward any longer. The weather was still so rainy, or sometimes snowy, that Joseph rarely got a clear enough view of the sky to work out much sense of the direction he was traveling in. But it seemed to him now that they had begun to sell him sidewise, shuttling him back and forth over the crest of these hills according to the lie of their own villages rather than in accordance with any need of his own, and his calculations appeared to show that there was never much change in latitude.

"I am going south," he told them, when his time was up at the next village. "I am returning to my family in the southern continent." But where he happened to want to go was no concern of theirs. "Do you understand me?" he said. "I must go south." They crossed their arms at him. They understood what he was saying, perhaps; but they did not care. This was the other side of that placid Indigene indifference. They felt no resentment over the conquest of their entire world by humans, perhaps, but they owed no obeisance, either. The next day, when they set out with him to take him to his newest home, the route that the wagon followed led unmistakably east.

Not to be going forward was the same thing as to be sliding backward. So Joseph knew that this phase of his journey, the phase in which he had tried to make his way back to his home across Manza as the chattel of helpful Indigenes, was coming to an end. They had ceased to be helpful, now. He would never reach Helikis if they went on shipping him around the central highlands forever in this lateral way. He saw that he was going to have to break away from them and proceed on his own.

But he hesitated to take the step. The notion of setting out through these mountains alone, in winter, with cold rain falling every day and now and then snow, was a troublesome one. What would he eat? Where would he sleep? How would he keep from freezing to death?

And also he wondered whether it might anger the last villagers in the sequence if he were to slip away from them before they had had a chance to strike a deal for him, thus cheating them of the opportunity to turn a profit, or at the worst break even, on their temporary ownership of him. Would they go in pursuit of him? He had never heard of Indigenes becoming angry over anything. But these Indigenes of the mountains were very little like the ones he had known in Keilloran, or in the Manza lowlands. They might not take his disappearance lightly. It was entirely possible that he would become the first Master to be a fugitive not just from rebel Folk but from Indigenes as well.

I will wait a little longer, he told himself. Perhaps the winter will end soon, or they will start selling me southwards again, or at least I will be sent the next time to some village in the foothills, so that when I escape I will be able to find my way down into the lowlands, where it is warmer and I will have some hope of foraging for food.

And indeed it began to seem as if they were moving him south again. There were two big leaps, one long ride that took him to a mountain-top village gripped by such terrible cold that not even snow would fall and the ground was locked in an iron rigidity and seemed to clang when you walked on it, and then another down the far slope to an easier place of leaping brooks and green gullies thick with ferns; and each of these places, the frostbound one and the ferny one, appeared to be well south of its predecessor. Joseph took heart from that. Two more such leaps and he might be out of the mountains altogether.

But he had rejoiced too soon. When he left the Indigenes of the fern-gully village, it was by way of a winding route up and up into the ridge above their sheltered district and down the other side, and then, all day long on a day of clear crisp weather and a second day just like it following, along a straight road with the sun sitting in the southern sky behind them like a great mocking eye. Joseph waited for the road to swing about, but never once did it deviate from that north-ward bearing. When at last they handed him over to his newest purchasers, he noted that the village to which he had been brought lay in a sloping saddle facing west, with mist-shrouded lowlands in the valley below, and a lofty chain of peaks rising like a wall behind him to the east. So he had gained a little by getting closer to the western side of the high country, where he expected that the descent into the lowlands would be easier, but he had lost a great deal through backtracking northward, and who was to say where they would send him after this? The earlier sidewise shuttling had been bad enough; but now he was going in circles. Regardless of the risks, it was time for him to take matters into his own hands.

It was the evening of Joseph's third day in this latest village. There was very little medical work for him here: a case of what looked like frostbite, and an inflamed jaw, and an infected hand. In general he found the place cheerless and unwelcoming. It was a small village and its people seemed sullen and morose, although Joseph had seen often enough before the unwisdom of trying to interpret the postures and facial expressions of Indigenes according to what he understood of human postures and expressions. He reminded himself that these people were not human and it was wrong to think of them as though they were.

But it was hard to regard them as anything but unfriendly. They never said anything to him except out of necessity, as when informing him of things he had to know in order to find his way around the village. Nor did they seem ever to look directly at him; instead they turned their heads sideways and gave him oblique slitted glances. They did appear to have some curiosity about him, but not of the kind that would lead to any sort of real communication between him and them. Perhaps they had never seen a human before, in this remote, isolated place. He was nothing but a freakish anomaly to them, an intruder from a part of the world they wanted nothing to do with. Well, that made it all the easier for him to leave with a clear conscience.

He thought he would try the combinant one more time before setting out. Joseph had not so much as touched it for many weeks, but it had navigational functions as well as being a communications device, and he had some hope that it might work better at this altitude than it had in the lowlands. He activated it and it gave him the same odd pink glow and meaningless sputtering sounds that he had been getting from it since the village of the Ardardin. But as he started to put it back in his pack a long double-jointed hand reached out from behind him and gently but firmly took the device from him.

He had not heard them come in, but three Indigenes had entered his room. Joseph thought he recognized the one who had taken the combinant from him as the head man of the village, but he was not sure, since they were so uncommunicative here; village chieftains in this region wore no special regalia, and it was too soon after Joseph's arrival for him to have learned to tell one villager from another.

It was holding the combinant in the palm of its hand and was prodding its buttons carefully with two fingers of the other.

"That's a communications device," Joseph said. "But it hasn't been working right for a long time."

The Indigene continued to poke at the combinant's control panel. It was as though Joseph had not said anything at all. Apparently the Indigene was trying to replicate the pink glow that Joseph had drawn from it.

"Do you want me to show you how to do it?" Joseph asked, holding out his hand. He did not think it was wise to try to take the device from the Indigene by direct action.

But the Indigene had found the right button. The pink glow appeared, and the sputtering began. That seemed to interest it very much. It brought the combinant up within a couple of inches of its flat-featured face and studied it with what looked like keen fascination; then it turned and displayed the little machine to its two companions; and then it began to turn the thing over and over in its hand, as if searching for some way to make it do something else besides glow and sputter.

This is very atypical of you, Joseph thought. You people are not supposed to have any interest in our machines. Indeed you scorn them, is that not so? You regard them as the illusory products of an illusory race.

But either he had misunderstood some of the things the Ardardin had been telling him, or it was an error to imagine that all Indigenes had the same set of philosophical beliefs, or else this mountaineer simply thought the combinant was a particularly pleasing trinket. The three of them were passing it around, now, each taking a turn at pushing its buttons. Joseph felt uneasy about that. The combinant had not been working properly for a long while, either because it was itself broken or the entire worldwide communications system had been brought down, and in any case he doubted that these people could do any further harm to it. But he did not like to see the device in their hands. You were told not to make any artifacts of human technology available to Indigenes. That was the rule. It had been explained to him, once: doing so might tend to dilute the purity of their culture, or some such thing. Although Joseph could not see how letting the inhabitants of this remote village play with a broken combinant could do any harm to the purity of Indigene culture, some vestige of his sense of himself as a Master recoiled from this violation of custom.

Besides, the combinant was *his*. He had little enough left of the life that once had been his in the days when he had been Joseph Master Keilloran. What if they found the device so interesting that they decided to keep it—looking upon it, say, as one additional benefit that they were getting in return for the trade-goods they had given the fern-gully people for Joseph?

And that was exactly what they seemed to intend. The three Indigenes turned and started to go from the room, taking the combinant with them.

"Wait a minute," Joseph said. "That instrument is mine. You may not have it."

They paused by the door and looked back at him. Their expressions, insofar as he could interpret them at all, appeared to register surprise that he had said something. They did not show any indication that they had understood what he said, although he was sure that they had.

He held out his hand. "Give it to me," he said, using the supplicatory mode. "I have need of it."

What an Indigene of the Ardardin's village would have replied, was, almost certainly, "I recognize your need," and then it would have handed the combinant over. But these people recognized nothing. Once more they turned to leave.

"No," Joseph said. "I must have it. Give it to me." Not using the supplicatory any more: this was a direct request. And, when he saw that they were paying no heed, he followed it with the same statement phrased in the rarely used mode reserved for outright commands, which in this context might well be construed as insulting. It made no difference. They did not care about his grammar; probably they were amazed that he could utter intelligible words at all. But his wishes, his pleas, his orders, were equally unimportant to them. They went from the room and his combinant went with them.

Let them have it, Joseph thought sullenly, when his first surge of anger and frustration had died away. It was broken anyway.

Although he knew it meant leaving the combinant behind, he was still resolved to make his escape. The dry weather of recent days was still holding. It was senseless to stay among the Indigenes any longer. Not a day, not an hour, not a moment. He would depart this very night.

With a sense of growing excitement, even jubilation, he made his preparations, stuffing his pack with as much dried meat and berries as it would hold, filling with fresh water the wine-flask from Getfen House that had served as his canteen during his days in the forest, rolling up the mantle of dark furs an earlier village had given him and tying it around his waist. He looked into the corridor. No one seemed to be on guard out there.

The night was clear and cold, though not as cold as some recent nights had been. The stars of the Manza sky, which once had looked very strange to him but by now were only too familiar, wheeled overhead. The only moon that was visible was fast-moving little Mebriel, hardly brighter than a star itself. A dull red glow in the east, behind the mountains, told Joseph that big Sanivark would probably be coming over the horizon soon, lighting everything up with its brick-red beams, but he hoped to have this place well to his rear before that happened.

A bonfire was burning in the village plaza. The sound of singing voices drifted through the air. The Indigenes seemed to gather there most nights after dark, heedless as ever of the cold. Joseph turned and headed in the other direction, down past the infirmary and the town midden. Earlier that day he had seen a path that went behind the midden and seemed to lead on downslope into the woods that lay west of town.

He passed a couple of shadowy figures as he went. They gave him quick glances, but no one stopped him, no one questioned him. He was not a prisoner here, after all. And the barrier of reserve that existed between these people and him protected him now. Still, he wished he had not been noticed. If his disappearance bothered them when they found him gone in the morning, this would give them a clue as to the direction he had taken.

The path was steeper than he had expected. The village's entire site sloped sharply to the west at something like a twenty-degree grade before the far side of the saddle-shaped valley in which the town was contained turned upward again, but the grade was irregular, flattening out in some places and dropping sharply in others. More than once Joseph found himself struggling down the side of what was essentially a huge ravine. The path quickly deteriorated too, now that he was some distance from town, so that in the moonlit darkness he could barely find it among all the brambles and woody briars that were encroaching on it, and on two occasions he wandered from it altogether and had to grope his way back. At all times he picked his way carefully, mindful of his agonizing stumble in the Getfen forest. Haste could be disastrous. His twisted knee had long since healed, but he knew that another such injury, out here by himself in these frosty woods, would mean the end of him.

Creatures hooted in the night. There were rustlings and cracklings all around him. He ignored all that. He forced himself steadily onward, moving as fast as he dared, guiding himself by a big icy-looking star that lay dead ahead. The only thing that mattered right now was putting distance between himself and the Indigene village.

It was hard work. Though Joseph had grown accustomed to the altitude after so many weeks in the mountains, he felt the strain of it nevertheless: his heart boomed in his chest and his breath came short, and for long stretches he found himself panting, which dried out his mouth and tempted him to dip into his precious water supply. He fought the temptation back. In this mountain saddle the drainage patterns were all wrong for streams, and he could not say when or where he would find his next source of fresh water: on the other side of the slope, no doubt.

But then the path showed signs of beginning to turn upward, and the ascent became a continuous one, which told him that he had finally reached the far side of the saddle, the shallow western rise that separated the village from the lowlands beyond. With his goal so close, Joseph stepped up his pace, pushing himself to the limits of his strength. The warmth of his own exertions protected him against the cold. He could feel streams of sweat running down the sides of his rib-cage, not an unpleasant sensation, as he forced himself up the steep trail. There would be time to rest later. He prayed for an easy descent into the lowlands once he was over the summit of the western ridge.

By the time Joseph attained it, though, he could see that no such easy descent was going to be granted him. Sanivark, emerging at last above the top of the mountains of the east with little Keviel trailing along behind, gleamed like a red lantern over his head, showing him the disheartening sight of a second saddle rolling just to the west of him, and what looked very much like a third one westward of that. Neither one had been visible from the village. He would have to cope with both of them, and who knew what obstacles beyond those, before he reached the lowlands.

He did not seem to be the object of any pursuit, at any rate. The village was only dimly visible, gratifyingly far behind him to the east—the smoke of its bonfire, the lights of a few of its houses—and there was no sign that anyone was moving toward him through the scrubby woods between there and here that he had just traversed. So he was free, no longer a commodity, no longer trade-goods being passed on from village to village. His only problem now was staying alive in these wintry woods.

He crouched for a time to the leeward of the saddle-top, catching his breath, letting his sweat dry, nibbling a bit of dried meat, studying the terrain ahead. But there was not going to be any rest for him. When he had stayed there long enough so that he was starting to feel the cold again, Joseph picked up and moved along, scrambling down into the second saddle and onward into the third, which turned out to be a low flattened basin offering no real challenge. The trail had given out, or else he had lost it, but that scarcely mattered. He was fully in the rhythm of it. He moved on and on. There were no more ridges: it was a straight downhill glide now into the misty lands below.

He thought several times of stopping to sleep, but no, he wanted to be out of the high country, entirely out, before he permitted himself to halt. Sanivark went sailing past him overhead, moving into the western sky and showing him his goal, a shrouded realm of drifting whiteness. The mists thinned as he went down toward it, and just as the pale strands of first light began coming over his shoulder he saw a green meadow not far below him, and a stream or perhaps a small river, itself nearly invisible but outlined by a long bank of fog that clung to it like cotton batting.

This was as far as he could go without resting. At the place where the last stretch of highland forest shaded into the meadow bordering the riverbank he found a deserted campsite that probably had been used by hunters in the autumn, and settled into it. There was a little cave that someone had roughly excavated out of the side of the hill, a stone fireplace with cold charcoal still in it and the charred bones of some fair-sized animal scattered about nearby, and a stack of firewood perhaps awaiting use by the returning hunters in the spring. Joseph dined on dried meat and berries and crawled into the cave just as the last few stars were disappearing from the rapidly bluing sky. He unwrapped his fur mantle and curled it around himself, tucked his hands into his robes, and closed his eyes. Sleep rolled over him like a tumbling boulder.

He awoke at midday. A great silence enfolded him, broken only by the screeching caws of the dark birds that were whirling in enormous circles above him in the cloudless sky. The mists had lifted and the sun was bright overhead. He dutifully said his morning prayers and breakfasted sparingly and sat for a long while looking back at the mountains out of which he had come, thinking about his zigzag route through the highlands these past weeks or months and wondering

whether in all that time he had succeeded in getting significantly closer to the Southland. He
doubted it. Certainly he was somewhat farther
south than on the day when he had stood staring
at the dismal blackened remains of Ludbrek
House, but a map, he suspected, would show him
that he had traveled no more than a finger's
breadth of the total distance separating him from
his father's distant lands.

By this time there would be no reason for anyone at home to think that he was still alive. The
Keillorans were basically optimistic people, but
they were not fools, and such a degree of opti-
mism would be nothing if not foolhardy. He was
here, and they were there, and there was so much
territory between that he knew he might just as
well start thinking of himself as irretrievably lost,
which was not quite the same thing as being
dead, but not all that far from it.

I am the only one in the world who knows
where I am, he thought. And all I know is that I
am *here*, though I have no way of knowing where
here is.

Joseph looked up at the blank blue screen that
was the sky.

"Father!" he cried, setting up echoes as his
voice reverberated off the mountains from which
he had just descended. "Father, it's me, Joseph!
Can you hear me? I'm in Manza, Father! I'm on
my way home!"

That was at least as useful as talking into a broken combinant, he told himself. And it was good to hear the sound of a human voice again, even if it was his own.

He went down to the stream, stripped, bathed. The water was so cold it felt like fire against his skin, but he had not been able to bathe very often in the mountain villages, and he forced himself through an elaborate ablution. He washed his clothes also, and set them out to dry in the sunlight, sitting naked beside them, shivering but strangely happy in the silence, the isolation, the brightness of the day, the fresh clear air.

And then it was time to get going. There was nothing like a road here for him to follow, not even a footpath, but the land was flat, and after his nighttime scramble through the mountain foothills this seemed almost preposterously easy. Just put one foot forward and then another, on and on, keep the mountains to your left and the stream to the right and the sun shining on your nose, and you will find that you are heading toward home, getting closer with every step you take.

No one seemed to live in this district. He wondered why. The soil seemed fertile enough, there was plenty of fresh water, the climate was probably all right. Yet he saw no sign that the Folk had farmed here, and none of the claimstones that would mark land belonging to one of the Great Houses, and no trace of a settlement of Indigenes, even. But of course this was a large continent and much of it, even after all these centuries of the human presence on Homeworld, was still as it had been when the first Folkish explorers had landed here.

A strange concept, *Folkish explorers*. Joseph had never examined the glaring contradictions in the term before. The Folk were such stolid, unadventurous, spiritless, passive people, or at least that was how he had always regarded them. Everyone did. One did not think of people like that as explorers. It was hard to imagine that any of them could have had enough fervor of the soul to get themselves out into spaceships and travel across the empty light-years and discover Homeworld, and yet they had. Hadn't achieved much once they got here, no, but they had managed to go looking for it, and find it, and settle it.

And yet, stolid and unadventurous and spiritless and passive though they might be, they had also found enough fervor within themselves just now to rise up here in the northern continent or perhaps throughout the entire world and kill most or all of the Masters, and set fire to their houses, and wreck their estates. That was something worth thinking about. Perhaps we have never understood much about the Folk at all, Joseph told himself. Perhaps they are almost as alien to us as the Indigenes or the noctambulos, or the alien races that live on the other worlds of the galaxy.

He went along steadily, marching from sunrise

to sundown, stopping to eat whenever he felt hungry, finding some cave or burrow or other sort of shelter for himself at night. The weather grew better every day. Sometimes there were brief rainstorms, mild and pleasant, nothing like the hard chill downpours of the high country. He often took off his clothes and stood naked in the rain, enjoying the sensation of cool clean water striking his skin.

This was beautiful country, still completely devoid of any sort of settlement. There was a springtime feel to the air. Green new growth was appearing everywhere. Dazzling carpets of tiny flowers, some pink, some yellow, sprang up after each rain-shower. They seemed to come straight out of the ground, without any leaves. Joseph made no attempt to keep track of the passing of the days. He still clung to the fantasy that if only he kept walking at this steady pace, ten miles a day, fifteen, however much he might be able to cover, he would come to the bottom of this continent sooner or later and cross over into Helikis, where, he wanted to believe, there had been no Folkish uprising and he would find people to help him get the rest of the way home.

He knew there was some element of folly in the belief that he had been clinging to all this while—without a shred of evidence to support it—that everything was still normal in Helikis. If there had been no rebellion in the southern continent, why had the southern Masters not sent aid to their beleaguered cousins in the north? Why were no military planes roaring northward overhead? Why no armies marching swiftly to set thing to rights? But he wanted to think that all was well in the Southland, because this whole long march of his would be pointless, otherwise. Joseph told himself that he had no knowledge about what was going on in most of the world, anyway. In all these months of wandering he had covered only a tiny area of the planet. There might be a tremendous civil war under way on a hundred different battlefields even now, while he, cut off from everything and everyone, plodded southward day by day in solitude through this quiet uninhabited region.

Uninhabited by Masters and Folk and Indigenes, at any rate. There was plenty of animal life. Joseph did not recognize any of the creatures he encountered as he went along, though some of them seemed to be northern variants of animals that were native to the southern continent. There was a plump round beast, quite large, with coarse red fur and a fat little comical tail, that seemed surely to be a relative of the benevongs of the south. There was another, cat-sized, with huge restless eyes and a formidable cloak of twitching blue spines, that beyond much doubt was the local version of the shy, easily frightened thorkins that he had sometimes seen digging for tasty roots along the banks of country streams. But the rest were completely new to him: a squat, broad-nosed climbing animal with brown and yellow spots; and a big, loose-jointed, thick-thighed creature whose tiny, pointed head seemed to have been borrowed from a much smaller animal; and a low-slung snuffling thing, long and sleek, that moved across the land in tightly clustered packs.

None of these showed the slightest fear of him, not even the one that looked like a thorkin. A thorkin of the Southland would have turned and bolted at the first sign of a human, but this animal simply stood its ground and stared. The sleek pack-creatures, who appeared to be browsing for insect nests in the ground, went right on about their business without paying heed to him at all. The big shuffling beast with the small head actually seemed to want to be friendly, wandering up so close that it was Joseph who backed uncertainly away.

One day he stumbled into a small encampment of poriphars in a clearing at the edge of a grove of handsome little white-barked trees, and understood why there were no Indigene villages in these parts. Indigenes would not trespass on the territory of other intelligent beings; and poriphars, like noctambulos and meliots and a couple of other native species, qualified as intelligent, if only just marginally. They were mere naked nomadic beasts, but it was known that they had a language; they had a tribal structure of some sort; they were advanced enough technologically to have the use of fire and simple tools. That was about all Joseph knew about them. A few wandering tribes of poriphars were found in Helikis, but they were mainly a northern species.

He came upon them suddenly, and they seemed as uncertain of how to regard the strange being who had materialized among them as Joseph was to deal with them. There were about a dozen of them, graceful impressive-looking creatures about his own size, with taut, muscular bodies that were densely covered with thick black-and-white-striped fur. Their long, narrow, leathery feet ended in powerful curving claws; their black, glossy hands were equipped with small, efficient-looking fingers. They had triangular faces with jutting wolfish snouts terminating in shiny black noses. Their eyes, large and bright and round, a deep blue-black in color, were protected by heavy brow-ridges.

The poriphars were sitting in a circle around a crude oven made of rocks, roasting spitted fish over the flames. When Joseph stepped out from behind a great gray boulder into their midst, very much to his surprise and theirs, they reacted with immediate uneasiness, moving closer to one another, bodies going tense, nostrils quivering. Their eyes were fixed closely on him, warily, as though a solitary human being, traveling on foot and carrying no visible weapons, might actually pose some threat to this band of strong, sturdy animals.

Slowly and clearly Joseph said, speaking in Indigene, "I am a traveler. There is no one else with me. I am going southward."

No response. The same wary glances.

"I am hungry. Can you give me some food?"

The same keen stares, nothing more.

The aroma of the roasting fish was overwhelming. It filled the air. Joseph felt famished, almost dizzy with hunger. He had eaten nothing but dried meat and berries for days, in decreasing quantities as his supplies began to run low. He had practically none left by now.

"Can you understand me?" he asked. He patted his abdomen. "Hunger. Food."

Nothing.

He had often heard that all the various intelligent life-forms of Homeworld were able to speak Indigene, but perhaps that was not true. Without much hope Joseph tried Folkish and then Master, with the same result. But when he patted his stomach again and pointed silently to one of the skewers of fish, then to his own lips, and pantomimed the act of chewing and swallowing, they seemed to comprehend at once. A brief debate ensued among them. Their language was one of rapid clicks and buzzing drones, probably impossible for human vocal apparatus to imitate.

Then one of the poriphars stood—it was a

head taller than Joseph; it probably could have killed him with one swipe of those sinewy arms—and yanked a skewer of fish from the fire. Carefully, using those agile little fingers with an almost finicky precision, it pried a thick slab of pale pinkish meat from the fish and handed it to him.

"Thank you," Joseph said, with great gravity.

He performed an elaborate salute, touching his forehead and his chest and bowing. Most likely the gesture had no meaning whatever for the poriphars, but it was the best he could do. He wished he had something to offer them in return, but he doubted that his remaining berries would interest them, and there was nothing else he could spare.

The temptation to cram the fish into his mouth and bolt it all down at once was a hard thing to resist, but Joseph ate as slowly as he could. It had a sweet, smoky flavor, heartbreakingly delicious. The poriphars remained quite motionless while he ate, watching him. Occasionally one of them made a clicking, buzzing comment. They still seemed uneasy. Their restiveness was an almost palpable thing.

Joseph had been alone for so many days that he wanted to stay for a while, somehow to talk with them, to tell them about himself and learn things about them, perhaps to find out about the nature of the route that lay ahead, or even about the civil war. But of course all that was impossible. There was no way to communicate. And he did not need a degree in alien psychology to understand that they had no interest in making his acquaintance, that the only thing they desired from him was that he remove himself from their presence without further delay.

Which he did, after making a final brief speech in Indigene on the off chance that they might indeed know something of that language. He apologized for having disturbed them and told them how grateful he was for their kindness in feeding a lone hungry wanderer, how he would if in any way he could repay their hospitality at another time. To this they made no reply, or showed any indication that they had understood. He walked away from them without looking back.

A couple of days later he saw a plane pass high overhead—the first manifestation of the outside world since he had fled from the Indigenes. Joseph stood staring up, wondering whether he was experiencing some hallucination brought on by hunger. The plane was so far above him, a mere dark winged speck in the sky, that he could hardly hear it at all, nothing more than a distant faint humming sound such as an insect might have made, nor could he identify it in any way. It was traveling in a northwesterly direction. Whose plane was it? Was it possible that they still could have regular commuter service between Helikis and Manza?

It seemed like a thousand years ago that he had made his own flight northward. Ten thousand; a million. The airstrip at Keilloran; the excitement of departure; his father and brothers and sisters loading him down with gifts to bring the Getfens; Anceph and Rollin climbing aboard with the luggage, and then Balbus, beckoning to him to follow. The flight had taken eleven hours, the longest flight of his life. How creaky he had felt when he disembarked at the Getfen airstrip! But then, his fair-haired laughing Getfen cousins all around him, sturdy Wykkin and bright-eyed Domian and lovely fragrant Kesti, and dark, stocky Gryilin Master Getfen behind them, his hosts for the summer, his new friends, the companions of his coming-of-age year—

Ten million years ago. A billion.

The plane, if a plane indeed was what it was, vanished from sight in the northern sky. Now that it was gone he began to doubt that he had really seen it. There must not be any planes flying any more, he told himself. If you wanted to go from one continent to another these days you would have to do it on foot, a journey that would take three years, or five, or forever. We have become prehistoric here. Something terrible has happened on Homeworld and a great silence has fallen over everything, he thought. The rebellious Folk have risen up in wrath and hurled the world back into medieval times—but not even the medieval time of Homeworld, but that of Old Earth,

the time of candlelight and horses and tourna-
ments of chivalry. What actually had horses been?
he wondered. Something like bandars, Joseph
guessed, swift high-spirited animals that you
rode from place to place, or set against one another in races.

The plane, real or not, had reminded him of
how easy it once had been to travel from one
place to another on Homeworld, and how difficult, how well-nigh impossible, it had become.
Heartsick, he thought of the vast curving breast
of the world that lay before him, the great impossible span of distance. What madness it had been
to think he could ever walk from Getfen to Keilloran! Joseph sank down against the ground,
forehead pressing against his knees. His head
swam with despair.

Up, he told himself sternly.

Up and get yourself moving. One step and another and another, and someday you will be
home.

Perhaps.

But the last of the food he had brought with
him from the Indigene village was gone. Joseph
found himself thinking longingly of the stewed
meat they ate in those villages, the porridges, the
milky wine. He had not much liked the wine
then, but now he tasted it in his mind and it
seemed heavenly, the finest taste in the universe.
He imagined a silvery shimmering in the air before him and a flask of the wine miraculously

dropping out of nowhere at his feet, and perhaps a pan of the braised illimani meat too. That did not happen. All the euphoria of those early springtime days when he had first come down out of the mountains had disappeared. The carpets of pretty pink flowers, the green blush of new foliage, the sweet fresh spring rain falling on his naked body—that was all so far behind him, now, that it seemed like something he had dreamed. I am going to starve to death, Joseph thought.

He dug along stream-banks in the hope of finding mud-crawlers, but mud-crawlers did not seem to live here. He did find roots and bulbs that looked as though they might be safe to eat, and nibbled on them experimentally, making mental notes about which ones went down easily and which upset his stomach. He chewed the tender new shoots of bushes for their sweet juice. He broke into a nest of sash-weevils and coolly, methodically, ate the little yellow grubs. They had almost no taste; it was like eating bits of straw. But there had to be some nourishment in them somewhere, for they were living things.

You must not let yourself die of hunger, he told himself. You are Joseph Master Keilloran and you are on your way home to your family, and you need to maintain your strength for the long journey that lies ahead.

He no longer bothered to wash very often. The

fresh, sparkling water of the streams felt too cold
against his skin, now that there was so little flesh
on his bones. His skin began to break out with little white-tipped red eruptions, but that seemed
the least of his problems. He stopped washing his
clothing, too, but for a different reason: the fabric
had grown so threadbare and tattered that Joseph
was afraid the robe would fall apart entirely if he
subjected it to the stress of washing it.

He threw rocks at basking lizards, but never
once did he hit one. They always seemed to come
awake the moment he raised his arm and go scur-
rying away with astonishing speed. He ripped
the bark from a tree and discovered brightly
striped beetles underneath, and in a kind of wondering amazement at his own boldness—or perhaps, Joseph decided, it was only his own
desperation—he put them into his mouth, one at
a time. He ate ants. He broke a branch from a little tree and swung it through the air, trying to bat
down insects with it, and actually caught some
that way. He was surprised to observe how easily
he could adapt to eating insects.

He talked to the animals that he met as he
went along. They came out and stared at him
without fear, and Joseph nodded to them and
smiled and introduced himself, and asked
whether they had heard anything about the war
between Folk and Masters, and invited them to
advise him on the edibility of the plants that
grew nearby. Since they were creatures that were

below the threshold of intelligence, they neither understood nor replied, but they did pause and listen. It occurred to Joseph that he should be trying to catch and kill some of them for their meat instead of holding these nonsensical conversations with them, but by this time he was too slow and weak to try that, and it seemed impolite, besides. They were his friends, companions of the way.

"I am Joseph Master Keilloran," he told them, "and I would be most grateful if you would send word to my family that I am on my way home to them."

He felt very giddy much of the time. His vision often became blurry. Hunger, he knew, was doing something to his brain. He hoped the damage would not be permanent.

One night Joseph was awakened by a blazing brightness on the horizon, a lovely red-and-yellow dome that quickly elongated to become a river of light climbing into the sky. Slowly he came to understand that it was a great fire somewhere very far off, and he wondered if the civil war was still going on, and, if so, who was attacking whom, and where. The brightness gave way to black smoke, and then he could see nothing at all.

Much later that same night, not long before sunrise, the thought came to Joseph as he lay in mazy suspension somewhere between sleep and wakefulness that if he were to hold his toes turned inward in a certain way as he walked he would be able to move two or even three times as fast as he usually did, and might even be able to leave the ground altogether and skate homeward two or three feet up in the air. It was an exciting idea. He could hardly wait for day to arrive, so he could put it to a test. But when he remembered it after he arose he saw the absurdity of it at once and was frightened to think that he had been able to entertain such a lunatic notion more or less seriously, even though he had not been fully awake at the time.

Whole days went by when Joseph found nothing to eat but ants. He did not even attempt to throw rocks at lizards any more, although they were abundant all around him, plump green ones with spiky red crests. Their meat, he imagined, was wonderfully succulent. But they were much too fast for him. And though he spent a great deal of time crouching beside streams trying to catch small darting fishes with his hand, they eluded him with ridiculous ease. He had stopped digging up roots or pulling green shoots from plants by this time, for he had begun to think they were poisoning him and was afraid to eat them.

He began to have headaches. His tongue seemed swollen and had a coppery taste. He could hear the blood pounding insistently in his temples. He shook constantly and walked with his arms wrapped tightly about his body as though he were still contending with the cold rain of the wintry highlands, though by all the outward signs he could tell that the days were growing steadily warmer, that it must be getting practically to be summer. Sometimes when Joseph had walked no more than half an hour he found it necessary to sit down and rest for ten or fifteen minutes, and occasionally longer. And then came a day when he could not continue at all after one of those rest-periods, when he simply settled down under a bush and let the time stretch on and on without getting up.

As he lay there he tried to conjure up a meal for himself out of nothing more than his imagination, a plate of sweet river-crabs followed by roast haunch of heggan in mint sauce, with baked compolls on the side, and a steaming brisbil pudding afterward. He had almost managed to delude himself into believing that he had really done it, that he had just enjoyed a rich, tasty dinner and was feeling much the better for it, when he regained enough clarity of mind to realize that it had been nothing more than a pleasant fantasy, that his stomach was still empty, that in fact he was on the verge of dying of starvation. He knew he was dying and almost did not care.

He lay back and closed his eyes. It seemed to him then that he heard the sounds of rumbling wheels nearby, of swiftly moving vehicles, as though there might be a highway just beyond the hedge across the way. But that had to be a delusion too. He had walked through this beautiful countryside for days, weeks, maybe even months, without ever finding any trace of civilized life other than the hunters' camp that he had come upon on his very first day down from the mountains. The nearest settlement of any kind was probably still a hundred miles away. He would not live to see it.

He realized then that he did care, at least a little, that his life was reaching its end.

How embarrassing it is, Joseph thought, to be dying like this, not even sixteen years old, the heir to House Keilloran transformed into a ragged bundle of skin and bones lying under a bush in some unknown corner of Middle Manza. He had always been so competent, so very good at looking after himself. What were they going to think back in Keilloran when the news finally reached them of what had happened to him? Martin would not weep, no. One quick wince, perhaps: that would be all the outward sign of emotion he would permit himself to show. His father had not even wept when his own beloved wife had died, so suddenly and senselessly, of the bite of that harmless-looking little red toad that had fallen from a tree and landed on her arm. Probably he had never wept in his life. But Joseph knew what her death had done to his father inside, and he knew what his own death would do to him, too.

And his brother Eitan, who was six years younger than Joseph was and had always worshipped him—Eitan would simply not be able to believe that his wondrous brother Joseph had perished in this idiotic way. Eitan would deny the news; he would be angered by it, he would pound the messenger furiously with his fists, he would turn to his father and say in that solemn old-man manner of his, "This is not true, Joseph would never have allowed such a thing to befall him."

And Rickard, three years older than Eitan—he would be angry too, but not for the same reason. Rickard, who now would have to become the heir to House Keilloran: how he would boil with rage at the realization that those responsibilities were unexpectedly going to be dumped upon him! Rickard was not the sort to run a Great House: everyone knew that, Rickard best of all. He was a clever boy, too clever for his own good, so bright that his intelligence worked against him. Rickard could always find ways to avoid handling anything difficult. Either he would sidestep any real challenge or he would simply allow it to flow around him like water around a boulder in a riverbed, whichever was easier. But it had never been necessary for him to be otherwise. He was only the second son. Joseph was the heir; Rickard knew he could look forward to a life of ease.

Perhaps Rickard would change, now that there

was no Joseph and he was going to be the first in line to inherit. Now that he could see the duties that went with being the Master of House Keilloran heading toward him like an avalanche. Joseph hoped so. Perhaps Cailin would help him. She was fourteen, old enough to understand these things, old enough to show Rickard that it would no longer suffice for him to slide by on mere cleverness, that he must take the trouble now to put that cleverness of his to responsible uses, inasmuch as his older brother was dead and he would someday be the Master of the House in his own right. She was a wise girl, Cailin, much undervalued by everyone, as girls tended to be. He wished now that he had treated her better.

Of course Joseph thought of his father, too, that stern, serious, studious man whom Joseph had never come to know as closely as he would have liked to. He never would, now. One thought led to another and he saw other and more ghostly members of his family standing before him, his mother the Mistress Wireille, who had betrayed them all by dying so young, and then his father's father, old Master Eirik, who had always seemed so forbidding of mien with his great white beard and jutting nose and tight-clamped scowling lips, but who actually had been the warmest and most kindhearted of men, the ruler of the House for sixty years and beloved by all. Joseph remembered how fond his

grandfather had been of telling tales of the Keilloran Masters of times gone by, the whole long
line, an earlier Joseph and an earlier Martin and
an earlier Eirik, far back into the first days of the
Masters of Homeworld, the same names over
and over, bold visionary men who had carved
out the family domain in the bounteous sub-
tropical Southland and ruled it with wisdom
and foresight and justice. Joseph, only a small
boy then, had felt an enormous sense of pride at
hearing those stories, at knowing that he was descended from that long line of Keillorans, that
one day he would sit where they had sat, and
would discharge the awesome duties of his post
in a way that showed that he was worthy of his
inheritance, and would in his turn continue the
line by engendering the Masters who would follow him—

"Easy with him," someone was saying. "Will
break in pieces if you handle him too rough, that
one."

"No meat on's bones, none. None. Half dead,
he is."

"Half and more. Easy, now. Up with him. Up."

His mind was still full of thoughts of his grandfather, and of his grandfather's grandfathers back
through time. It seemed to him that one of the
voices he was hearing, a deep, gruff one, was his
grandfather's voice, the voice of Eirik Master
Keilloran, who had made a special journey to
Middle Manza to rescue his errant grandson.

Could that be? His grandfather was dead these ten years past, was he not? Perhaps not. Perhaps that was he, right here, now, his father's father, that wonderful fierce-looking old man. Who would scoop him up, take him in his arms, stride easily from province to province with him until he was home again in Keilloran.

"Grandfather?" Joseph said. He did not open his eyes. "Is that really you, grandfather?"

There was no answer. He was not at all sure that he had actually spoken aloud.

But it definitely was true that he was being lifted, carefully, very carefully, cradled like a dangling cloak across someone's outstretched arms. The stirring of fresh air around Joseph's head brought him back a little way into conscious awareness, and he opened his eyes a bit, peering out through slitted lids. There were two men, neither of them his grandfather, though one, the one with the deep, gruff voice, was indeed old and bearded. But his beard was an untidy straggling thing and he was a short, heavy-set man wearing a tight yellow jerkin and loose-fitting trousers that flared at the cuffs, Folkish clothes, and his face, framed by his long unkempt grayish hair, was a pure Folkish face, coarse-featured, heavy-jawed, bulbous-nosed. The other man, the one who was carrying him, looked much younger, and Folkish also. And Folkish was what they were speaking, though it was a strangely slurred Folkish, very nasal, not at all familiar.

Joseph realized that he himself, when he had cried out a moment ago to his grandfather, would surely have spoken in Master. So if he really had spoken aloud they must know what he was, and thus all of his months of strenuous travail had been in vain. He had been captured by the rebels anyway, and now, he assumed, they were going to put him to death.

Well, what did that matter? He would not have lived more than another day or two anyhow, even if they had not found him. But if they meant to kill him, why were they going to all the trouble of picking him up and carrying him somewhere? They could finish him off with one quick twist of his skinny neck, the way the noctambulo had killed the mud-crawlers in the Getfen forest.

Perhaps he had not really said anything out loud, then. So they had no hint of who or what he might be, other than some pathetic starving wretch asleep under a bush, a lost soul in need of help. For the first time since the really serious weakness and dizziness had come over him Joseph felt a faint glimmering hope that he might actually survive a little longer.

They were both holding him, the older man gripping him by the ankles, the other under his arms, as they swung him upward and gently lowered him into a vehicle of some sort, not an open wagon of the kind he had grown accustomed to during his travels between one Indigene village and the next, but an actual truck. They tucked him in so that he was sitting upright. Joseph leaned back and drew shallow breaths and waited for the next thing to happen.

"Have a bit of bread, will you?" the older one asked.

Joseph only nodded. His mind felt so muzzy that he did not want to attempt framing a sentence in Folkish just yet, and he was afraid to answer in Master.

The other one took Joseph's hand and pressed something into it: a torn-off chunk of bread, it was, hard, grayish, much the same sort of rough peasant stuff that the Getfen woman—what was her name? Joseph was unable to remember, though he remembered her clearly enough—had given him the night that all this began. Hungry as he was, Joseph stared at it a long while before he put it to his lips. He was not sure that he could get it down. The thought came to him of that old Folkish man he had found cowering in the subcellars of Ludbrek House—Waerna, that was his name, he could at least remember that one—and how, offered food and drink for what perhaps was the first time in many days, the old man had looked at it timidly, afraid to try to eat. Now he was as close to starvation as Waerna had been then, floating in a dreamy half-world where swallowing a bite of bread was, perhaps, an impossible task. He knew he had to try. His two Folkish rescuers were softly urging him, in their odd, slurred Folkish, to have a little. But when Joseph attempted it he was unable to manage even one bite. The bread seemed as hard as stone against the tips of his teeth, and when he touched his tongue to it, purely to feel the flavor of it, disgust rose in him and something squirmed within his gut like a wild animal struggling to break free. Joseph turned his head aside, wincing.

"Very thirsty," he said. "Drink—first. Can't—eat."

He said it in Folkish. Did they understand him? Yes. Yes. The older one put a flask to his lips. Water, it was. Joseph drank, cautiously at first, then more deeply. That was better. Once again he attempted the bread, and was able this time to take a tiny bite. He chewed at it unendingly, got it down at last, felt it almost immediately trying to come back up. Somehow he held it down. Had another bite. Another. Better, yes.

The younger one said, "A bit of meat, now?"

The mere idea made Joseph feel ill. He shook his head.

"You wouldn't be wanting wine just now either, then."

"No. No."

"They can see after him in town," the older one said. "We needs be going now."

Joseph heard the sound of the truck's engine starting up. He remembered then the things he had been carrying, his few possessions, his pack, his utility case, the fur mantle that he had brought with him from the Indigene village. He did not want to leave those things behind, forlorn and abandoned under that bush. "Wait," Joseph said. "There were some things of mine there—my belongings—"

The younger man grunted something and jumped down from the truck. When he returned, only a few moments later, he was carrying everything with him. With curious delicacy he spread Joseph's mantle out over his knees, and gave him the other things, not without a puzzled frown as he handed over the utility case. Then the truck started up.

Joseph realized from the swiftness of the man's return that his recent resting-place must have been no more than a few yards off the road that they were traveling now. The traffic-sounds that he had heard while lying in his stupor had been no illusions, then. He had managed to make his way nearly back to civilization, or civilization's edge, anyway, though the last of his energy had left him before he had actually reached it, and he would have died under that bush if these men had not found him. They must have gone off a short way into the underbrush to relieve themselves, Joseph thought, and by that little happenstance alone had his life been saved.

If indeed it had been saved. His weakened body might not recover, he knew, from the stresses of his long solitary march. And even if he did regain some measure of health, it was still not at all clear what was going to happen to him now, a fugitive Master who has fallen into the hands of the Folk.

four

THEY DROVE FOR WHAT MIGHT HAVE BEEN HOURS. Joseph drifted in and out of consciousness. From time to time he heard one of the men speaking to him, and he answered as well as he could, but it was hard for him to remember, a moment later, what they or he had said. Had they asked him where he was heading? Had he told them? He hoped that they were going south, in any event, and tried to reckon their direction from the position of the sun as he glimpsed it through the truck's little side window.

He was not sure at first how to interpret what he saw. The sun seemed to be in front of them as they journeyed down the highway, and that felt wrong, somehow. But then Joseph reminded himself that in this hemisphere the sun was supposed to be in the southern part of the sky. So that was all right. If they were traveling toward the sun, they must be going south. He could see it out of the right-hand window, which meant that this must be afternoon, since the sun moved across the sky from east to west, and west had to be to the right if they were going south. Yes? Yes. His mind felt very clear, icy-cold, and yet it was so very hard to think properly: everything was a terrible effort. I have damaged myself through lack of food, Joseph told himself again. I have made myself stupid, perhaps permanently so. Even if I do get back to House Keilloran eventually I will no longer be qualified to do a Master's work, and I will have to step aside and let Rickard inherit the House, and how he will hate that! But what else can I do, if I have become too stupid to govern the estate?

It was a painful thing to consider. He let himself glide into sleep, and did not awaken again until the truck had come to a halt and the two men were lifting him out of it, treating him as they had before, as though he were very fragile, as though any but the gentlest handling might shatter him.

Joseph could barely stand. He leaned against the younger of his two rescuers, locking his arm inside the man's, and tried as well as he could to stay upright, but he kept swaying and beginning to topple, and had to be pulled back again and again to a standing position.

They had reached a village: a Folkish village,

Joseph supposed. Its layout was nothing like that of the Indigene villages in which he had lived for so many months. This was no dense, dark warren in the Indigene style, tight rows of conical mud-and-wattle houses crowded together in hivelike fashion around a central plaza of ceremonial buildings with the village's communal growing-fields beyond. Here Joseph saw scatterings of small squarish wooden buildings with thatched roofs and stubby stone chimneys rising above them, set widely apart, each house with a low picket fence around it and its own pleasant little kitchen-garden in front and what looked like stables for domestic animals to the rear. Untidy grassy strips ran between the villagers' dwellings. Dusk was beginning to descend. Burning stakes set into the ground provided illumination. To one side ran a canal, spanned here and there by arching wooden bridges. Off the other way there was a big domed building standing by itself that was surmounted by the Folkish holy symbol, the solar disk with rays of sunlight streaming from it, marking it as the village's house of worship. The closest thing to a main plaza was the expanse of bare, skinned ground where the truck had halted, but this was a mere parking area that could not have had any ceremonial significance. Vehicles of all kinds were scattered about it, wagons and carts and trucks and harvesting-machines.

His arrival, he saw, was causing a stir. Little

groups of curious villagers came out of the houses to inspect him. Most of them hung back, pointing and murmuring, but one, a short, spraddle-legged man with the widest shoulders Joseph had ever seen, scarcely any neck, and a blunt bullet-shaped head, came right up to him and gave him a long moment of intense, piercing scrutiny. "This is Stappin," whispered the man who was holding him up. "Governor of the town, he is." And indeed Joseph was readily able to discern the aura of authority, strength, and imperturbable self-confidence that this man radiated. They were traits that he had no difficulty recognizing. His father had them—the Master of any Great House would—and Joseph had seen them in the Ardardin, too, and in some of the other Indigene chieftains along the way. They were necessities of leadership. The aim of Joseph's entire education had been to enable him to develop those traits in himself.

"Why, is just a boy!" Stappin said, after studying Joseph for a time. "Looks old, he does. But those are young eyes. —Who are you, boy? What are you doing here?"

Joseph dared not admit that he was a Master. But he had failed to prepare himself for this moment. He said the first thing that leaped into his mind, hoping that it was the right thing: "I am Waerna of Ludbrek House."

There was no reason why they would ever have heard that name all the way down here. But if by some chance they had, and said that they knew Waerna of Ludbrek House and he was an old man, Joseph intended simply to tell them that he was the grandson of the Waerna they knew, and had the same name.

Stappin did not react to the name or his implied claim of Folkish blood, though. Joseph went on, "When the estate where I lived was destroyed in the rebellion, I fled into the mountains. Now I have no home at all."

The words drained the last of his stamina. His knees turned to water and he slumped down, sagging against the man who held him. Everything became unclear to him after that, until he opened his eyes and discovered that he was inside one of the cottages, lying in an actual bed— no piles of furry skins here—with an actual blanket over him and a pillow under his head. A Folkish woman was looking down at him with motherly concern. By the sputtering light of candles set in sconces against the walls Joseph saw four or five other figures in the room, a boy or youngish man, a girl, and several others lost in the shadows.

The woman said, "Will you take some tea, Waerna?"

He nodded and sat up. The blanket slipped away, showing him that they had removed his clothes: he saw them now, his filthy Indigene robes, lying in a heap beside the bed. It appeared that they had bathed him, too: his skin had a fresh, cool feeling that it had not had in many days.

The woman put a mug of warm tea in his hand. Joseph drank it slowly. It was very mild, faintly sweet, easy to swallow. Afterward the woman watched him for a time, to see how well he kept it down. He was managing it. Something was cooking in another room, some soup or stew simmering over a fire, and the smell of it made him a little uneasy, but the tea seemed to have settled his stomach fairly well.

"Would you like something else to eat?" the woman asked.

"I think so," Joseph said. The woman turned and said something to the girl, who went out of the room. Joseph was afraid that she was going to bring him whatever it was they were cooking in there, which he knew he would not be able to deal with, but when she came back a little while later she was bearing two slices of bread on a plate, and a mug of warm milk. She knelt beside the bed to offer them to him, smiling encouragingly. He nibbled at the bread, which was soft and airy, much easier to get down than the hard crust he had been offered in the truck, and took a sip or two of the milk. The girl kept looking at him, still smiling, holding out the plate of bread in case he should feel capable of eating more.

He liked the way she smiled. It was a pretty smile, he thought. She looked quite pretty herself, as Folkish girls went: her face very broad, as they all tended to be, strong bones, a wide nose, full lips, but her skin was pale and clear and her hair, straight and cropped short, was a soft golden color. So far as he was able to tell she was about his age, or perhaps a year or two older. I must be feeling better already even to be noticing these things, he told himself.

It troubled him that when he sat up like this the whole upper part of his body was bared to her, and she could see how scrawny he had become. That embarrassed him. He looked like a dead man, a skeleton that somehow still was covered with skin. But then he shivered, and the woman—was she the girl's mother?—noticed that at once and put a wrap around his shoulders, a woolen thing, coarse and heavy, that felt unpleasantly scratchy against his skin but did at least hide his shrunken arms and hollow chest from view as well as keeping him warm. He took a few more bites of the bread and finished the milk.

"More?" the woman asked.

"I think not. Not just yet."

They were being very kind to him. Didn't they suspect, from his slender build and finely formed features and whatever hints of a Master accent in his voice he was unable to conceal, that he was a member of the enemy race? Apparently not. They would know nothing of what a southern Master accent sounded like here, anyway; and as for his long limbs and his tapering nose and his thin lips, well, there had been more than a little interbreeding down through the centuries, and it was not all that uncommon for members of the Folk to show some physical traits of the ruling class. It did seem that they accepted him for what he claimed to be, a young man of their own kind, a refugee from a far-away destroyed House.

"You should rest again now," the woman said, and they all went out of the room.

He wandered off into a dreamless dozing reverie. Later, he could not possibly have said how much later, the boy or young man who had been in his room before came in with a bowl of the stuff they had been cooking and a plate of a grayish mashed vegetable, and Joseph tried without success to eat some. "I'll leave it in case you want it," the boy said. Again Joseph was alone.

Some time later he awoke with a full bladder, stumbled out of bed in the darkness with no good idea of where he ought to go, and tripped over some small piece of furniture, sending himself sprawling with a crash into something else, a little bedside table on which they had left a pitcher of water for him. The pitcher, landing on what seemed to be a stone floor, made a sound as it broke that he was certain would wake the whole household, but no one came. Joseph crouched where he had fallen, trembling, dizzy. After a few moments he rose unsteadily and tiptoed out into the hall. Because they had left him naked below the waist, and he did not want to reveal his emaciated thighs and belly to anyone he might encounter out there, especially not the girl, he took the coverlet from his bed and wrapped it around his hips. In the hallway there was just enough moonlight coming in so that he could see other bedrooms, and hear the sound of snoring coming from one or two of them. But he could not find anything that might be a lavatory.

He needed very badly to go by this time. A door presented itself that turned out to be the main door of the house, and he went outside, into the yard, moving steadily but with an invalid's slow, cautious pace. All was silent out there. The whole village seemed to be asleep. The night was warm, the air very still. The two smaller moons were in the sky. A big brown dog lay curled up against the picket fence. It opened one yellow eye and made a soft, short growling sound, but did not otherwise react to Joseph's presence. He walked past it, following along the line of the fence until he judged he was sufficiently far from the house, and opened the coverlet and urinated against a bush. Because all of his bodily functions had become so deranged, it took him an incredibly long time to do it, what seemed like hours. How strange, he thought, to be standing here like this in the yard of a Folkish house, peeing outdoors by moonlight, peeing slowly and endlessly the way an old man does. But all of this is a dream, is it not? It must be. It must.

He found his way back to his own bedroom without incident and dropped at once into deep sleep, the first really sound sleep he had had in more weeks than he could remember. When he awoke, it was long after daylight: floods of golden sunshine were pouring into the room. Someone had come in while he slept, picked up the overturned table, removed the fragments of the broken pitcher. The bowl of stew and the plate of mashed vegetable were still sitting on the cupboard where the boy who had brought them had left them. A stab of hunger pierced through him suddenly and he sprang from the bed, or tried to, but dizziness instantly overcame him and he had to sit again, trembling a little, racked by little shuddering spasms. When the shuddering stopped he got up again, very carefully this time, slowly crossed the room, ate a few spoonfuls of the vegetables, sipped at the stew. He was not as hungry as he had thought he was. Still, he was able to keep the food down, and after a little while he managed to eat some more of it.

They had put out clothing for him, good honest Folkish dress—brown cotton leggings, a singlet of gray wool, a leather vest, a pair of open sandals. Nothing fit him very well: the leggings were too short, the singlet too tight, the vest too loose across the shoulders, the sandals too small. Probably most or all of these things belonged to the boy of the house. But wearing them, ill-fitting or not, was better than going about naked, or wrapping himself in his bed-sheet, or trying to get back into his filthy Indi-gene robes.

The woman who had cared for him last night came into the room. He saw that she was forty or so, plump, with weary dark-shadowed eyes but a warm, ingratiating smile. The girl and the young man who had been in the room last night were with her again. "I am Saban," the woman said. "My daughter Thayle. Velk, my son." Velk ap-peared to be eighteen or twenty, short, strongly built, dull-eyed, probably not terribly bright. Thayle did not seem as pretty as she had last night, now that Joseph could see the Folkish stockiness of her frame, but she looked sweet and cheerful and Joseph liked her smooth clear skin and the bright sheen of her yellow hair. He doubted that she was any older than sixteen, per-haps even a year or two younger; but it was very hard to tell. The Folk always looked older than they really were to him, because they tended to be so sturdily built, so deep-chested and thick-shouldered. Saban indicated a third person stand-ing in a diffident slouch farther back in the room and said, "That is my man, Simthot." About fifty, shorter even than his son, a burly man with pow-erful arms and shoulders, deeply tanned skin, the creases of a lifetime of hard work furrowing his expressionless face. "You are a guest in our house as long as you need to stay," said Saban, and

Simthot nodded emphatically. He appeared to be accustomed to letting his wife do the talking for him.

"I feel much better this morning," Joseph told her. "It was good to sleep in a comfortable bed again, and to be able to eat a little food. I thank you for all your kindnesses."

Was that too formal, too Master-like? Even though he spoke in Folkish, he was afraid of betraying his aristocratic origins by expressing himself too well. He wondered if a Folkish boy of fifteen or sixteen would ever be as articulate as that.

But Saban showed no sign of suspicion. She told him only that she was pleased that the night's rest had done him good, and warned him not to try to recover too quickly. The town governor, she said, would come here later in the day to speak with him. Meanwhile, she suggested, he ought to get back into bed.

That seemed wise to him. He no longer felt as though he were on the brink of death, but he knew he had a long way to go before he had some semblance of vigor again.

Thayle brought him tea with honey in it, and stood by his bedside while he drank it. When he was done Joseph asked her for more of the bread she had given him the night before, and she brought that too, and watched him in a kind of placid satisfaction as he nibbled at it. Like her mother, she appeared to be taking an almost maternal interest in his welfare.

He needed to urinate again, and perhaps even to move his bowels, something he had not succeeded in doing in many days. But he still did not know where to go. Though Joseph would not have hesitated to ask a servant for the location of the nearest privy, if he were a guest in some Great House, he felt oddly inhibited about asking the girl. He was not even sure of the word for it in Folkish; that was part of the problem. But he knew he was being ridiculous. After a time he said, feeling heat rise to his cheeks, "Thayle, I have to—if you would please show me—"

She understood immediately, of course. He would not let her help him rise from the bed, though there was a bad moment of vertigo when he did, and he refused her arm as they went from the room. The lavatory was at the back of the house. Because he knew she was waiting for him outside to guide him back to his room, he tried to be as quick about things as he could, but his body was still not functioning normally, and he could not look her in the eye when he finally emerged a long time afterward. All she said was, "Would you like to go outside for some fresh air and sunshine?"

"I'd like that very much, yes," he told her.

They emerged into the kitchen-garden. The warm sunlight felt good against his face. She stood very close beside him, as though afraid he might be too weak to stand on his own for long.

The firm curve of her breast was pressing into his side. Joseph was surprised to observe how much he liked that. He was actually beginning to find her attractive despite or perhaps even because of her Folkish look, which was somewhat unsettling, though in an interesting way. I suppose I have been away from my own people too long, he thought.

He guessed that it was probably about noon. Very few townsfolk were around, just some very small children playing in the dust and a few old people busy on the porches of their houses. The rest were working in the fields, Joseph assumed, or accompanying their herds through the pastures. A peaceful scene. The dog that had been sleeping out here last night was still curled up on the ground, and again it gave him a quick one-eyed inspection and a soft little growl before subsiding into sleep. It was not easy to believe that elsewhere on Homeworld a bloody war was going on, estates being pillaged and burned, people driven into exile.

"What is this village called?" Joseph asked, after a little while.

"It's a town, not a village," Thayle said.

Evidently that was an important distinction. "This *town*, then."

"You don't know? Its name is Eysar Haven."

"Ah. Eysar Haven."

"Originally it was called something else, though that was so long ago that nobody remem-

bers what. But then the name was changed to
Eysar Haven, because he actually came here once,
you know."

"He? Eysar, you mean?"

"Yes, of course, Eysar. Who else? He was really
here. Some people don't even believe that Eysar
truly existed, that he's just a myth, but it isn't so.
He was here. He stayed for weeks and weeks,
while he was making the Crossing. We know that
to be a fact. And after he left the town was named
for him. It's wonderful to think that we walk on
the very same ground that Eysar's feet once
touched, isn't it?"

"Yes. It certainly is," said Joseph carefully.

He felt that he was in dangerous territory here.
There was a note of reverence and awe in
Thayle's voice. Eysar must be some great Folkish
hero, whose name was known to one and all in
the Folkish world. But Joseph had never heard of
him. *He stayed for weeks and weeks, while he was
making the Crossing.* What could that mean? A
Master's education did not include a great deal of
Folkish history, nor Folkish mythology, for that
matter. For all Joseph knew, Eysar had been a
great Folkish king in the days before the Conquest, or the leader of the first Folkish expedition
to land on Homeworld, or perhaps some sort of
charismatic wonderworking religious leader. The
thought that the Folk once had had great kings of
their own, or glorious heroes, or revered religious
leaders, and that they still cherished the memory

of those great men, was a little startling to him, simply because it had never occurred to him before. And certainly it would not do at all for Thayle to find out that he had no knowledge of who this Eysar was, or the Crossing, or, for that matter, of any significant datum of Folkish life or culture.

He searched for a way to change the subject. But Thayle did the job for him.

"And where is it you come from?" she asked. "Ludbrek House, you said. Where is that?"

"Up in the north. On the other side of the mountains."

"That far? You've come a very great distance, then. It's hard to believe anyone could travel as far as that on foot. No wonder you suffered so much. —That's a strange name for a town, Ludbrek House."

"That's not the town name. It's the name of the Great House that ruled the district."

"A Master-house?" Thayle said. "Is that what you mean?"

She spoke as though the system of Great Houses with satellite towns of Folk around them was nearly as unfamiliar to her as the deeds of Eysar were to him.

"A Master-house, yes," he said. "We all belonged to Ludbrek House, many hundreds of us. But then the rebels burned it and I ran away. You don't belong to any House here, then, is that right?"

"Of course not. You are among cuylings here. You mean you didn't realize that?"

"Yes—yes, of course, I don't know what I could have been thinking—"

Cuylings.

That word was new to him also. It must refer to free Folk, Folk who had managed to stay clear of the rule of the Masters, holding themselves somehow apart from the dominant economic structure of the world. Again Joseph saw how little he knew of these people, and what risks that posed for him. If he allowed this conversation to go on much longer she was bound to find out that he was an impostor. He needed to interrupt it.

He shook his head as though trying to clear it of cobwebs, and swayed, and gave a deliberate little lurch that sent him stumbling into her. As he came up against her he began to let himself fall, but she caught him easily—he was so light, so flimsy—and held him, her arm encircling his ribcage, until he had found his footing again. "Sorry," Joseph muttered. "Very dizzy, all of a sudden—"

"Maybe we should go inside," she said.

"Yes. Yes. I guess I'm not strong enough yet to spend this much time on my feet."

He leaned on her shamelessly as they returned to the house. She would be more likely to overlook his little lapses of knowledge if she could ascribe them to his general state of debilitation and exhaustion. He clambered gladly into his bed.

When she asked him if he wanted anything to eat, Joseph told her that he did, and she brought him some of last night's stew, which he ate with steadily increasing enthusiasm. Then he told her that he wanted to sleep for a while, and she went away.

But he was wide awake. He lay there thinking over their conversation—Eysar, cuylings, the Crossing—and remembering, also, the interesting sensations that the pressure of Thayle's breast against his side had evoked in him. He enjoyed her company. And she seemed eager to make herself responsible for his welfare. Joseph saw that it would be only too easy to give himself away, though. There were only great gulfs of ignorance in his mind where the most elementary facts of Folkish life and history ought to be.

Stappin, the town governor, came to Joseph late that afternoon. Joseph was still in bed, sitting up staring idly at nothing at all, wishing he dared to take one of his books from his pack and read it, when the intense little man with the astonishingly broad shoulders and the bullet-shaped head entered his room. Joseph was instantly ill at ease. If he had come so close to revealing the truth about himself to Thayle in the course of the most casual sort of conversation, what chance did he have of concealing it from this hard-eyed, ruthless-looking man, who plainly had come here for the purpose of interrogating him? And what would happen to him, he wondered, once Stappin discovered his secret?

The governor had been doing a little research, too. He wasted no time on pleasantries. And he let it be known right away that he had his suspicions about Joseph's story. "Ludbrek House, that is where you came from, is what you told us yesterday. How can that be? There are people here who have heard of that place. They tell me that Ludbrek House is such a very great distance from here. Beyond the mountains, it is."

"Yes," Joseph said impassively. He met the stony little eyes with an even stare. I am Joseph Master Keilloran, he told himself, and this man, formidable as he is, is only the governor of a Folkish town. With a little care he would get through this. "On the other side, in High Manza."

With a little care, yes.

But he had let the words "High Manza" slip out without thinking. He regretted that at once. Did the Folk, he wondered, really use that term for the northern third of the continent, or was that in fact purely a Master designation?

With his very first statement he had quite possibly placed himself in peril. He saw that he must be more sparing in his replies. The less he said, the less likely was it that he would stumble into some blunder that would disclose the truth about himself. It had been a mistake to remind himself a moment ago that he was Joseph Mas-

ter Keilloran: right now he was Waerna of Ludbrek House, and he must be Waerna down to his
fingertips.

But Stappin did not seem to be bothered by the
phrase itself, only by the improbability of the
journey. All he said was, "That is many hundreds
of miles. It was winter. It rains up there in the
winter, and sometimes there is snow, also. There
is little to eat. No one could survive such a journey."

Joseph indicated his emaciated form, his wild
tangled beard. "You can see that I very nearly did
not."

"No. You could not have survived, not on your
own. Someone must have helped you. Who was
that?"

"Why, it was the Indigenes," Joseph said. "I
thought you knew that!"

Stappin appeared genuinely startled. "They
would not have done that. The Indigenes are concerned only with the Indigenes. They will have
nothing to do with anyone else."

"But they did," Joseph said. "They did! Look,
look there—" He indicated the ragged Indigene
robes that he had been wearing when he arrived
in Eysar Haven. Saban or Thayle had washed
them and stacked them, neatly folded, in a corner
of the room. "That cloth—it is Indigene weave.
Look at it, Governor Stappin! Touch it! Can it be
anything other but Indigene weave? And that fur

mantle next to it. They gave it to me. They took me in, they fed me, they moved me from village to village."

Stappin spent some time digesting that. It was impossible to tell what was going on behind those cold, hard eyes.

Then, unexpectedly, he said, "Why is it you speak so strangely?"

Joseph compelled himself to meet the governor's gaze steadily, unflinchingly. "What do you find strange about my speech, Governor Stappin?"

"It is not like ours. Your tone of voice. The way you put your words together."

Calm, he thought. Stay calm. "I am of Ludbrek House in High Manza, and this is the way we speak there. Perhaps a little of the Masters' way of speaking has come into our speech and changed it. I could not say."

"Yes. Yes. I forget: you are stendlings, there."

Another new word. From the context Joseph guessed it was the antithesis of "cuyling," and meant—what? Serf? Slave? Vassal? Something on that order.

He simply shrugged. He was not going to get into a discussion of a word whose meaning was uncertain to him.

"And how came it to pass," Stappin said, and there was still an ugly little suspicious edge to his voice, "that you and the Indigenes became such great friends?"

"The uprising happened," Joseph said. "That was the first thing."

He studied Stappin carefully. By now Joseph had concluded that these cuyling Folk of Eysar Haven not only had taken no part in the rebellion, but that they must know very little about it. Stappin did not question his use of the term. He did not react to it in any way. He remained standing as he was, motionless beside Joseph's bed, legs far apart, hands balled into fists and pressing against his hips, waiting.

"It was in the night," Joseph said. "They came into the Great House and killed all the Masters there." He searched about in his memory for the names old Waerna had mentioned, the dead Masters, the leader of the rebels, but he could not remember them. If Stappin queried him about that, he would have to invent the names and hope for the best. But Stappin did not ask for names.

"They killed everyone, the men and the women both, and even the children, and they burned their bodies, and they burned the house also. The place is a complete ruin. There is nothing left there but charred timbers, and all of the Masters of Ludbrek House are dead."

"Did you help to kill them?"

"I? No, not I!" It was easy enough to sound genuinely shocked. "I must tell you, Governor Stappin, I was of the Folk of Ludbrek House. I could never have struck a blow against the Masters of the House."

"A stendling, yes," Stappin said. His tone did not seem so much one of contempt as of simple acknowledgment; but, taken either way, it left Joseph with no doubt of the word's meaning.

"It would not be in my nature to turn against my Masters that way," Joseph said. "If that is a mark against me, I am sorry for that. But it is the way I am."

"I say nothing about that." And then, with an odd little flicker of his eyes: "What work did you do, when you were at Ludbrek House?"

Joseph was unprepared for that. But he did not hesitate to answer. I must not lose my way, he told himself. "I was in the stables, sir," he said, improvising dauntlessly. "I helped care for the bandars and the ganuilles."

"And where were you while they were killing the masters and burning the house?"

"I was hiding, sir. Under the porch that faces the garden. I was afraid they would kill me too. I have heard that many Folk who were loyal to their Houses were killed by the rebels, everywhere in High Manza, and elsewhere too, perhaps."

"When the killing was over, what did you do then?"

"There was no one in sight when I came out. I fled into the forest and lived on my own for a few days. Then I met a noctambulo in the woods who took me to a nearby village of Indigenes. I had hurt my leg and was unable to walk, and the Indigenes took me in and helped me."

There still was obvious skepticism in the governor's expression. These stories must seem like children's fairy-tales to him, Joseph thought. Since everything Joseph was telling him now was the absolute truth, though, he began to feel that he had passed a critical stage in the interrogation. So long as he had been making things up, or borrowing pieces of the other Waerna's account of the uprising, there was always the risk that Stappin would catch him out in a lie. But from this point on he would not be making things up. Sooner or later Stappin would have to accept his narrative as the truth.

He said, "When I recovered, I went into the service of the Indigenes. That may sound strange, yes. But I have some skills at healing the sick, from my work with the stables. When they discovered that, the Indigene villagers used me as a doctor for their own people for a time." Joseph went on to explain how they had sold him, finally, to others of their kind, and how he had been passed from village to village in the high country while the winter rainy season came and went. Here, too, the governor would not be able find any chink of falsity in his tale, for it was all true. "At last," he said, "I grew tired of living among the Indigenes. I wanted to be back among my own people. So I escaped from the village where I was, and came down out of the mountains. But I did not know that the land down here was as empty as it proved to be. There were no Great Houses, no villages of the Folk, not even any Indigenes. I used up the food I had brought with me and after a time I could find nothing anywhere to eat. There were many days when I ate nothing but insects, and then not even those. I made myself ready for death. Then I was found by two men of Eysar Haven, and the rest you know."

He sat back, wearied by the long speech, and tried to ready himself for what Stappin was likely to ask him next, which he supposed would be a question about what he planned to do now. It would hardly be prudent to say that he was heading south, for what reason would he have for wanting to go in that direction? The best thing to reply, he guessed, was that he had no plan at all, that with his House destroyed he was without affiliation, without purpose, without direction. He could say that he had not taken the time to form any plan yet, since he would be in no shape to go anywhere for weeks. Later, when he was healthy again, he could slip away from Eysar Haven and continue on his way to Helikis, but that was nothing he needed to tell Governor Stappin.

The question that he had been expecting, though, did not come. Stappin confronted him again in inscrutable silence for a time, and then said, with a tone of finality in his voice, as though he had reached some sort of verdict within himself, "Once again your luck has held, young Waerna. There will be a home for you here. Saban and Simthot are willing to give you shelter in their house as a member of their own family. You will work for them, once you have your strength again, and in that way you will pay them back the cost of your lodging."

"That seems quite fair, sir. I hope not to be a burden on them."

"We do not turn starving strangers away in Eysar Haven," said Stappin, and began to move toward the door. Joseph, thinking that the interview was at its end, felt a sudden great relief. But the governor was not done with him yet. Pausing at the threshold, Stappin said suddenly, "Who was your grandfather, boy?"

Joseph moistened his lips. "Why, Waerna was his name also, sir."

"Is a Folkish name, Waerna. I mean your *real* grandfather, the one whose blood runs in your veins."

"Sir?" said Joseph, baffled and a little frightened.

"Don't play with me. There's Master blood in you, is it not so? You think I can't see? Look at you! That nose. Those eyes. Small wonder you stayed loyal to your House when the uprising came, eh? Blood calls out to blood. As much Master blood in you as there is Folk, I'd venture. *Stendlings!*" There was no doubting the contempt in his voice this time.

And then he was gone, and Joseph sank back against his pillow, numb, empty.

But he was safe. Despite their suspicions, they

had taken him in. And in the days that followed, his strength began quickly to return. They fed him well; Joseph felt guilty about that, knowing that he would never stay here long enough to repay Saban and Simthot for what they were providing for him, but perhaps he could do something about that when, if, he reached his homeland again. Meanwhile his only consideration must be to make himself ready for a continuation of his journey. As Joseph grew accustomed to regular meals again, he ate more and more voraciously each day. Sometimes he ate too much, and went off by himself to hide the nausea and glut that his greed had caused in him. But his weight was returning. He no longer looked like a walking skeleton. Thayle trimmed his hair, which was shaggy and matted and hung down to his shoulders, now, cutting it back to the much shorter length favored by the people of Eysar Haven. Then Velk brought him a mirror and a scissors, so that Joseph could trim his beard, which had become a bedraggled disorderly black cloud completely enveloping his face and throat. He had not seen his own reflection in months, and he was horrified by what the mirror showed him, those knifeblade cheekbones, those crazily burning eyes. He scarcely recognized himself. He looked five years older than he remembered, and much transformed.

No one said anything to him, yet, about working. Once he was strong enough to go out on his own, he spent his days exploring the town, usually by himself, sometimes accompanied by Thayle. He found it very pleasant to be with her. Her strapping Folkish physique, the breadth of her shoulders and her wide staunch hips, no longer troubled him: he saw that he was adjusting his ideals of feminine beauty to fit the circumstances of his present life. He did indeed find her attractive, very much so. Now and again, as he lay waiting for sleep, he let his mind wander into thoughts of what it would be like to press his lips against Thayle's, to cup her breasts in his hands, to slide himself between her parted thighs. The intensity of these fantasies was something utterly new to him.

Not that he attempted at all to indicate any of this to Thayle. This journey had changed him in many ways, and the uncertainties he once had had about girls now struck him as a quaint vestige of his childhood; but still, it seemed very wrong to him to be taking advantage of the hospitality of his hosts by trying to seduce the daughter of the household. His times alone with Thayle were infrequent, anyway. Like her father and brother and sometimes her mother, she went off for hours each day to work in the family fields. It was high summer, now, and the crops were growing quickly. And gradually Joseph learned that Thayle was involved with one of the young men of the town, a certain Grovin, who was almost certainly her lover and possibly her betrothed. That was something else to consider.

Joseph saw him now and then in the town, a lean, sly-faced sort, perhaps eighteen or nineteen, quick-eyed, mean-looking. He was not at all surprised, though he found it a little embarrassing, to find himself taking a dislike to Grovin. But he had no direct encounters with him.

The town itself was a modest little place, no more than two or three thousand people in all, Joseph guessed, although spread out over a fairly extensive area. All the houses were in one place, all the public buildings in another, and the farmland was beyond—the entire town holdings divided into small family-held plots, nothing communally operated as among the Indigenes, though Joseph gathered that all the townsfolk worked together at harvest-time, moving in teams from plot to plot.

This must have been the way the Folk lived before we came here, Joseph thought. A simple life, a quiet life, raise your crops and look after your cattle and have your children and grow old and give way to the next generation. That was the way the Folk of the Great Houses lived as well, he supposed, but everything they did was done in the service of their Masters, and although a wise Master treated his Folk well, the fact remained that they spent their lives working for their Masters and only indirectly for themselves.

Stendlings. A whole planet of stendlings is what

we have turned them into, sparing only these few cuyling towns here and there in the outback. Joseph still could not see that there was anything seriously wrong with that. But obviously Governor Stappin and the citizens of Eysar Haven might have something different to say on that subject.

There was a statue in the middle of the little group of public buildings that formed the center of the town: a man of middle years, a very Folkish-looking man, thick-thighed and heavy-chested with his hair coming down over his forehead in bangs, carved from gray granite atop a black stone pedestal. He had not been very deftly portrayed, but there seemed to be wisdom and benevolence and much warmth in his expression as he stood there eternally looking out over the heart of the town.

Joseph could find no inscription on the base of the statue to indicate the identity of the man whom it represented. He did not dare ask any of the people strolling nearby. But certainly this must be Eysar, Joseph thought, since this town is named for him. Everyone would know what Eysar looked like: it is not necessary to put a label on his statue. He wondered if he would ever find out who Eysar was.

These were warm, lazy days. Joseph felt almost strong enough to set out for home once more, but the concept of "home" had become such a vague, remote thing in his mind that he saw no urgency in resuming his trek. Who could tell what new hardships awaited him once he took his leave of Eysar Haven? He knew what it was like, now, to starve. Here he was fed well, he had a soft place to sleep, he felt a certain warmth toward Saban and her family. It struck him as quite a plausible choice to remain here a while longer, working with Thayle and Velk and Simthot in the family fields, helping with the harvest, living as though he were really and truly the Folkish boy Waerna of Ludbrek House, now adopted into citizenship at the cuyling town of Eysar Haven.

The Master within him knew that this was foolishness, that it was his duty to get out of here as soon as he was capable of it and take himself onward toward Helikis, toward Keilloran House, toward the father and brothers and sisters who probably had never ceased mourning the loss of him and whose lives would be brightened beyond all measure by his return. It was only the weariness in him speaking, the damage that his time of eating roots and ants had caused, that made him think of lingering here. It was a sign that he was not yet healed.

But he let the days slide easily by and did not force himself to wrestle with the problem of becoming Joseph Master Keilloran again. And then, one warm humid summer evening at dusk, when he was walking through the fields with Thayle, amidst the ripening heads of grain, the whole thing was abruptly thrust upon him once more, out of nowhere, striking like a sudden lightning-bolt, an earthquake, a cataclysmic volcanic eruption.

He had just said, "Look how full these heads are, Thayle, how dark. It will be harvest-time in another month or so, won't it? I'll be able to help you with it by then."

To which she replied sweetly, "Will you be staying here that long, then, Waerna? Are you not beginning to think of returning to your own people?"

He gave her a puzzled look. "My people? I have no people anymore. The Folk of Ludbrek House have scattered in every direction, those that are still alive. I don't know where anyone is."

"I'm not talking about the Folk of Ludbrek House. I mean your real people."

The quiet statement rocked him. He felt like a small boat suddenly adrift in a stormy sea.

"What?" said Joseph, as casually as he could. He could not make himself look at her. "I'm not sure that I understand what—"

"I know what you are," Thayle said.

"What I am?"

"What you are, yes." She caught him by the sleeve and pulled him around to face her. She was smiling. Her eyes were shining strangely. "You're a Master, aren't you, Waerna?"

The word struck him with explosive force. He felt his heart starting to race and his breath came short. But Joseph struggled to permit nothing more than a look of mild bemusement to appear on his face. "This is crazy, Thayle. How could you possibly think that I'm—"

She was still smiling. She had no doubt at all of the truth of what she was telling him. "You have a Master look about you. I've seen some Masters now and then. I know what they look like. You're tall and thin: do you see anybody tall and thin in Eysar Haven? And darker than we are. You have the darkest hair I've ever seen. And the shape of your nose—your lips—"

Her tone of voice was a gentle one, almost teasing. As though this were some sort of game. Perhaps for her it was. But not for him.

"So I have some Master blood in me." Joseph kept his voice level, which was not an easy thing to manage. "Stappin said something about it to me, weeks ago. He noticed it right away. Well, it's probably true. Such things have been known to happen."

"*Some* Master blood, Waerna? *Some?*"

"Some, yes."

"You know how to read. I know that you do. There are books in that pack you were carrying when you came here, and one night when I was outside the house very late I looked in your window and you were awake and reading one. It's a Master book. What else could it be? And you were reading it. You look like a Master, and you read like a Master, and you have a little case that's

full of Master tools. I've looked at them while I
was cleaning your room. I've never seen anything
like them. And your books. I held the book-thing
right in my hand and pressed the button, and
Master words came out on the screen."

"I dwelled among Masters at Ludbrek House.
They taught me to read so I could serve them
better."

She laughed. "Taught a stable-boy to read, so
he could be a better stable-boy?"

"Yes. And the utility case that you saw—I stole
that when I fled from Ludbrek House. The books,
too. I swear to you, Thayle, by whatever god you
want me to swear by—"

"No." She put her hand over his mouth. "Don't
lie, and don't blaspheme. That'll make everything
worse. I know what you are. It has to be true. You
hadn't ever heard of Eysar, and you don't know
the names of our holidays, and there are a thousand other things about you that just aren't right.
I don't know if anyone else here has seen it, but I
certainly have."

He was stymied. He could bluff all he liked,
but nothing he could ever say would convince
her. She thought that she knew what he was, and
she was sure that she was right, and she *was* right,
and Joseph would have to be the best actor in the
world to make her believe now that he was of the
Folk. Even that might not be good enough. She
knew what he was. His life was in her hands.

He wondered what to do. Run back to the

house, collect his things, get himself away from this place while he still could? He did not feel ready for that, not now, not so suddenly. Night was coming on. He had no idea which way to go. He would have to live off the land again, at a time when he was still not entirely recovered from his last attempt at that.

Thayle said, as though reading his mind, "You don't need to be afraid of me, Waerna. I'm not going to tell anyone about you."

"How can I be sure of that?"

"It would be bad for you, if I did. Stappin would never forgive you for lying to him. And he couldn't let a runaway Master live among us, anyway. You'd have to leave here. I don't want that. I like you, Waerna."

"You do? Even though I'm a Master?"

"Yes. Yes. What does your being a Master have to do with it?" That strange glow was in her eyes again. "I won't say a word to anyone. Look, I'll swear it." She made a sign in the air. She uttered a few words that Joseph could not understand. "Well?" she said. "Now do you trust me?"

"I wish I could, Thayle."

"You can say a thing like that, after what you just heard me swear? I'd be furious with you, if you were Folk. But what you just said would tell me you're a Master if nothing else I knew about you did. You don't even know the Oath of the Crossing! It's a wonder no one else here has caught on to you before this." Joseph realized that somewhere in the last moments Thayle had taken both his hands in hers. She stood up on tiptoe, so that her face was very close to his. Softly she said, "Don't be afraid of me, Waerna. I won't ever bring you harm. Maybe the Oath of the Crossing doesn't mean anything to you, but I'll prove it to you another way, tonight. You wait and see."

Joseph stared at her, not knowing what to say.

Then she tugged at him. "Let's go back, all right? It's getting near time for dinner."

His mind was swirling. He wanted very much to believe that she would not betray him, but he could not be sure of that. And it was deeply troubling to realize that his secret was in her hands.

The evening meal was a tense business for him. Joseph ate without saying a word, looking down into his plate most of the time, avoiding the glances of these people with whom he had lived for weeks, people who had taken him in, cared for him, bathed him when he was too weak, fed him, clothed him, treated him as one of their own. He was convinced now that they all knew the truth about him, had known it a long while, not just Thayle but her brother also, and Simthot, and Saban. He must have given himself away a hundred times a day—whenever he failed to recognize some reference that any of the Folk from anywhere on Homeworld would have understood, whenever he said something in what he hoped was idiomatic Folkish that was actually phrased in a way that nobody who was truly of the Folk would ever phrase it.

So they knew. They had to know. And probably they were in constant anguish over it, debating whether to tell Stappin that they were sheltering a member of the enemy race here. Even if they wanted to protect him, they might fear that they were endangering their own safety by holding back on going to the governor and reporting what they knew. Suppose Stappin had already worked out his real identity also, and was simply waiting for them to come to him and report that the boy they were harboring was actually a fugitive Master? The longer they waited, the worse it would be for them, then. But possibly they were just biding their time until some appropriate moment, some special day of the Folkish year that he knew nothing about, when you stepped forward and denounced the liars and impostors in your midst—

In the evenings Saban and Simthot, and sometimes Velk as well, would settle in the front parlor to play a game called weriyel, which involved making patterns with little interlocking pieces of carved bone on a painted board. Joseph had explained, early on, that this game had not been known to him in his days at Ludbrek House, and they had seemed to take that at face value; Velk had taught him the rules, and some evenings he played with them, although he had not yet developed much skill at it. Tonight he declined to join them. He did not want to remind them of how badly he played. He was sure that his lack of knowledge of the rules of weriyel was one more bit of evidence that he was no true man of the Folk.

Thayle never took part in the weriyel games. Most evenings she went out—to be with her lover Grovin, Joseph assumed. He did not really know, and he scarcely felt free to ask her. Lately he had taken to imagining the two of them going off to some secluded grove together and falling down to the ground in a frenzied embrace. It was not a thought that he welcomed in any way, but the harder he tried to rid his mind of it, the more insistently it forced itself upon him.

Though darkness was slow to come on these summer nights and it was much too early to think about going to sleep, Joseph, uncomfortable now in the company of his hosts, retired early to his room and sprawled glumly atop his bed, staring upward, hands locked behind his head. Another night he might have spent the time reading, but now he was fearful of that, not wanting Saban or Velk to come in without warning, as they sometimes did, and find him with the little reader in his hands. It was bad enough that Thayle, spying on him late at night through the window—and why had she done that?—had seen him reading. But it would be the end of everything for him here if one of the others actually walked in and caught him at it.

Joseph saw no solution for his predicament other than to leave Eysar Haven as soon as possible. Tomorrow, even, or perhaps the day after: pack his belongings, say his farewells, thank Saban and her family for their hospitality, head off down the road. There was no need for him to sneak away, as he had done when leaving the Indigenes. These people did not own him. He was merely a guest in their midst. And, though Joseph had agreed to repay them for his lodgings by helping them with the harvest, they would very likely be happy enough to see him get on his way without waiting around for harvest-time, suspecting what they surely did about his real identity. It was the only sensible thing to do: go, go quickly, before the anomaly of a Master dwelling in a Folkish town became too much for anyone to tolerate.

Finally it was dark enough to try to sleep. He got under the covers. But he was still all awhirl within, and he lay stiffly, hopelessly awake, shifting from one position to another and finding none to his liking. There was not going to be any sleep for him at all this night, Joseph decided.

But he must have fallen asleep somewhere along the way, because he heard the door of his room opening and sat up, groggy and confused as one is when one is abruptly awakened, with the fragments of an exploded dream still floating through his mind. Someone had come in. Joseph could see very little, what might have been a figure at his threshold, a mere outline, darkness against darkness. "Who's there?" he asked.

"Shh! Quiet!"

"Thayle?"

"Shh!"

Footsteps. A rustling sound, as of garments being thrown aside. This was beyond all belief. I am still asleep, Joseph thought. I am dreaming this. He was aware of movements close by him. His coverlet being drawn back. She was joining him in bed. A warm body up against his flesh, too warm, too real, to be a phantasm of the night.

"Thayle—what—?"

"I told you I'd show you tonight that you could trust me. Now be quiet, will you? Please!" Her hands were moving boldly over his body. Joseph lay still, astonished, wonderstruck. So it was going to happen at last, he realized, the thing that he had read about in so many books and plays and stories and poems, the thing that he knew he would experience eventually, but which he had not thought would be coming to him so soon, here, now, tonight. Perhaps it had been inevitable that his first time would be with a girl of the Folk. He did not care about that. He did not care about anything, just now, except what was unfolding in this bed. Her touch drew shivers from him. He wished he could see her, but there were no moons tonight, not even much starlight, and he dared not break the flow of events to light a lamp, nor did he think she would want him to.

"You can touch me," she said. "It's allowed."

Joseph was hesitant about that for a moment, but only for a moment. His hand hovered over her, descended, found her. A thigh, this was. A hip. That sturdy body, that strong wide-hipped Folkish body, here against him, naked, willing. The fragrance of her flesh, delighting him, dizzying him. He slid his hand upward, meeting no discouragement, until he found her breasts. Carefully he closed his fingers over one of them. It was a firm, heavy, resilient globe; it filled his entire hand. He could feel the little hard node of her nipple pressing against his palm. So that is what breasts feel like, Joseph thought. He had expected them to be softer, somehow, but perhaps the softness happened later, when a woman was twenty or twenty-five, and had had some babies. He wriggled around to a better position and glided across the valley of her chest to the other breast, and caressed them both for a while. She seemed to like it that he was touching her breasts. Her lips sought his, and found them, and he was astounded to find her tongue slipping between his lips. Is that what people did when they kissed? Tongues? He felt impossibly innocent. Surely she must realize, by this time, how totally innocent he was. But that was all right, Joseph thought, so long as she does not laugh, so long as she leads me along step by step, so long as she teaches me what to do. As she was doing.

On his own initiative he moved his hand lower, sliding it down her body, reaching her belly, now, the deep indentation of her navel, halting there, running the hand from side to side, from one hard upjutting hipbone to the other. Then, emboldened, he went onward, found the soft, dense patch of hair at the meetingplace of her thighs, touched it, stroked it. She seized two of his fingers and thrust them inward. He felt moisture. Warmth.

And then everything was happening very quickly. He was on her, searching, thrusting, suddenly inside her, enveloped in that moist softness, the tender velvety secret place between her legs, moving. It was an astounding sensation. No wonder, no wonder, that themes of desire and passion were so central to all those books, those plays, those poems. Joseph had always supposed it would be something extraordinary, the act itself, but he had never really imagined—how could he?—the actual intensity of the feeling, that sense of being inside another human being, of being so intimately linked, of having these exquisite ecstatic feelings spreading outward from his loins to the entirety of his body. They built and built with irresistible force, sweeping him away within moments: he wanted to hold back, to savor all this a little longer, but there was no way he could do that, and as the spasms rocked him like a series of detonations Joseph gasped and shuddered and pressed his face down beside Thayle's cheek and clung to her strong sturdy body until it was over, and then he was lying stunned against her, limp, sweaty, drained, trembling, ashamed.

Ashamed?

Yes. In that first moment of return from his climax it astonished him how quickly he had traveled from unthinkable ecstasy to dark, exhausted, bewildered guilt. The whole descent had taken mere instants. Now that Joseph was able to think coherently again, his thoughts all were bleak ones. He had not expected that. There had been no chance to expect anything. But now, now, in the surprisingly harsh and chilly aftermath, looking back at that frenzy of eager grappling, he could not help but focus on the question of what sort of pleasure there could have been in it for her. Could there have been any, any at all? She had merely served as the instrument of his own delight. He had simply entered her, moved quickly, used her for his own gratification. Master and peasant girl, the old, old story, disgusting, shameful. He had never hated himself so much as in that moment.

He felt impelled to say something, and could not, and then did. "It all went so fast," Joseph said, speaking into his pillow, his voice rough and frayed, sounding unfamiliar in his own ears. "I'm sorry, Thayle. I'm sorry. I didn't want—"

"Shh. It was fine. Believe me, Waerna."

"But I would rather have—I would have liked to—

"*Shh!* Be still, and don't worry. It was fine. Fine. Just lie here beside me and relax." Soothingly she stroked Joseph's back, his shoulder, his arm. "In a little while you'll be ready to go again."

And he was. This time it all went much less frenziedly for him. There was none of the crazy heedless swiftness of before. He felt almost like an expert. He had always been a quick learner. He knew now what to expect, had a better understanding of how to pace himself, how to hold himself back. Thayle moved skillfully beneath him, a steady pumping rhythm, delightful, amazing. Then the rhythms grew more irregular and she dug her fingertips hard into his shoulders, clung to him, rocked her hips, arched her back, threw back her head, and he knew that something was happening within her, something awesome, something convulsive, although he was not entirely sure what it was; and a weird throaty sound emerged from her, deep, throbbing, not even really a human sound, and Joseph knew that her big moment must have arrived. Somewhere within it he had his own, not as overwhelming as before, not nearly, but nonetheless an immensely powerful sensation.

There was no guilt or shame this time, none of the terrible bleakness of that earlier aftermath. He felt only a calm sense of accomplishment, of achievement, an awareness of pleasure given and received. It seemed to Joseph that he had crossed some border in this past hour, stepping over into a strange and wonderful new land from which there would be no returning.

They lay tangled together, spent and sticky, breathing hoarsely, saying nothing for a long while.

"It was my first time," he said finally.

"I know."

"Ah. Was it that easy to tell, then?"

"Everybody has a first time sometime. It's not anything you need to explain. Or to apologize for."

"I just want to thank you," Joseph said. "It was very beautiful."

"And for me also. I won't ever forget it." She giggled. "Grovin would kill me if he found out. He thinks he owns me, you know. But no one owns me. No one. I do as I please." She drew a little playful line along Joseph's jaw with the tip of one finger. "Now we each have a secret against each other, do you see? I could tell Stappin that you're a Master, but I won't. And you could tell Grovin that I've been to bed with you."

"But I won't."

"No. Neither of us will say anything to anybody. We've put each other in each other's hands. —But now tell me your real name. You can't be a Waerna. Waerna isn't a Master name."

"Joseph," he said.

"That's a strange name. *Joseph. Joseph.* I've never heard a name like that before."

"It's an ancient name. It goes back to Old Earth. My father has an Earth name too: Martin."

"Joseph. Martin."

"I'm not from Ludbrek House, either. Not from Manza at all. I'm Joseph Master Keilloran of House Keilloran in Helikis."

It was strange and somehow wonderful to speak the full name out loud, here in this little Folkish town, in this Folkish house, lying here naked in the arms of this naked Folkish girl. It was the final nakedness, this last stripping away of all concealment. Thayle had never heard of House Keilloran, of course, had barely heard of Helikis itself—a far-off land, that was all she knew, somewhere down in the southern part of the world—but she said the name three or four times, Joseph Master Keilloran of House Keilloran in Helikis, Joseph Master Keilloran of House Keilloran in Helikis, as though the words had some magical potency for her. She had some difficulty pronouncing Joseph's surname correctly, but he saw no point in correcting her. Joseph felt very drowsy, very happy. Idly he stroked her body in a tender but nonsexual way, his hand traveling lightly along her flanks, her belly, her cheeks, a purely esthetic enjoyment, simply enjoying the smoothness of her, the firmness of her skin and the taut flesh and muscle beneath it, the way he might stroke a finely carved statuette, or a thoroughbred racing-bandar, or a perfectly thrown porcelain bowl. He did not think there was any likelihood that he could feel desire again just yet, not so soon after those two cataclysmic couplings. But then his hands were going to her breasts, and then to her thighs, and to his surprise and delight he felt himself awakening to the pull of her body one more time, and she made a little chuckling sound of approval and drew him down into her once more.

Afterward she kissed him gently and wished him pleasant dreams, and gathered up her scattered clothing and went out. When she was gone Joseph lay awake for a while, reliving all that had taken place, playing it back in his mind with the utmost vividness, watching it all in wonder, amazement, even disbelief. He tumbled then into sleep as into a crevasse on some lofty snowy mountain slope and was lost in it, dreamless, insensate, until morning.

There was no possibility after the experiences of that night of his leaving Eysar Haven of his own volition, regardless of the risks involved in his staying. Thayle had tied him to it with unbreakable silken bands. His only thought now was of when she would enter his bed again.

But that did not happen immediately. Often in the days that followed Joseph would glance toward her and see that she was covertly looking at him, or that she was smiling warmly in his direction, or even winking and blowing him a kiss; but though he lay awake for a long while each night hoping for the sound of the opening door, the footsteps approaching his bed, the rustle of clothing being shed, four nights went by before she finally did come back. It was an eternity. "I thought you were never going to be with me again," he said, as his hands moved toward her breasts. She said something about needing to take care that her parents did not discover what was going on under their own roof. No doubt that was so. But also it had occurred to Joseph that Thayle probably was in the habit of spending several evenings a week with Grovin, and would not want to come to him while her body was still sweaty and slippery from another man's passions. He tried not to think about that; but it was a time of agony to him, those nights that he waited in vain for her, imagining that at this very moment she might be with Grovin, doing with him the same things that he so desperately wanted her to be doing once more with him.

Twice during those days his path and Grovin's crossed in town, and both times Grovin gave him hard, sour looks. Joseph asked Thayle about that, wondering whether Grovin suspected something, perhaps the truth about Joseph's identity or else the possibility that he and Thayle were taking advantage of his presence in her family's house to do the very thing that they were in fact doing. But she assured him that neither could be true. "If he so much as dreamed you were a Master, he'd have taken it up with Stappin already. And as for suspecting you and me—no, no, he's so confident of himself that it would never occur to him. If he thought anything was going on between us he'd have let me know about it by now."

"Then why does he look at me that way?"

"He looks at everybody that way. It's just the way he is."

Maybe so. Still, Joseph did not much like it.

The summer days floated along in a golden haze of mounting heat. The harvest season approached. Joseph lived for the nights of Thayle's visits. Helikis might have been a continent on another planet for all that it entered his mind.

They were friends as well as lovers, by this time. In the intervals between their bouts of lovemaking they talked, lying side by side looking toward the ceiling instead of at each other, sometimes for hours. She revealed a lively, questing intelligence: that came as a surprise to Joseph. It fascinated Thayle that he should be a Master. In this district of cuyling Folk, where the nearest Great Houses were far off beyond the mountains, Masters were unfamiliar, exotic things. She understood that most of the rest of the world was divided up into huge feudal estates on which her people had for many hundreds of years lived, essentially, as property, until the recent outbreak of violent revolution. She had heard about that, anyway. But she seemed to have no inward grasp of what it was like. "You *own* the Folk who live on your land?" she asked. "How is that, that one person can own others?"

"We don't exactly own them. We provide for them; we make sure everyone is housed, that nobody goes hungry, that there's work for everybody, that good medical care is available. And in return for that they work the lands, and look after the livestock, and do what needs to be done in the factories."

"But everyone is housed here in Eysar Haven, and everyone has work to do, and nobody goes hungry, and all of that. Why would we need Masters here?"

"You don't, I suppose. But the Folk of other places aren't as self-sufficient as the people of the cuyling towns are."

"You mean, they came to your ancestors and said, 'Please rule us, please be our Masters?' They *wanted* your people to take charge of their lives for them?"

"Well, in a manner of speaking—"

"No. Actually they were conquered, weren't they? There was a thing called the Conquest, when the Masters came out of the sky and seized the land and *forced* everyone to submit to them. Except for a few like us, off in places of the world that nobody seemed to want to bother conquering. Isn't that so, Joseph?"

He could not deny that. He would not even try. It would not be known as the Conquest, he thought, if it had not been a conquest. And yet— yet—it had always been his understanding that the Masters had imposed the system of Great

Houses upon the Folk for the good of the Folk themselves, not just for their own, and that the Folk had learned to see the wisdom of that system. It had been his understanding, too, that the Folk were an inherently weak breed, nothing more than creatures of a docile domesticated sort that had been waiting for leadership to be provided for them.

But it was impossible for Joseph to say any of that to her. How could he let this girl—this woman, really—for whom he now felt such desire, such need, such love, even, and from whom he had received such delights and hoped to receive more, think that he looked upon her not as a human being but as a kind of domesticated beast? Not only would telling her that be a hideous impossible insult, but he knew it was not even true. Everything about her demonstrated that. Everything he had seen about Eysar Haven demonstrated that. These people were quite capable of functioning on their own. And perhaps that had been true of all the other Folk, too, once upon a time, back before the Conquest.

It was clear to him now that the Conquest had been a conquest indeed, in fact as well as name. The Folk had been doing well enough before the first Masters came to Homeworld. They lacked the force and drive of Masters, perhaps, but was that a sin? Had they deserved to lose control of their own lives, their own world, for such failings? The Masters had *subjugated* the Folk. There was no other applicable word. Even if the bloody rebellion that had driven Joseph himself into these wanderings across the face of the continent of Manza had not taught him by now how resentful of Master rule the Folk were, or some of them, anyway, this stay in Eysar Haven and these late-night conversations with Thayle would have shown him that. It all seemed obvious enough to him now; but it was devastating to him to be forced to see how much he had simply taken for granted, he with his fine Master mind, his keen, searching intellect.

She challenged him in other areas, too.

"Your father, the Master of House Keilloran— how did he get to be the Master of the House?" She still could not pronounce the name correctly, but Joseph let that go. "Did everybody who lives there choose him for that?"

"His father was Master of the House before him," Joseph told her. "And his father before that, going back to the beginning. The eldest son inherits the title."

"That's all?" Thayle said. "He is allowed to govern thousands and thousands of people, Masters and Folk alike, simply because he's his father's son? How strange. It seems very foolish to me. Suppose there's someone else better suited to govern, somebody who's smarter and wiser and more capable in every way. Everyone can see that, but he won't be allowed, will he? Because he's not the eldest son of the eldest son.

That's a stupid system, I think." Joseph said nothing, and Thayle was silent a moment, too. Then she said, "What happens if there's more than one son? That wouldn't be very unusual, would it?"

"The eldest son always inherits."

"Even if the second or even third son is plainly better qualified. Or the second or third *daughter*, for that matter. But I suppose daughters don't figure into this."

"Only the eldest son," Joseph said. "He's specially trained for the job from childhood on. Since it's known that he's going to inherit, they see to it that he's been properly taught to do what must be done."

"But no matter how well they teach him, he isn't necessarily the smartest member of his family, is he? Even if it is agreed that you have to limit the title to a single family just because that family happens to have grabbed power first, you could have generation after generation where the new Master isn't even the best qualified person among his own people. Do you think that's so good, Joseph?"

This is a girl of the Folk who is asking me these questions, he said to himself. This is a docile, ignorant creature, a peasant, a person incapable of serious thought.

There was another long silence.

Thayle said then, "Are you the eldest son, Joseph?"

"Yes. Yes, I am."

"You will inherit the title, then, and be Master of House Keilloran. By right of birth alone, nothing else."

"If I live to get home, yes. Otherwise my brother Rickard will be. He won't like that, if things happen that way. He never expected to rule and he's not well prepared for doing it."

"But he'll become the Master anyway, because he'll be the eldest available son."

"Yes. Yes."

"By right of birth alone. Not necessarily because he'll be a good Master."

He wished she would stop pounding at him. "Rickard will be a good Master if the title comes to him," Joseph said stubbornly. "I'm sure that he will. I know that he will." But he could not hide the lack of conviction in his voice. He was amazed at how, within the space of fifteen minutes, Thayle had undermined every assumption he had ever held about the relationship of Master to Folk, about the method by which the Great Houses chose their leaders, about the merit of his own automatic succession to the powers of head of the House. He felt as though this bed on which the two of them were lying had turned somehow into a flimsy raft, on which he was being borne down some turbulent river toward a steep cataract that lay only a short distance ahead.

Joseph let the silence stretch and stretch until it was nearing the breaking-point, but still he could not bring himself to speak. Whatever he might say would be wrong.

"Are you angry with me?" Thayle asked him finally.

"No. Of course I'm not."

"I've offended you. You thought I was criticizing you."

"You have a different way of looking at things, that's all. I was just thinking about everything you said."

"Don't think too much. Not now." She reached across to him. Gratefully he surrendered to her embrace. They began to move in the way that was already beginning to become familiar to them. Joseph was glad to be able to lose himself in the unthinking pleasures that her supple body offered.

The next morning after breakfast, the hour when nearly everyone had gone off to the day's work in the fields and Joseph was alone in the house, he was startled to hear her voice, calling to him from outside, a low, sharp whisper: "*Joseph! Joseph!*"

That surprised him, that she should be calling him by his real name. But at this time of the day there was no one around but old people and small children to hear her do it.

And the fact of Thayle's presence here at this time of day made his heart leap. She must have sneaked back from the fields so that they could be together. It was exciting to think that she would want him that much. And there was another thing: they had never made love by daylight. That would be something new, different, wonderful, a revelation.

He rushed out onto the porch to greet her and lead her to his bedroom.

But then he saw her. How she looked. "Thayle?" he said, in a small, bewildered voice. "What happened, Thayle? Was there an accident?"

"Oh, Joseph—oh—oh, Joseph—"

She looked horrifying. Her clothing was torn and dirty. One sleeve dangled by threads. Thayle herself looked bruised and hurt. Her lower lip had a bloody cut on it and it was beginning to turn puffy. Another narrow trail of blood ran down from one of her nostrils. Her left eye was swelling shut. She held her hand pressed to her cheek: that seemed to be swelling up also. One of her sandals was missing. Her expression was a strange one: blank, frozen, dazed.

Joseph gathered her in without asking questions, held her close against himself, gently stroked her back and shoulders. She began to sob quietly. For a few moments she accepted the comfort he was offering her, and then she pulled back from him, looking up into his eyes, searching for words. "You have to leave," she said. "Right now. There's no time to waste."

"But what—what—?"

"Grovin. He knows. He was hiding outside

your window last night. He heard us . . . everything."

"And he beat you?" Joseph asked, incredulous. "He did this?" It had never occurred to him that a man would strike a woman, any woman, let alone his own lover. But then he reminded himself that these people were Folk, and that not very long ago the Folk had risen up and slaughtered their Masters as they sat in their manor-houses, and plenty of their own kind as well.

"He did it, yes." She made it sound almost unimportant. "Come on, Joseph! Come *on*. Get your things. I've taken a truck. We need to get you away from here, fast. I told you he'd kill me if he found out I was going to bed with you, and he will, he will, if you stay here any longer. And he'll kill you too."

It was still hard for Joseph to get his mind around all that Thayle was telling him. He felt like a sleepwalker who has been unceremoniously awakened. "You say he overheard us?" he asked. "The lovemaking, you mean, or the things we were discussing, too? Do you think he knows I'm a Master?"

"He knows, yes. Not because he overheard our conversation. I told him. He suspected that you were, you know. He's suspected all along. So he asked me what I knew about you, and then he hit me until I told him the truth. And hit me again afterward. —Oh, please, Joseph, don't just stand there in that idiotic way! You have to get moving.

Now. This very minute. Before he brings Stappin down on you."

"Yes. Yes." The stasis that had enfolded him these past few minutes began to lift. Joseph rushed into his room, grabbed up his few possessions, bundled them together. When he emerged he saw that Thayle had had the presence of mind to assemble a little packet of food for him. He was going to be alone again soon, he realized, trekking once more through unknown regions of this unfriendly continent, living off the land.

The thought of parting from her was unbearable.

What was running through his mind now were thoughts not of the dangers he would be facing out there, or of the trouble Grovin could cause for him before he managed to leave, but only of Thayle's lips, Thayle's breasts, Thayle's open thighs, Thayle's heaving hips. All of which had been his this brief while, and which now he must leave behind forever.

When they emerged from the house they found Grovin waiting outside, standing squarely in their path. His face was cold and mean, a tight, pinched-looking, furious face. He glared at them, looking from Thayle to Joseph, from Joseph to Thayle, and said, "Going somewhere?"

"Stop it, Grovin. Let us pass. I'm taking him to the highway."

He ignored her. To Joseph he said, icily, fiercely, "You thought you had a sweet little deal, didn't you? They fed you, they gave you a soft place to sleep, and they gave you something soft to sleep with, too. Wasn't that nice? But what are you doing here, anyway, you lazy parasite? Why aren't you dead like the rest of your kind?"

Joseph stared. This was his rival, the man who had hurt Thayle. What was he supposed to do, hurt this man in return? Something within him cried out that he should do it, that he should beat Grovin to his knees for having dared to take his hand to her. But nothing in his education had prepared him for doing anything like that. This was not like punishing an unruly field-hand, which any Master would do without thinking twice about it; this was something else, a private quarrel over a woman, between two people who also happened to be of two different races.

Nothing in his education had prepared him, either, for the spectacle of an angry Folker hurling abuse at him this way. That was not a thing that ought to be happening. It was a phenomenon on the order of water running uphill, of the sun rising in the west, of snow falling in the middle of summer. Joseph did not know what to say or do. It was Thayle, instead, who took it upon herself to step forward and push Grovin out of the way; but Grovin merely grinned and seized her by one wrist and flung her easily from him, sending her spiraling down into a heap on the ground.

That could not be allowed. Joseph dropped the things he was carrying and went toward him, not sure of what he was going to do but certain that he had to do something.

He had fought before, roughhousing with other Master boys his age, or even with Anceph or Rollin, but it had been clearly understood then that no one would be hurt. This was different. Joseph clenched his hand into a fist and swung at Grovin, who slapped the fist aside as though it were a gnat and punched him in the pit of the stomach. Joseph staggered back, amazed. Grovin came after him, growling, actually growling, and hit him again, once on the point of his left shoulder, once on the side of his chest, once on the fleshy part of his right arm.

Being hit like this was as surprising as first sex had been, but not at all in the same way. The flying fists, the sudden sharp bursts of pain, the absolute *wrongness* of it all—Joseph was barely able to comprehend what was taking place. He understood that it was necessary to fight back. He could do it. Grovin was slightly built, for a Folker, and shorter than Joseph besides. Joseph had the advantage of a longer reach. And he was angry, now, thinking of what Grovin had dared to do to Thayle.

He struck out, once, twice, swinging hard, missing the first time but landing a solid blow on Grovin's cheekbone with the second blow. Grovin grunted and stepped backward as though he had been hurt, and Joseph, heartened, came striding in to hit him again. It was an error.

He managed to hit Grovin once more, a badly placed punch that went sliding off, and then the other, crouching before him like a coiled spring, came back at him suddenly with a baffling flurry of punches, striking here, here, there, spinning Joseph around, kicking him as he was turned about, then hitting him again as Joseph swung back to face him. Joseph staggered. He moved his arms wildly, hoping somehow to connect, but Grovin was everywhere about him, hitting, hitting, hitting. Joseph was helpless. I am being beaten by a Folker, Joseph thought in wonder. He is faster than I am, stronger than I am, in every way a better fighter. He will smash me into the ground. He will destroy me.

He continued to fight back as well as he could, but his best was not nearly good enough. Grovin danced around him, hissing derisively, laughing, punching at will, and Joseph made only the foggiest of responses. He was faltering now, lurching and teetering, struggling to keep from falling. Grovin took him by the shoulders and spun him around. And then, as Joseph turned groggily back to face him and began gamely winding up for one last desperate swing, Grovin was no longer there. Joseph did not see him at all. He stood blinking, bewildered.

Thayle was at Joseph's side. "Hurry, Joseph! Hurry, now!"

Her eyes were bright and wild, and her face was flushed. In her hand she was gripping a thick, stubby piece of wood, a club, really. She looked at it, grinning triumphantly, and tossed it away. Joseph caught sight of Grovin a short distance off to the left, kneeling in a huddled moaning heap, shoulders hunched, head down, rocking his head from side to side. He was holding both hands clapped to his forehead. Blood was streaming out freely between his fingers.

Joseph could not believe that Thayle had done that to him. He could not have imagined a woman clubbing a man like that, not under any circumstances, any at all.

But these people are Folk, Joseph reminded himself. They are very different from us.

Then he was scooping up his discarded possessions and running, battered and dizzy and aching as he was, alongside Thayle toward the truck that was parked at the edge of the clearing, a truck much like the one in which his two rescuers had brought him to Eysar Haven many weeks before. He jumped in beside her. She grasped the steering-stick and brought the truck to a roaring start.

Neither of them spoke until they were well outside the town. Joseph saw that it was not easy for Thayle to control the vehicle, that it took all her concentration to keep it from wandering off the road. Plainly she was not an experienced driver. But she was managing it, somehow.

It did not seem to him that the fight had caused him any serious injury. Grovin had hurt him, yes.

There would be bruises. There would be painful places for some days to come. But his disorientation and bewilderment in the final stages of the battle, that weird helplessness, he saw now, had been the result more of simply finding himself personally involved in violence, finding himself in actual hand-to-hand combat, than of any damage Grovin had been able to inflict. Of course, it might all have become much worse very soon. If Grovin had succeeded in knocking him down, if Grovin had begun to kick him and stomp on him, if Grovin had jumped on him and started to throttle him—

Thayle's intervention had saved his life, Joseph realized. Grovin might well have killed him. That might even have been what he was trying to do.

The truck rolled onward. Joseph was the first to break the long silence, with a question that had been nibbling at his soul since they had boarded the truck. "Tell me, Thayle, are we going to stay together?"

"What do you mean, Joseph?" She sounded very far away.

"Just what I said. You and me, together, on the whole drive south. To the Isthmus. To Helikis, you and me, the whole way." He stared urgently at her. "Stay with me, Thayle. Please."

"How can I do that?" That same distant tone, drawing all the life out of him. Her hand went idly to the cut and bruised places on her face, touching them lightly, investigating them. "I can take you as far as the crossroads." They had already left the town behind, Joseph saw. They were back in forested territory again, on a two-lane road, not well paved. "Then I have to go back to Eysar Haven."

"No, Thayle. Don't."

"I have to. Eysar Haven is where I live. Those are my people. That is my place."

"You'll go back to *him*?"

"He won't touch me again. I'll see to that."

"I want you to come with me," Joseph said, more insistently. "Please."

She laughed. "Yes, of course. To your great estate in the south. To your grand home. To your father the Master of the House, and your Master brothers and sisters, and all the Folk who belong to you. How can I do that, Joseph?" She was speaking very quietly. "Ask yourself: How can I possibly do that?"

It was an unanswerable question. Joseph had known from the start that what he was asking of her was madness. Come strolling into Keilloran House after this long absence, blithely bringing with him a Folkish girl, his companion, his bed-mate, his—beloved? There was no way. She could see that even more clearly than he. But he had had to ask. It was a crazy thing, an impossible thing, but he had had to ask. He hated having to leave her.

A second road had appeared, as roughly made as the one they were on, running at right angles to it. Thayle brought the truck erratically to a halt. "That's the road that runs toward the south," she told him. "Somewhere down that way is the place where your people live. I hope you have a safe journey home." There was something terribly calm and controlled about her voice that plunged him into an abyss of sadness.

Joseph opened the door and stepped down from the truck. He hoped that she would get out too, that they could have one last embrace here by the side of the road, a hug, at least, so that he could know once more the feeling of her strong body in his arms, her breasts pressing up against him, the warmth of her on his skin. But she did not get out. Perhaps that was the very thing that she wanted to avoid: to be drawn back into the whole unworkable thing, to have him reawaken in her something that must of necessity be allowed to sleep. She leaned across, instead, and took his hand and squeezed it, and bent toward him so that they could kiss, a brief, awkward kiss that was made all the more difficult for them by the cut on her lip, and that was all there was going to be.

"I won't ever forget you," Joseph said.

"Nor I," she told him. And then she was gone and he was alone again.

He stood looking at the truck as it swung around and disappeared in the distance, praying that she would change her mind, that she would halt and come back and invite him to clamber up alongside her and drive off toward Helikis with him. But of course that did not happen.

Soon the vehicle was lost to view. He was alone in the stillness here, the frightening quiet of this empty place.

five ————————————————————

LOOKING OFF TOWARD THE BLANKNESS ON THE HORI-
zon where the dark dot that was the truck had
been before it passed from sight, Joseph felt as
though he had just awakened from a wonderful
dream, where only bits and pieces of recollection
remain, and shortly even those are gone, leaving
only a vague glow, an aura. Fate had taken him
to Eysar Haven; fate had put him into the house
where Thayle lived; fate had sent her into his
bed, and now he was changed forever. But all
that was behind him except the memories. He
was on his own again in unfamiliar territory,
with the same inconceivable journey of thousands of miles still ahead of him, even after having come all this distance since his escape from
Getfen House.

He took stock of the situation in which he

found himself now: dense woodlands, late summer, the air hot and torpid, no sign of a human presence anywhere around, no houses, no cultivated fields or even the remnants of them, nothing but the poorly maintained road along which he was walking. Were there other cuyling towns nearby? He should have asked her while he had the chance. How far was he from the Isthmus? From the nearest Great House? Would he find encampments of the rebels ahead? Was the rebellion still going on, for that matter, or had it been quelled by armies out of Helikis while he was spending the summer mending in Eysar Haven? He knew nothing, nothing at all.

Well, he would learn as he went, as he had been doing all along. The important thing now was simply not to let himself starve again. He knew only too well what that was like.

And the provisions Thayle had thrown together for him would last him no more than a day or two, he guessed. After that, unless he could learn to turn himself into an effective hunter or found a new set of hospitable hosts, it would be back to eating ants and beetles and bits of plants again.

He started off at a swift pace, but soon realized he could not maintain it. Although he had returned nearly to full strength during his time in Eysar Haven, he had also softened there from inactivity. His legs, which had turned to iron rods during the endless days of his solitary march down from the mountains, were mere muscle and bone again, and he felt them protesting. It would take time for them to harden once more. And he was beginning to feel stiff and sore, already, from the beating that Grovin had given him.

The land changed quickly as Joseph proceeded south. He was not even a day's walk beyond the place where Thayle had left him and he was no longer in good farming territory, nor did his new surroundings offer the possibilities for shelter that a forest might provide. The woods thinned out and he began to ascend a sort of shallow plateau, hot and dry, where little twisted shrubs with sleek black trunks rose out of red, barren-looking soil. It was bordered to east and west by low, long black hills with ridges sharp as blades, and streaks of bright white along their tops, blindingly reflective in the midday sun, that looked like outcroppings of salt, and perhaps actually were. The sky was a bare, dazzling blue rind. There were very few streams, and most of those that he found were brackish. He filled his flask at one that was not, but he realized that it would be wise to use his water very sparingly in this region.

There was a vast, resounding quietude here. It was not hard to think of himself as being all alone in the world. No family, no friends, not even any enemies; no Masters, no Folk, no Indigenes, no noctambulos, nothing, no one: only Joseph, Joseph, Joseph, Joseph all alone, walking ever onward through this empty land. It was completely new to him, this solitary kind of life. He could not say that he disliked it. There was a strange music to it, a kind of poetry, that fascinated him. Such great isolation had a mysterious purity and simplicity of form.

Despite the increasing bleakness of the landscape, Joseph moved through his first hours in it in an easy, almost automatic way. He barely took notice of its growing harshness, or of the growing weariness of his legs; his mind was still occupied fully with thoughts of Thayle. He thought not only of the warmth of her embrace, the smoothness of her skin, the touch of her lips against his, and the wondrous sensations that swept through him as he slid deep within her, but also of their discussions afterward, the things she had said to him, the things she had forced him to think about for the first time in his life.

He had always assumed—unquestioningly— that there was nothing remarkable about his being a member of the ruling class by mere right of birth. That was simply how things were in the world: either you were a Master or you were not, and it had been his luck to be born not only a Master but a Master among Masters, the heir to one of the greatest of the Great Houses. "Why are you a Master?" Thayle had asked him. "What right except right of conquest allows you to rule over other people?" Those were not things that one asked oneself, ordinarily. One took them for

granted. One regarded one's rank in life as a matter of having been endowed by a stroke of fate
with certain great privilege in return for a willingness to shoulder certain great responsibilities,
and the inquiry stopped there. "You are Joseph
Master Keilloran," they had told him as soon as
he was old enough to understand that he had
such a thing as a name and a rank. "Those people
are the Folk. You are a Master." And then he had
devoted the succeeding years of his boyhood to
the study of the things he would have to know
when he came—by inheritance alone, by simple
right of birth—into the duties of the rank for
which destiny had chosen him.

Out here everything was different. The identity that had been automatically his from the
hour of his coming into the world had been taken
from him. For these past months he had been
only what he could make of himself—first a fugitive boy searching frantically for safety and
gladly accepting the aid that a passing noctambulo offered him; then a valued tribal healer and
the friend, no less, of an Indigene chieftain; then
a fugitive again, a pathetic one, living along the
desperate borderlands of starvation; then the
welcome guest of a Folkish family who nursed
him back to health as though he were of their
own blood, and the lover, even, of the girl of that
family. And now he was a fugitive again. He was
created anew every day out of the context of that
day.

How upside-down everything has become, Joseph thought. At home I never had to worry about where my next meal would come from, but I was aware constantly that when I grew up and succeeded my father I would have to bear the enormous responsibilities of running a Great House—instructing the overseers on what needed to be done, and by whom, and checking the account books, and looking after the needs of the Folk of my House, and many such things like that. Out here there are no responsibilities to think about, but there is no assurance that I will have anything to eat the day after tomorrow, either.

It was a dizzying business. There once had been a time when his life had been all certainty; now it was a thing of perpetual flux. Yet he did not really regret the transformations that had been worked upon him. He doubted that many Masters had been through experiences such as he had had on this journey. He had had to cope with unexpected physical pain and with severe bodily privation. His stay among the Indigenes and his conversations with the Ardardin had taught him things about that race, and the relationship of the Masters to it, that would stand him in good stead once he returned to civilization. Likewise his time at Eysar Haven, both the things he had learned in Thayle's eager arms and the things she had forced him to confront as they lay side by side quietly talking afterward. All that had been tremendously valuable, in its way. But it will have been a mere waste, Joseph told himself, if I do not survive to return to House Keilloran.

Darkness came. He found a place to sleep, a hollow at the side of a little hill. It would do. He looked back nostalgically to his bed at Eysar Haven, but he was amazed how quickly he could become accustomed to sleeping in the open again. Lie down in the softest place you can find, though it is not necessarily soft, curl into your usual sleeping position, close your eyes, wait for oblivion—that was all there was to it. A hard day's walking had left him ready for a night's deep sleep.

In the morning, though, his legs ached all the way up to his skull, and he was aching from the effects of Grovin's blows, besides. Not for another two days would any of that aching cease and his muscles begin to turn to iron again. But then Joseph felt himself beginning to regain the hardness that had earlier been his and before long he felt ready to walk on and on, forever if need be, to Helikis and beyond, clear off the edge of the world and out to the moons.

The road he had been following veered sharply left, vanishing in the east, a dark dwindling line. He let it go. South is my direction, Joseph thought. He did not care what lay in the east. And he needed no road: one step at a time, through glade and valley, past hill and dale, would take him where he wanted to go.

As the food Thayle had given him dwindled toward its end, he began to think more seriously about the newest metamorphosis in his steady sequence of reinvention, the one that must transform him into a hunter who lived off the land, killing for his food.

Though he was traveling now through a harder, more challenging environment than any he had encountered before, it was by no means an empty one. Wherever he looked he saw an abundance of wild animals, strange beasts both large and small, living as they had lived for millions of years in this unaccommodating land for which neither Masters nor Folk nor Indigenes had found any use. In a glade of spiky gray trees he saw a troop of long-necked red-striped browsing beasts that must have been thirty feet tall, munching on the twisted thorny leaves. They looked down at him with sad, gentle gray eyes that betrayed little sign of intelligence. A brackish lake contained a population of round shaggy wading animals that set up a rhythmic slapping of the surface of the water with their flat, blunt, hairless tails, perhaps because they were annoyed by his presence, as he passed them by. There was a squat, heavy, ganuille-like beast with an incongruous nest of blunt horns sprouting above its nostrils, and small, frisky, stiff-tailed tawny animals with dainty, fragile legs, and slow-moving big-headed browsers nibbling on the unpromising saw-edged reddish grass

that grew here, and paunchy, jowly, furry creatures with ominous crests of spikes along their
spines, creatures that walked upright and, judg-
ing by the way they paused in their wanderings
to contemplate the stranger in their midst, might
very well be at the same level of mental ability as
the poriphars, or even beyond it.

Joseph knew that he would have to kill some
of these creatures in order to survive. The noctambulo was not here now to do his hunting for
him. Nor were there any streams conveniently
provided with mud-crawlers, or with those tasty
white tubers he remembered from his earliest
days on the run, and it was not very likely that
he would be able to find any of the small scrab-
bling creatures the noctambulo had so easily
snatched up with quick swipes of its scooplike
paws.

So he would have to do it himself. He had no
choice. The idea of killing anything bigger than a
mud-crawler seemed disagreeable to him, and he
wondered why. At home and at Getfen House he
had hunted all manner of animals great and
small, purely for pleasure, and had never given
the rights and wrongs of it a thought; here he
must hunt out of necessity, and yet something
within him balked at it. Perhaps it was because
this was no hunting preserve, but the homeland
of wild creatures, into which he was coming un-
invited, and with murder on his mind. Well, he
had not asked to find himself here. And he, just

like any of the animals here that fed on the flesh of other beasts, needed to eat.

That night, camping among some many-branched crooked-trunked trees that had covered the ground with a dense litter of soft discarded needles, Joseph dreamed of Thayle. She was standing gloriously naked before him by moonlight, the white light of Keviel, that made her soft skin gleam like bright satin and cast its cool glow on the heavy globes of her breasts and the mysterious triangular tangle of golden hair at the base of her belly, and she smiled and held out her hands to him, and he reached for her and drew her down to him, kissing her and stroking her, and her breath began to come in deep, harsh gusts as Joseph touched the most intimate places of her body, until at last she cried out to him to come into her, and he did. And waited to go swimming off to ecstasy; but somehow, maddeningly, he awoke instead, just as the finest moment of all was drawing near, Thayle disappearing from his grasp like a popping bubble.

"No!" he cried, still on the threshold between dreaming and wakefulness. "Come back!" And opened his eyes and sat up, and saw white Keviel indeed crossing the sky overhead, and realized that he was in fact not alone. But his companion was not Thayle. He heard a low snuffling sound, and picked up a smell that was both sharp and musty at the same time. Elongated reddish-green eyes were staring at him out of the moonlit darkness. He could make out a longish thick-set body, a flattened bristly snout, tall pointed ears. The creature was no more than seven or eight feet away from him and slowly heading his way.

Joseph jumped quickly to his feet and made shooing gestures at the beast. It halted at once, uncertainly swinging its snout from side to side. His eyes were adapting to the night, and he saw that his visitor was an animal of a sort he had noticed earlier that day, fairly big, slow-moving grazing beasts with thick furry coats reminiscent of a poriphar's, black with broad white stripes. Unlike the poriphars they had seemed harmless enough then, in all likelihood mainly herbivorous, equipped with nothing that looked dangerous except, perhaps, the strong claws that they used, most likely, for scratching up their food out of the ground.

Groping in his utility case, Joseph located his pocket torch and switched it on. The animal had settled down on its haunches and was looking at him in a matter-of-fact way, as though it were puzzled at finding Joseph here, but only mildly so. It did not seem like a particularly quick-witted creature. "You aren't by any chance an intelligent life-form, are you?" Joseph said to it, speaking in Indigene. It continued to stare blandly at him. "No. No. I didn't really think you were. But I thought it was a good idea to check." Probably this was one of its preferred feeding areas, a place where it liked to dig by night for nuts hidden beneath the fallen needles, or insects that dwelled just underground, or some other such easy prey.

"Am I in your way?" Joseph asked. "I'm sorry. I just needed a place to sleep. If this place belongs to you, I'll go somewhere else, all right?"

He expected no reply, and got none. But the animal did not leave, either, and as it began to resume its snuffling search for dinner Joseph saw that he was going to have to find another camping-ground for himself. He was hardly likely to be able to fall asleep again here, not with a thing this size, be it harmless or not, prowling around so close by him. Gathering up his belongings, he moved a dozen yards away and settled down again, but that was no better; soon the animal was coming in his direction once more. "Go away," Joseph told it. "I don't want to be your friend. Not right now, anyway." He made the shooing motions again. But it was hopeless. The animal would not leave, and Joseph was wide awake, probably irreparably so, besides. He sat up unhappily the rest of the night, watching the beast poking unhurriedly about among the needles.

Dawn seemed to take forever to arrive. From time to time he fell into a light doze, not really sleep. Somewhere in the night, he realized, the striped beast had wandered away. Joseph offered a morning prayer—he still did that, though he was not sure any longer why he did—and sorted through his bag of provisions, calculating how much he could allow himself for breakfast. Not

very much, he saw. And the remainder would go
at lunchtime. This was the day when he would
have to start hunting for his food, or scratch
around in the needles on the ground for whatever
it was that the striped creature had been looking
for, or else prepare himself for a new descent into
famine.

Hunting it would be. Barren-looking though
the land appeared, there were plenty of animals
roaming hereabouts, a whole zoo's worth of
them, in fact. But he had nothing with him in the
way of a real weapon, of course. What did castaways without weapons do when they needed to
catch something to eat?

A sharpened stake in a pit, he thought. Cover it
with branches and let your quarry tumble down
onto it.

It seemed an absurd idea even as Joseph
thought of it, but as he set about contemplating it
as a practical matter it looked sillier and sillier to
him. A sharpened stake? Sharpened with what?
And dig a pit? How, with his bare hands? And
then hope that something worth eating would
obligingly drop into it and neatly skewer itself?
Even as he looked around for something he could
use as a stake, he found himself laughing at his
own foolishness.

But he had no better ideas at the moment, and
a stake did turn up after a lengthy search: a slender branch about five feet long that had snapped
free of a nearby tree. One end of it, the end where

it had broken off, was jagged and sharp. If only he could embed the stake properly in the ground, it might actually do the trick. But now he had to dig a hole as deep as he was tall, broad enough to hold the animal he hoped to catch. Joseph scuffed experimentally at the ground with the side of his sandal. The best he could manage was a faint shallow track. The dry, hard soil would not be easy to excavate. Perhaps he could find some piece of stone suitable for digging with, but it would probably take him a month to dig the sort of pit he needed. He would starve to death long before that. And he had wasted the whole morning on this ridiculous project, without having moved so much as an inch closer to his destination.

The last of his food went for his midday meal, as he knew it would. A prolonged search afterward for edible nuts or even insects produced nothing.

What next? He reached once more into his recollection of old boys' adventure books. String a snare between two trees, he supposed, and hope for something to get entangled in it. He did have a reel of metallic cord in his utility case, and he spent a complicated hour rigging it between two saplings a short distance above the ground. The black-and-white burrowing animal of the night before came snuffling around while he worked. Joseph was fairly sure it was the same one. By daylight it looked larger than it had seemed in the night, a short-legged, fleshy, well-built creature that weighed at least as much as he did. Its thick white-striped pelt was quite handsome. The animal seemed entirely unafraid of him, coming surprisingly close, now and then pushing its flat bristly snout against the cord that Joseph was trying to tie to the saplings and making the task harder for him. "What is this?" Joseph asked it. "You want to help? I don't need your help." He had to shove it out of the way. It moved off a short distance and looked back sadly at him with a glassy-eyed stare. "You'd like to be my friend?" Joseph asked. "My pet? I wasn't really looking for a pet."

Finally the job of fashioning the snare appeared to be done. Joseph stepped back, admiring his handiwork. Any animal that ran into it with sufficient velocity would find itself caught, he hoped. Those lively little tawny-skinned animals that went frisking swiftly around the place in groups of five or six: they were just reckless enough, possibly, to be taken that way.

But they were not. Joseph hid himself behind a big three-sided boulder and waited, an hour, two hours. It was getting on toward twilight now. In this early dusk his snare would surely be invisible: he could barely see it himself, looking straight toward the place where he knew it to be. From his vantage-point behind the boulder he caught a glimpse of his furry striped friend browsing around nearby, scratching up large rounded seeds out of the ground and munching on them in a noisy crunching way. But he doubted that that would bother the little tawny animals. And at last they came frolicking along, a good-sized herd of them, a dozen or more this time, tails held stiffly erect, ears pricked up, nostrils flaring, small hooves clacking as they skipped over the rocky soil. They were moving on a path that seemed likely to take them straight toward Joseph's trap. And indeed it was so. One by one they danced right up to it, and one by one as they reached it they launched themselves into the air in elegant little leaps, soaring prettily over the outstretched cord with two or three feet to spare and continuing on beyond, switching their tails mockingly at him as they ran. They went over his snare like athletes leaping hurdles. Scarcely believing it, Joseph watched the entire troop pass by and prance out of sight.

He waited half an hour more, hoping some less perceptive animal might come by and fall victim to the snare, one of the many wandering beasts of these unpromising fields. That did not happen. Darkness was coming on and he had nothing whatever to eat. In the morning things would be no better. He was looking at starvation again, much too soon. None of the parched, gnarly plants that grew in this dry land looked edible to him, though the grazing animals plainly did not mind them. He could not bring himself to eat the three-sided saw-edged blades of tough red grass that grew in sparse clumps everywhere around. There were no likely roots or tubers, no snails, perhaps not even ants. Somewhere beyond those white-edged hills there might be a land of tender fruits and sweet, succulent, slow-moving land crabs, but he might not live long enough to reach it, if indeed any such place existed. Nor could he hope that Folkish rescuers would come conveniently to his rescue a second time when he collapsed once again by the wayside in the last stages of hallucinatory exhaustion.

I must find something that I can kill and eat, Joseph thought, and find it quickly.

There was a familiar snuffling sound off to his left.

No, Joseph thought, aghast. I can't! And then, immediately afterward: Yes! I must!

His new friend, his self-appointed companion. This slow-moving musky-smelling seed-eating thing, so trusting, so unthreatening. It was not just any animal; somehow this day it had turned into an animal that he felt he knew. That is sheer imbecility, he told himself. An animal is an animal, nothing more. And he was in dire need. But could he kill it, this harmless, friendly creature? He must. There was nothing else. Nothing. Nothing. Nothing. It was a horrifying idea, but so too was starving. He had experienced starvation once already, and once was more than enough: the steady melting away of his flesh, the shriveling of his muscles, the weakening of his bones, the blurring of his vision, the swollen tongue, the taste of copper in his throat, the quivering legs, the headaches, the giddiness, the craziness.

He picked up a wedge-shaped rock, a large one, the biggest one that he could hold. The animal was looking at him in a vague incurious way. Clearly it did not have the slightest awareness of Joseph's intentions. Joseph prayed that there was little or no intelligence behind those dull eyes. Did you ever really know how intelligent any creature might be? No. You never did, did you? He thought of the poriphars who had shared their food with him beside that stream in the lovely springtime country just below the mountains. No one doubted that they were intelligent beings. Stand this creature on its hind legs and it would look a little like a poriphar, Joseph thought: a distant cousin, possibly. He hoped it was only a coincidental resemblance. "Forgive me," he said foolishly, taking a deep breath, and raised the rock in both hands and brought it down as hard as he could across the striped animal's wide flat forehead.

The impact barely seemed to register on it. It stared stupidly at Joseph and took a couple of wobbly uncertain steps backward, but did not undertake any real retreat. Joseph hit it again, and again. And again. He went on and on, to little apparent avail. The animal, staggering now, made a sorrowful rumbling noise. I must be unrelenting, Joseph told himself, I must be ruthless, it is too

late to stop. I must carry this through to the end.
He struck it once more and this time the thing fell,
toppling heavily, landing on its side and moving
its feet through the air in a slow circular path. The
rumbling continued. There was a breathy whimper now, too. The reddish-green eyes remained
open, peering at him, so Joseph thought, with a
reproachful stare.

He felt sick. It was one thing to hunt like a gentleman, with a weapon that spat death cleanly
and quickly from a distance. It was another thing
entirely to kill like a savage, pounding away
brutishly with a rock.

He went to his utility case and found his little
knife, and knelt, straddling the creature, feeling
strong spasms of some sort going through its
back and shoulders, and, weeping now, drove the
blade into the animal's throat with all his
strength. The rear legs began to thrash. But the
knife was barely adequate to the task and it all
took very much longer than Joseph expected. I
must be unrelenting, Joseph told himself a second
time, and clung to the animal, holding it down
until the thrashing began to diminish.

He rose, then, bloodied, sobbing.

Gradually he grew calm. The worst part of it is
over, he thought. But he was wrong even about
that, because there was still the butchering to do,
the peeling back of the thick pelt with the knife
that was scarcely more than a toy, the slitting of
the belly, the lifting out of the glistening abdomi-

nal organs, red and pink and blue. You had to get the internal organs out, Anceph had taught him long ago, because they decayed very quickly and would spoil the meat. But it was a frightful task. He was shaken by the sight of the animal's inwardness, all that moist shining internal machinery that had made it a living, metabolizing thing until he had picked up his rock and begun the ending of its life. Now those secret things were laid bare. They all came spilling forth, organs he could not begin to identify, the sacred privateness of the creature he had killed. Joseph gagged and retched and turned away, covered with sweat, and then turned back and continued with what he had to do. Twice more he had to pause to retch and heave as he went about the work, and the second time the nausea was so intense that it was necessary for him to halt for some five or ten minutes, shaking, sweating, dizzied. Then he forced himself to continue. He had arrogated unto himself the right to take this innocent creature's life; he must make certain now that the killing had not been without purpose.

When he was done he was slathered with gore, and there was no stream nearby in which he could bathe himself. Unwilling to squander his small supply of drinking-water, Joseph rubbed himself with gritty handfuls of the sandy soil until his hands and arms seemed sufficiently clean. Then he searched in his utility case for his firestarter, which he had not used in such a long time that he was not at all sure it still worked. The thought that it might be necessary for him to eat the meat raw brought Joseph to the edge of nausea again. But the firestarter worked; he built a little bonfire of twigs and dried leaves, and skewered a steak and roasted it until the juices dripped from it; and then, the culminating monstrous act, he took his first bite. The meat had something of the same sharp and musky taste that he had smelled in the animal's pelt, and swallowing it involved him in a mighty struggle. But he had to eat. He had to eat *this*. And he did. He ate slowly, sadly, chewing mechanically, until he had had his fill.

It was dark, now, and time for sleep. But he did not want to use the same campsite that he had used the night before. That would summon too many memories of the animal that had visited him there. Instead he settled down not far from the dying ashes of his fire, though the ground was bare and uneven there. While he lay waiting for sleep to take him Joseph remembered a time he had gone with Anceph on a three-day hunting trip in Garyona Woods, he and Rickard and some of their friends, and on the second morning, awakening at daybreak, he had seen Anceph crouching over the faintly glowing coals of their campfire, staring at small plump animals, vivid red in color, that seemed to be leaping around and across them. "Ember-toads," Anceph explained. "You find droves of them in the morning whenever there's a fire burning down. They like the warmth, I suppose." He was holding a little net in one hand; and, as Joseph watched, he swept it swiftly back and forth until he had caught a dozen or more of the things. "Plenty of good sweet meat on their legs," said Anceph. "We'll grill 'em for breakfast. You'll like the way they taste." He was right about that. Rickard refused indignantly even to try one; but Joseph had had his fill, and recalled to this day how good they had been. He wondered if there would be ember-toads hopping about what was left of his fire in the morning, but he did not think there would—they were found only in Helikis, so far as he knew—and indeed there was nothing but white ash in his fire-pit when he woke. No ember-toads, not here, and the body of good-natured Anceph, who knew so much about hunting and all manner of other things, lay in some unmarked grave far to the north at Getfen House.

The task for this morning was to cut and pack however much of the striped creature's meat he could carry with him when he resumed his march. Joseph could not say how long the meat would last, but he wanted to waste as little of it as necessary, and perhaps in this dry climate it would be slow to spoil.

He got down to the job quickly and in a businesslike manner. It did not make him suffer as the killing and the first stage of the butchering had made him suffer: this part of it was just so much work: unpleasant, messy, slogging work, nothing more. He was greatly relieved not to feel any but the faintest vestige of last night's grief and shame over the killing of that harmless, friendly animal. Everything has to die sooner or later, Joseph told himself. If he had hurried the event along for the striped animal, it was only because his own life would have been imperiled if he could not quickly find food, and in this world those who are quicker and stronger and smarter end up eating those who are not: it was the rule, the inflexible rule of the inflexible universe. Even Thayle, who thought it was wrong that the Masters should have set themselves up as overlords over the Folk, did not see anything wrong with eating the flesh of the beasts. It was a normal, natural thing. He had eaten plenty of meat in his life, just like everyone else, without ever once weeping over it before; the only difference this time was that the act of slaughtering it himself had brought him that much closer to the bloody reality of what it meant to be a carnivore, and for a moment in his solitude here he had let himself give way to feelings of guilt. Some part of him, the Master part that had been so rarely in evidence these recent days, found that unacceptable. Guilt was not a luxury he could afford, out here in this lonely wilderness. He must put it aside.

Joseph spent the first half of the morning cutting the meat up into flat strips, letting all residual blood drain away, and carefully wrapping them in the thick, leathery leaves of a tree that grew nearby. He hoped that that might preserve it from decay for another few days. When he had loaded his pack with all that it could hold, he roasted what was left of the meat for his midday meal, and set out toward the south once more. After a few dozen steps something impelled him to look back for one last glance at his campsite, and he saw that two scrawny yellow-furred beasts with bushy tails were rooting around busily in the scattered entrails of the animal he had killed. Nothing goes to waste, Joseph thought, at least not in the world of nature. Man is the only animal that countenances being wasteful.

The day was uneventful, and the one after that. Though there was no actual path for him to follow, the land was gently undulating, easy enough to traverse. Far off in the distance he saw mountains of considerable size, purple and pink in the morning haze, and he wondered whether he was going to have to cross them. But that was not something to which he needed to give much thought at the moment. The immediate terrain presented no problems. Joseph's thighs and calves had shed the stiffness of a few days before, and he saw no reason why he could not cover twenty miles a day, or even thirty, now that he was in the rhythm of it.

He was pleased to see that the territory through which he was passing grew less forbidding as he continued onward: before long the soil became blacker and richer, the vegetation much more lush. Soon the ominous sharp-ridged salt-encrusted black hills dropped away behind him. There was more moisture in the air, and better cloud-cover, so that he did not have to endure the constant pounding presence of the summer sun, although by mid-morning each day the heat was considerable. He found water, too, a thin white sheet of it that came sluicing down over a mica-speckled rock-face from some clifftop spring high above, collecting in a shallow basin at the foot of the cliff; he stripped gladly and washed himself from head to toe, and drank deep, and refilled his flask, which had gone so low that he had been permitting himself only the most niggardly sips at the widest possible intervals. A bush not far away was bowed down under heavy clusters of fat, lustrous, shining golden berries that looked too attractive not to be edible. Joseph tried one and found it full of sweet juice, soft as honey. He risked a second, and then a third. That had become his wilderness rule, three berries and no more, see what happens next. By the time he had built a fire to roast his evening meat, no harmful effects had manifested themselves, so he allowed himself another dozen with his meal. When he resumed his journey after breakfast he took three big clusters with him, but later he saw that the bush was common all along his path, wherever a source of water was to be found, and he did not bother carrying such a large supply. Within a couple of days, though, the berry-bushes were nowhere to be seen, and when he tried a smaller, harder red berry from a different bush it burned his mouth, so that he spat it quickly out. Even that one taste was enough to keep him awake half the night with a troublesome griping of the abdomen, but he felt better in the morning.

An hour into his morning march Joseph came up over a gentle rise in the land and saw a road cutting through the valley below him, looping down from the northeast and aligning itself with the route that the position of the sun told him he must take. Quite possibly it was the same road that Thayle had left him on, the one that he had abandoned when it seemed to turn eastward. It did at least look similar to that one, rough and narrow and badly in need of maintenance. There was no traffic on it. He had never realized how sparsely populated so much of the northern continent was.

After only a few days back in the purity of the wild Joseph felt a strange reluctance to set foot again on anything so unnatural as an asphalt highway. But the road did seem to run due south from where he was, and therefore was probably his most direct course toward the Isthmus. There was no harm in following it by day, he thought. He would go off into the bush each evening when it came to be time to settle down for the night.

It was not pleasing to be walking on a paved

surface again, though. The highway felt harsh, even brutal, against his sandaled feet. He was tempted to go take the sandals off and go barefoot on it. I am becoming a creature of nature, he thought, a wild thing, a beast of the fields. My identity as a civilized being is dropping away from me day by day. I have become a shaggy animal. If I ever do get home, will I be able to turn myself back into a Master again? Or will I slip away from House Keilloran when no one is looking, and go off by myself to forage for berries and roots in the wilderness beyond the estate?

There were traces in this district of former settlement: a scattering of small wooden houses of the sort he had lived in at Eysar Haven, but isolated ones, set one by one at goodly distances from each other at the side of the road. They were the homes of individual Folkish farmers, he supposed, who had not wanted to live in a village, not even a cuyling village. None of them was occupied, though there was no sign of any destruction: apparently their owners had just abandoned them, he could not tell how long ago. Perhaps the war had come this way, or perhaps those who had lived here had just gone away: it was impossible to tell.

Joseph prowled around in one that had a wire bird-coop alongside the main building, the sort in which thestrins or heysir would have been kept. There was at least the possibility that some remnants of the farmer's flock might still be in residence there. His supply of meat was nearly at its end and it would be splendid to dine on roast thestrin tonight, or even an omelet of heysir eggs. But Joseph found nothing in the coop except empty nests and a scattering of feathers. Inside the farmhouse itself a thick layer of dust coated everything. The building had been emptied of virtually all it had once contained except for some old, shapeless furniture. Joseph did discover a single incongruous unopened bottle of wine standing at the edge of a kitchen counter. He had nothing with which to open it, and finally simply snapped its neck against the side of the rust-stained sink. The wine was thin and sour and he left most of it unfinished.

That night a light rain began to fall. Joseph decided to sleep inside the house, but he disliked the confined feeling that sleeping indoors produced in him, and the drifting clouds of dust that he had stirred up were bothersome. He slept on the porch instead, lying on some bedraggled old pillows that he found, listening to the gentle pattering sound of the rain until sleep took him.

The morning was bright, clear, and warm. He allowed himself a quick, minimal breakfast and set out early, and soon was beyond the last of the abandoned farmhouses. He was moving into a terrain that was neither forest nor meadow, dominated by immense stately trees with steeply upturned branches, each standing in splendid isolation, far from its nearest neighbor, amidst a field of dense, rubbery-looking pink-leaved grass. A myriad of small round-bodied hopping creatures with fluffy grayish fur moved about busily below the trees, probably searching for seeds.

The sight of them in such a multitude made Joseph, who had begun to see that he would need to restock his food supply in another day or two, feel a burst of sudden hunger. He yearned for a rifle. The best he could hope for, though, was to try to bring one down with a well-aimed rock. But as he crept up on one group of them with what he hoped was something like stealth they melted away before him like winter fog in the bright morning sun, easily and unhurriedly drifting out of his range as Joseph approached them, and resumed their explorations at the far side of the field. A second group did the same. Joseph gave the enterprise up without casting a single stone.

His mood was cheerful, nevertheless. This was an inviting kind of countryside and he did not doubt that he would find something to eat somewhere, sooner or later, and his body felt so well tuned now, so smoothly coordinated in every function, that there was real joy to be had from striding along down the empty road at a brisk pace. The sun stood high in the sky before him, showing him the way to Helikis. Joseph felt that it did not matter if it took him another whole year to get home, three years, ten years:

this was the great adventure of his life, the unexpected epic journey that would shape him forever, and however much time it required would
be the span that his destiny had marked out for
it to last.

Then he came around a curve in the road, still
moving jauntily along, whistling, thinking pleasant thoughts of his nights with Thayle, and discovered that the road just ahead was full of
military-looking vehicles, perhaps half a dozen of
them, with a crowd of armed men standing
alongside them.

A roadblock, Joseph realized. A checkpoint of
some kind. And he had walked right into it, or
nearly so.

Had they seen him? He could not tell. He
halted quickly and turned about, meaning to slip
back the way he had come, thinking to hide himself in the woods until they moved along, or, if
they didn't move along, to take up a lateral trail
that would get him around them. He succeeded
in covering about a dozen paces.

Then a voice from somewhere above him, a
crisp, flat, nasal voice, said in Folkish, "You will
stay exactly where you are. You will lift your
hands above your head."

Joseph looked up. A stocky helmeted man in a
drab uniform stood on the hillside overlooking
the highway. He had a rifle in his hands, aimed
at the middle of Joseph's chest. Several other men
in the same sort of uniform were jogging around

the bend in the road toward him. They were armed also.

Any movement other than one of surrender would be suicidal, Joseph saw. He nodded to the man on the hillside and held up his hands.

They came up to him and formed a little cluster about him. Rebel soldiers, he supposed, five of them altogether. Not one came up much higher than his shoulders. All five had the same flat broad noses, narrow grayish eyes, yellowish hair that looked as though it had been cut by snipping around the edges of an inverted bowl. They might almost have been five brothers.

He heard them chattering quickly in Folkish, arguing over him, trying to decide who and what he was. The prevailing belief among them seemed to be that he was a spy, although for whom they thought he might be spying was not something Joseph was able to determine. But one of them thought he was a wandering wild man of the woods, a harmless crazy simpleton. "Only a crazy man would come along this road right now," he said. "And look how filthy he is. Did you ever see anyone who looked as filthy as this one?" Joseph took some offense at that. It was only a few weeks since he had last trimmed his beard and his hair, and not a great many days had gone by since he had last washed himself, either. He thought he appeared respectable enough, considering his recent circumstances. Yet these soldiers, or the one who had said it, at least, saw him quite differently. This latest sojourn in the wilderness must have left him far more uncouth-looking than he suspected.

He said nothing to them. That seemed the wisest policy. And they made no attempt whatever to interrogate him. Perhaps at their level of authority they had no responsibility for questioning prisoners. Instead they merely bundled him unceremoniously into one of the vehicles parked by the side of the road and headed off with him toward the south.

A sprawling encampment lay ten minutes down the road: wire-mesh walls encircling dozens of flimsy-looking, hastily flung-up huts, with scores of Folkish soldiers wearing the rebel uniform moving around busily within it. At the gate Joseph's five warders surrendered him, with a muttered explanation that Joseph could not hear, to two others who seemed to be officers of a higher rank, and they gestured to Joseph to follow him within.

Silently, he obeyed. Any kind of resistance or even a show of reluctance to cooperate was likely to prove foolhardy. They conveyed him down an inner avenue between rows of the little huts and delivered him to one of the larger buildings, which, Joseph saw, was provided with an attached and fenced-in yard of considerable size: a compound for prisoners, he supposed. Wordlessly they directed him within.

It was a long windowless structure, a kind of

dormitory, dark inside except for a few feeble lamps. The air inside was stale-smelling and stifling. Simple iron-framed cots were arranged along the walls. Most were empty, though half a dozen were occupied by Folk, all of them men, most of them sitting slumped on the edges of their cots staring off into nothingness. Joseph saw no one among them who might have been a Master. A door on the right led to the fenced-in outside area.

"This will be yours," said one of his guards, indicating an empty cot. Wordlessly he held out his hand for Joseph's pack, and Joseph surrendered it without offering objection, though he bitterly regretted being parted from his utility case and everything else that had accompanied him through all these many months of wandering. He owned so little that he could carry it all in that single pack, and now they were taking it away from him. The officer sniffed at the pack and made a face: the last of the wrapped meat was within, probably beginning to go bad. "They will come to speak with you in a little while," the guard said, and both men turned and went out, taking the pack with them.

Not a single one of the slump-shouldered Folkish men sitting on the cots looked in his direction. They seemed as incurious about him as the cots themselves. Joseph wondered how long it was that they had been interned here, and what had been done to them during their stay.

After a little while he went out into the adjoining yard. It was a huge, barren, dreary place, nothing but bare dusty sun-baked ground, not even a blade of grass. At the far end Joseph saw what looked like a brick-walled washhouse and a latrine. There were some more Folkish men in the yard, each one keeping off by himself in a little zone of isolation, holding himself apart from any of the others, immobile, looking at nothing, almost as though he was unaware that anyone else was with him out there. All of them stood in a manner that gave them the same odd slumped, defeated look as the men on the cots inside. Joseph was surprised to see three Indigenes also, a little silent group huddled together in one corner. He wondered how this incomprehensible civil war could have managed to involve Indigenes. He understood nothing. But he had been on his own for more than a year, he calculated: from mid-summer in High Manza to late summer, or even early autumn, wherever he was now. A great deal must have happened in all that time, and no one here was going to explain it to him.

There seemed to be no harm in trying to find out, though. He went up to the nearest of the Folkers, who paid no more attention to the approaching Joseph than a blind man would, and said softly, "Pardon me, but—"

The man glared at Joseph for an instant, only an instant, a quick, hot, furious glare. Then he turned away.

"I'm sorry," Joseph said bewilderedly. It did not seem at all remarkable to him just then to be apologizing to a Folker. "I'm new here. I only wanted to ask you a few things about—"

The man shook his head. He seemed both angry and frightened. He moved away.

Joseph got the same reaction from the next two men that he tried. And when he went toward the trio of Indigenes, they drifted silently away from him the way those little hopping creatures in the field had. He gave the project up at that point. It is not the done thing here, Joseph realized, to have conversations with your fellow inmates. Perhaps conversation was prohibited; perhaps it was just risky. You never knew who might be a spy. But again he wondered: spying for whom? For whom?

Noon came and went. In early afternoon three Folkish orderlies arrived with food for the prisoners' meals, carrying it in big metal tubs slung between two sticks: cold gluey gruel, some sort of stewed unidentifiable meat that had the flavor of old cardboard, hard musty bread that was mostly crust. The inmates lined up and sparse portions were ladled out to them on tin plates. They were given wooden spoons to use. Hungry as he was, Joseph found it hard to eat very much. He forced himself.

The hours went by. The sun was strong, the air humid. He saw armed sentries marching about outside the wire-mesh fence. Within the compound no one spoke a word to anyone else. At sundown one of the guards blew a whistle and everyone who was in the yard went shuffling inside, each to his own cot. Joseph had forgotten which cot was his: he picked one at random in a row of empty ones, half hoping that someone else would challenge his taking of it so that he could at least hear the sound of a human voice again, but no one raised any objection to his choice. He sprawled out on it for a while; then, not finding it comfortable to lie on the thin, hard mattress, he sat up like the others, slumped on the edge of his cot. When it was dark the orderlies returned with another meal, which turned out to be the same things as in the earlier one only in smaller portions. Joseph could not bring himself to eat very much of it. He hardly slept at all.

The second day went by very much like the first. The food was, if anything, just a little worse, and there was even less of it. The silence in the yard grew so intense that it began to resound within Joseph's head like a trumpet-call. For hour after hour he paced along the fenced border of the compound, measuring off its dimensions in footsteps. He envisioned his spending the next thirty years, or the next fifty, doing nothing but that. But of course he would not last fifty years on the sort of food that they served the prisoners here.

The question is, Joseph thought, will I starve to death before I go insane, or afterward?

It seemed foolish even to think of attempting to

escape. And trying to stand upon his rights as a Master was an even sillier idea. He had no rights as a Master, certainly not here, perhaps not anywhere any more. More likely than not they would kill him outright if they found out who he really was. Better to be thought to be a vagabond lunatic, he thought, than the scion of one of the Great Houses of Helikis. But why was he here? What was the point of rounding up vagabond lunatics? Did they mean simply to intern their prisoners purely for the sake of interning them, so that they would not intrude on whatever military action might be going on in this part of the world? Why not just shoot us, then? he wondered. Perhaps they would; perhaps they were merely waiting for the order to come from some other camp. Joseph began to think he might almost prefer to be shot to having to spend an indefinite length of time here.

But on the third morning a guard entered the compound and indicated, in the curt wordless way that seemed to be the usual way of communicating with prisoners in this place, that Joseph was to follow him.

The guard marched him up the middle of the camp, turned left down an aisle of important-looking structures that were guarded by strutting sentries and appeared more solidly constructed than those Joseph had seen so far, and delivered him to a smallish building at the end of the row.

A Folkish officer with an air of great confidence and power about him that reminded Joseph of Governor Stappin of Eysar Haven was sitting behind a desk that had the contents of Joseph's pack spread out on it: his utility case, his books, his flask, and all the rest. His shoulders were immensely broad, even as Folkish shoulders went, and he had his shirt open to the waist in the muggy heat, revealing a dense, curling thatch of reddish-gold hair. The hair of the officer's head was of the same color and curling texture, but it was receding badly, laying bare the great shining dome of his forehead.

"Well," he said, glancing from Joseph to the assortment of objects on his desk, and then to Joseph again. "These things are very interesting. Where did you get them?"

"They were given to me," said Joseph.

"By whom?"

"Different people. It's hard to remember. I've been traveling so long."

"Traveling from where?"

"From the north," Joseph said. He hesitated a moment. "From High Manza," he added.

The officer's gaze rested coldly on Joseph. "From where in High Manza, exactly?"

"A place called Getfen House, it was." It was Joseph's intention to tell as few lies as possible, while revealing as little as he could that might be incriminating.

"You came from a Great House?"

"I was there just a little while. I was not a part of House Getfen at all."

"I see." The officer played with the things on the desk, inattentively fondling Joseph's torch, his cutting-tool, his book-reader. Joseph hated that, that this man should be touching his beloved things. "And what is your name?" the officer asked, after a time.

"Joseph," Joseph said. He did not add his title or his surname. It would not do to try to masquerade as Waerna of Ludbrek House any longer, for that had not worked particularly well at Eysar Haven and was unlikely to do any better for him here, and he preferred to use his real name rather than to try to invent anything else. They would not necessarily recognize "Joseph" as a Master name, he thought, not if he held back "Master" and "Keilloran" from them.

But the name did seem odd to the Folkish officer, as well it should have. He repeated it a couple of times, frowning over it, and observed that he had never heard a name like that before. Joseph shrugged and offered no comment. Then the officer looked up at him again and said, "Have you taken part in any of the fighting, Joseph?"

"No."

"None? None at all?"

"I am not a part of the war."

The officer laughed. "How can you say that? Everyone is part of the war, everyone! You, me, the Indigenes, the poriphars, everyone. The animals in the fields are part of the war. There is no hiding from the war. Truly, you have not fought at all?"

"Not at all, no."

"Where have you been, then?"

"In the forests, mostly."

"Yes. Yes, I can see that. You have a wild look about you, Joseph. And a wild smell." Again the officer played with the things from the utility case. He ran his fingertips over them, almost lovingly, and smiled. "These are Master things, some of them. You know that, don't you, Joseph?" Joseph said nothing. Then the officer said, switching for the first time from Folkish to Master, and with a sudden ferocity entering his voice, "What you are is a spy, are you not, Joseph? Admit it. Admit it!"

"That is not so," said Joseph, replying in Folkish. There was no harm in revealing that he understood Master—there was no Folker who did not—but he would not speak it here. "It is just not so!"

"But what else can you be but a spy?"

"It is not so," Joseph said again, more mildly. "I am not in any way a spy. I told you, I am not a part of the war. I know nothing whatever about what has been going on. I have been in the forests."

"A mere wanderer."

"A wanderer, yes. They attacked Getfen House,

where I was staying, and I went into the forests. I could not tell you what has happened in the world since."

"You did not fight, and you are not a spy," the officer said musingly. He drummed on his desktop with the fingers of one hand. Then he rose and came around the desk to where Joseph was standing. He was surprisingly tall for a Folker, just a few inches shorter than Joseph, and the immense width of his shoulders made him seem inordinately strong, formidably intimidating. He stared at Joseph for an interminable moment. Then, almost casually, he placed his right hand on Joseph's right shoulder and with steady, inexorable pressure forced Joseph to his knees. Joseph submitted without resisting, though he was boiling within. He doubted that he could have resisted that force anyway.

The Folkish officer held him lightly by his ear. "At last, now, tell me who you are spying for."

"Not for anybody," Joseph said.

The fingers gripping his ear tightened. Joseph felt himself being pushed forward until his nose was close to the floor.

"I have other things to do today," the officer said. "You are wasting my time. Tell me who you're working for, and then we can move along."

"I can't tell you, because I'm not working for anyone."

"Not working for the traitors who come in the

night and attack the camps of patriots, and strive to undo all that we have worked so hard to achieve?"

"I know nothing about any of that."

"Right. Just an innocent wanderer in the forests."

"I wanted no part of the war. When they burned Getfen House I ran away. I have been running ever since."

"Ah. Ah." It was a sound of annoyance, of disgust, even. "You waste my time." Now he was twisting the ear. It was an agonizing sensation. Joseph bit his lip, but did not cry out.

"Go ahead, pull it off, if you like," he said. "I still couldn't tell you anything, because I have nothing to tell."

"Ah," said the officer one more time, and released Joseph's ear with a sharp pushing motion that sent him flat on his face. Joseph waited for—what, a kick? A punch? But nothing happened. The man stepped back and told Joseph to rise. Joseph did, somewhat uncertainly. He was trembling all over. The officer was staring at him, frowning. His lips were moving faintly, as though he were framing further questions, the fatal ones that Joseph was dreading, and Joseph waited, wondering when the man would ask him what he had been doing at Getfen House, or what clan of the Folk he belonged to, or which towns and villages he had passed through on his way from High Manza to here. Joseph did not dare answer the first question,

324   Robert Silverberg

could not answer the second, and was unwilling to
answer the third, because anything he said linking
him to Eysar Haven or the Indigene villages might
lead to his unmasking as a Master. Of course, the
man could simply ask him outright whether he
was a Master, considering that he looked more like
one than like any sort of Folker. But he did not ask
him that, either: he did not ask any of those obvious things. A course that seemed obvious to
Joseph was apparently not so to him. The officer
said only, "Well, we are not torturers here. If you're
unwilling to speak, we can wait until you are. We
will keep you here until you beg us to question
you again, and then you will tell us everything.
You can go and rot until then." And to the guard
waiting at the door he said, "Take him back to the
enclosure."

Joseph did not bother counting the days. Perhaps a week went by, perhaps two. He was feverish some of the time, shaking, sometimes
uncertain of where he was. Then the fever left
him, but he still felt weak and sickly. The strength
that he had regained at Eysar Village was going
from him again, now that he had to depend on
the miserable prison-camp food. He was losing
what little weight he had managed to put on in
the weeks just past. Familiar sensations re-
asserted themselves: giddiness, blurred vision,
mental confusion. One afternoon he found himself once again quite seriously considering the
proposition that as the starvation proceeded he

would become completely weightless and would be able to float up and out of here and home. Then he remembered that some such thought had crossed his mind much earlier in the trek, and he reminded himself that no such thing must be possible, or else he would surely have attempted it long before. And then, when he felt a little better, Joseph was amazed that he had allowed himself even to speculate about such an idiotic thing.

Several times on his better days he approached men in the enclosure to ask them why they were here, who their captors were, what was the current state of the civil war. Each time they turned coldly away from him as though he had made an obscene proposal. No one ever spoke to anyone in this compound. He called out to the three Indigenes that he was a friend of the Ardardin and had worked as a doctor among the people of the mountains, but they too ignored him, and one day they were removed from the enclosure and he never saw them again.

I will die in this place, he thought.

It is an absurd end to my journey. It makes no sense. But what can I do? Confess that I'm a spy? I am not a spy. I could give them no useful information about my spying even if I wanted to.

I suppose that I can confess that I am a Master, Joseph thought, and then they can take me out and shoot me, and that will be the end. But not yet. I am not quite ready for that. Not yet. Not yet.

Then one morning a guard came for him, very

likely the same one who had come for him that other time, and gave him the same wordless gesture of beckoning as before, and led him up the long aisle of important-looking structures to the office of the burly man with thinning reddish-gold hair who had interrogated him earlier. This time the man's desk was bare. Joseph wondered what had become of his possessions. But that probably did not matter, he thought, because this time they would ask him the fatal questions, and then they would kill him.

The officer said, "Is your name Joseph Master Kilran?"

Joseph stared. He could not speak.

"Is it? You may as well say yes. We know that you are Joseph Master Kilran."

Joseph shook his head dazedly, not so much to deny the truth, or almost-truth, of what the man was saying, but only because he did not know how to react.

"You are. Why hide it?"

"Are you going to shoot me now?"

"Why would I shoot you? I want you to answer my question, that's all. Are you Joseph Master Kilran? Yes or no."

It would be easy enough to answer "No" with a straight face, since he was in fact not Joseph Master Kilran. But there could be no doubt that they were on to the truth about him, and Joseph saw no advantage in playing such games with them.

He wondered how they had found him out.

Were descriptions posted somewhere of all the missing Masters, those who had escaped being slain when the Great Houses of Manza were destroyed? That was hard to believe. But then he understood. "Kilran" was his clue: Thayle had never managed to pronounce his surname accurately. This man must have recognized all along that he was a Master. Probably in the past few days they had sent messengers to the people of all the towns in the vicinity, including the people of Eysar Haven, asking them whether any fugitive Masters had happened to come their way lately. And so they had learned his name, or something approximating his name, from Thayle. It was a disquieting thought. Thayle would never have betrayed him, he was sure of that: but he could easily picture Grovin betraying *her*, and Governor Stappin forcing a confession out of her, by violent means if necessary.

It was all over now, in any case.

"Keilloran," Joseph said.

"What?"

"Keilloran. My name. 'Kilran' is incorrect. I am Joseph Master Keilloran, of Keilloran House in Helikis."

The officer handed Joseph a writing-tablet. "Here. Put it down on this."

Joseph wrote the words down for him. The officer stared at what Joseph had written for a long moment, pronouncing the words with his lips alone, not uttering any of it aloud.

"Where is House Keilloran?" he asked, finally.

"In the southern part of central Helikis."

"And what was a Master from the southern part of central Helikis doing in High Manza?"

"I was a guest at Getfen House. The Getfens are distant kinsmen of mine. *Were*."

"After Getfen House was destroyed, then, what did you do, where did you go?"

Joseph told him, a quick, concise summary, the flight into the forest, the aid that the noctambulo had given him, the sojourn as a healer among the Indigenes. He did not care whether the officer believed him or not. He told of his escape in the mountains, of his trek back to the lowlands and his time of starvation, of his rescue by the inhabitants of a friendly cuyling town. He did not name the town and the officer did not ask him for it. "Then I left them and was heading south again, still hoping to find my way back to Helikis, when I was captured by your men," Joseph concluded. "That's the whole story."

The officer, tugging obsessively at the receding curls of his forehead, listened with an apparent show of interest to all that Joseph had to say, frowning most of the time. He took extensive notes. When Joseph fell silent he looked up and said, "You tell me that you are a visitor from a far-off land who happened by accident to be in Manza at the time of the outbreak of the Liberation." It was impossible for Joseph not to hear the capital letter on that last word. "But why should

I accept this as true?" the man asked. "What if you are actually a surviving member of one of the Great Houses of Manza, a spy for your people, lying to me about your place of origin? One would expect a spy to lie."

"If I'm from one of the Great Houses of Manza, tell me which one," said Joseph. He had started speaking in Master, without giving it a thought. "And if I'm a spy, what kind of spying have I been doing? What have I seen, except some Indigene villages, and one town of free Folk who were never involved in your Liberation at all? Where's the evidence of my spy activities?" Joseph pointed to the officer's desk, where his belongings once had lain. "You confiscated my pack, and I assume you've looked through it. Did you find the notes of a spy in it? My records of troop movements and secret strategic plans? You found my school textbooks, I think. And some things I wrote down about the philosophical beliefs of the Indigenes. Nothing incriminating, was there? Was there?"

The officer was gaping at him, big-eyed. Joseph realized that he was swaying and about to fall. In his weakened condition an outburst like this was a great effort for him. At the last moment he caught hold of the front of the officer's desk and clung to it, head downward, his entire body shaking.

"Are you ill?" the officer asked.

"Probably. I've been living on your prison-camp food for I don't know how many days. Before that I was foraging for whatever I could find in the wilderness. It's a miracle I'm still able to stand on my own feet." Joseph forced himself to look up. His eyes met the officer's. —"Prove to me that I'm a spy," he said. "Tell me which House I come from in Manza. And then you can take me out and shoot me, I suppose. But show me your proof, first."

The officer was slow to reply. He tugged at his hair, chewed his lower lip. Finally he said, "I will have to discuss this with my superiors." And, to the guard who had brought him here: "Return him to the compound."

Shortly past midday, before Joseph had even had a chance to confront whatever unsavory stuff they intended to give the prisoners for their afternoon meal, he was back at the big officer's headquarters again. Two other men in officers' uniform, senior ones, from the looks of them, were there also.

One, a hard-looking man who had a terrible scar, long healed but still vivid, running across his jutting cheekbone and down to the corner of his mouth, pushed a sheet of paper toward Joseph and said, speaking in Master, "Draw me a map of Helikis. Mark the place where you come from on it."

Joseph made a quick sketch of the continent, and drew a cross a little past midway down to indicate the location of Keilloran House.

"What is your father's name?"

"Martin Master Keilloran."

"And his father?"

"Eirik Master Keilloran."

"Your mother's name?"

"Wireille. She is dead."

The scar-faced officer looked toward the other two. Something passed between them, some sign, some wordless signal, that Joseph was unable to interpret. The officer who had twice interrogated him gave a single forceful nod. Then the second man, the oldest of the three, turned to Joseph and said, "The free people of Manza have no quarrel with the Masters of Helikis, and they are not interested in starting one now. As soon as it is practical you will be taken to the border, Joseph Master Keilloran, and turned over to your own kind."

Joseph stared. And blurted: "Do you seriously mean that?"

At once he saw the flash of anger in the scar-faced officer's eyes. The ugly scar stood out in a blaze of red. "We of the Liberation have no time for jokes." The words were spoken, this time, in Folkish.

"I ask you to forgive me, then," Joseph said, in Folkish also. "I've been through a great deal this past year, very little of it good. And I was expecting you to say that you were sentencing me to death."

"Perhaps that is what we should do," the scar-faced man said. "But it is not what we *will* do. As I said: you will be taken to the border."

Joseph still had difficulty in believing that. It was all some elaborate ruse, he thought, a ploy intended to soften him up so that they could come at him in some unexpected way and extract the truth from him about his espionage activities. But if that was so, they were going about it in a very strange way. He was transferred from the prisoners' compound to a barracks at the other side of the camp, where, although he was still under guard, he had a small room to himself. His pack and everything that had been in it were restored to him. Instead of the abysmal prisoner food he was given meals that, although hardly lavish, were at least nourishing and sound. It was the quality of the food that led Joseph at last to see that what was going on was something other than a trick. They did not want to send him back to Helikis as a creature of skin and bone. They would fatten him up a little, first, to indicate to the Masters of Helikis that the free people of Manza were humane and considerate persons. Perhaps they would even send the camp barber in to cut his hair and trim his beard, too, and outfit him with a suit of clothes of the sort a young Master would want to wear, too. Joseph was almost tempted to suggest that, not in any serious way, to one of his jailers, a young, easy-going Folker who appeared to have taken a liking to him. But it was not a good idea, he knew, to get too cocky with his captors. None of these people had any love for him. None would be amused by that sort of presumptuousness.

The fact that they were calling their uprising the Liberation told Joseph what their real attitude toward him was. They hated Masters; they looked upon the whole race of them as their enemies. They were not so much offering him assistance in getting back to his home as they were merely spitting him out. He was no concern of theirs, this strayed Master out of the wrong continent, and very likely if all this had been happening six or eight months before they would simply have executed him the moment they had realized what he was. It was only by grace of whatever political situation currently existed between the liberated Folk of Manza and the Masters who must still be in power in Helikis that he had been allowed to live. And even now Joseph was still not fully convinced of the sincerity of the scarfaced man's words. He did not plan to test them by trying to enter into any sort of easy intimacy with those who guarded him.

Four days went by this way. He saw no one but his jailers in all this time.

Then on the fifth morning he was told to make himself ready for departure, and half an hour later two soldiers, uncongenial and brusque, came for him and escorted him to a waiting car, where a third man in Liberation uniform was at the controls. His two guards got in beside him. He was not riding in any clumsy jolting wagon this time, no open wooden cart, no farm truck. The vehicle was a smooth, sleek car of the sort that a Master might use, and probably once had.

The road went due westward, and then a little to the north. Joseph was in the habit by this time of determining his course by the position of the sun. Neither of his guards said a word, to each other or to him. After several hours they stopped for lunch at an ordinary public roadhouse: he was leaving the wilderness world behind, reentering the one he had once known, prosperous-looking farms on all sides, fields awaiting harvest, farm vehicles moving up and down the roads, everything seeming quite as it should but obviously under Folk control, no sign of a Master presence anywhere. The guards, silent as ever, watched him closely while they ate; when he asked to go to the restroom, one of them went with him. Joseph clearly saw that they had been ordered to prevent him from escaping, if that was what he had in mind, and probably they would shoot him if they thought that that was what he was trying to do. So, just as he still did not completely believe that he was being released, they did not completely believe that he was not a spy.

An hour more of driving, after lunch, brought them to an airfield, a smallish one that nevertheless must have been a reasonably important commercial field before the Liberation but now looked somewhat run down. A solitary plane, with dull-toned Liberation emblems painted over whatever insignia it had borne before, was waiting on the runway. The sight of it was another powerful reminder for Joseph of the modern civilized world that was somewhere out there, that he once had lived in and would be returning to now. He wondered how easy it was going to be to fit himself back in. His guards led him aboard, taking him to a seat in the front of the cabin, where he could not see any of his fellow passengers.

Joseph wondered if this was actually a flight to Helikis. Could that be possible? Had everyone on Homeworld already settled into such a complacent acceptance of the new order of things in liberated Manza that normal air traffic between the continents had resumed?

He had his answer soon enough. The plane took off, soared quickly to its cruising altitude, moved off on a southerly course. Joseph, sitting in the middle of a group of three seats, leaned forward across the guard at his right to stare out the window, looking hopefully for the narrowing of the land below that would tell him that they were nearing the sea and approaching the Isthmus, the little bridge of land that separated the two continents. But he saw no coastline down there, only an immense expanse of terrain, most

of it divided into cultivated patches, reaching to
each horizon. They were still in Manza. And now
the plane was starting to descend. The flight had
lasted perhaps two and a half hours, three at
most. They had gone only a relatively short distance, at least as aerial journeys went, though
Joseph knew now that it would have taken him
several lifetimes to cover that relatively short distance on foot, as he had with so much bravado
intended to do. And he was still a long way from
home.

"Where are we landing?" Joseph asked one of
his guards.

"Eivoya," the guard said. The name meant
nothing to Joseph. "It is where the border is."

It hardly seemed worthwhile to seek a more
detailed explanation. The plane touched down
nicely. Another car was waiting for Joseph at the
edge of the runway. Once again the two guards
took seats on either side of him. This time they
drove about an hour more: it was getting to be
late in the day, and Joseph was growing very
tired, tired of this long day's traveling, tired of sitting between these two uncommunicative men,
tired of having things happen to him. He realized
that he was probably as close to home as he had
been in over a year, and that this day he had covered a greater distance toward that goal than he
had managed to cross by his own efforts in all the
time since the burning of Getfen House. Yet he
felt no sense of mounting jubilation. He still did

not know what further obstacles lay between him and Keilloran. He might not even get there at all. And he was weary to the bone. This is what it feels like to be old, he thought. To cease to care, even about things that you have sought to achieve. I have aged seventy years in just these few months.

The car pulled up at the edge of what looked like an untilled field. There was nothing in view anywhere around, no farms, no buildings. He saw a few trees a long way off. There was a scattering of gray clouds overhead.

"This is where you get out," said the guard to his left. He opened the door, stepped out, waited.

"Here?" Joseph asked.

The guard nodded. He scowled and made an impatient backhanded gesture.

It made no sense. Here, in the middle of nowhere? This forlorn weedy field looked like exactly the sort of place where you would choose to take a prisoner to be executed, but if all they had wanted to do was kill him, why had they bothered to go through all this involved business of loading him on cars, flying him south, driving him around in the countryside? They could much more easily have shot him back at the camp. It would have caused no stir. Tens of thousands of Masters had been massacred in Manza already; the death of one more, even a stranded visitor from Helikis, would hardly make much difference in the general scheme of things.

"Out," the guard said again. "This is wasting time."

Very well, Joseph thought. Whatever they wanted. He was too tired to argue, and begging for his life was unlikely to get him anywhere.

The Folker pointed out into the field. "There's the border marker, out there ahead of you. Now run. Run as fast as you know how, in the direction that I'm pointing. I warn you, don't go in any other direction. Go! Now!"

Joseph began to run.

They will shoot me in the back before I have gone twenty paces, he told himself. The bolt will pass right through my pack, into my body, my lungs, my heart, and I will fall down on my face here in this field, a dead man, and they will leave me here, and that will be that.

"Run!" the guard called, behind him. "*Run!*"

Joseph did not look back to see if they were aiming at him, though he was sure that they were. He ran, ran hard, ran with all the determination he could summon, but it was a tough sprint. The ground was rough beneath his feet, and not even these last few days of decent meals had brought him back to anything like a semblance of strength. He ran with his mouth open, gulping for air. He felt his heart working too quickly and protesting it. Several times he nearly tripped over the extended ropy stem of some treacherous low-growing shrub, lurched, staggered, barely managed to stay upright. He thought back to that time, what seemed like a hundred years ago, when he had lurched and staggered and stumbled and fallen in the forest near Getfen and had done that terrible injury to his leg. He did not want that to happen again, though it was strange to be fretting about anything so minor as an injured leg when two men with guns might be taking aim at him from behind.

But the shot that he had expected did not come. A few moments more and he ascended a little rise in the field, and when he came down the far side he saw a broad palisade standing before him, a row of stout logs tightly lashed together set in the ground, and he realized that he had arrived at the dividing point that set the two worlds apart, the boundary between the territory of the Liberation and that which must still remain under the sovereignty of his own people.

There was a gate in the palisade and a guardpost above it. The grim faces of four or five men were looking out at him. Joseph thought he saw the metal face of a gun facing him also.

Bringing himself to a stumbling halt a few dozen yards before the palisade, he raised his arms to show that he intended no harm. He hoped that they were expecting him.

"Masters!" he cried, in his own language, with what was nearly his last gasp of breath. "Help me! Help! Help!"

Then the ground came rushing up toward him

and Joseph seized it and held it, because everything was whirling around. He heard voices above him, saw booted feet standing beside him. They were lifting him, carrying him through the gate.

"What place is this?" he asked, speaking through a thin mist of exhaustion.

"House Eivoya," someone said.

"You are Masters?"

"Masters, yes."

He was lying in a bed, suddenly. There were bright lights overhead. They were washing him. Someone was doing something to his arm, attaching something to it. Someone else was wrapping a kind of collar around his left ankle. Joseph had the impression that they were explaining to him the things that they were doing to him, step by step, but none of it made much sense, and after a time he gave up trying to follow it. It was easier to go to sleep, and he did. When he awoke, sleep still seemed the easier choice, and he glided back into it. The next time he awakened there were two people in the room, a man and a woman, older people, both of them, watching him.

The woman, he discovered, was his doctor. The man introduced himself as Federigo Master Eivoya, of House Eivoya. "And what is your name?" the man said.

"Joseph. Joseph Master Keilloran. Am I still in Manza?"

"Southern Manza, yes. Just north of the Isthmus. —Can you tell me your father's name, Joseph?"

"You don't believe I am who I say I am? Or are you just trying to see whether my mind still works?"

"Please."

"Martin is his name. Martin Master Keilloran. My mother was Mistress Wireille, but she's dead. My brothers' names—"

"You don't need to go on."

"So you believe me?"

"Of course we believe you. We needed to know, and now we do."

The woman said, "You'll want to rest for a while. You're half starved, you know. They treated you very badly in that prison camp, didn't they?"

Joseph shrugged. "I was in pretty bad shape when I got there. They didn't make things any better for me, though."

"No. Of course not."

She gave him something to make him sleep again. He dreamed of Thayle, tiptoeing into the room, climbing naked into the bed beside him, taking his thin ruined body into her arms, holding him against the warmth of her, her firm abundant flesh. He dreamed he was in the village of the Ardardin, discussing the difference between the visible world and the invisible one. At last it all was clear to him. He understood what the Ardardin meant by the axis of the worlds upon which all things spin, and the place where mundane time and mythical time meet. He had never really managed to grasp that before. Then he was back in the forest with the noctambulo, who was reciting noctambulo poetry to him in a low monotonous voice, and then he was in his own room at Keilloran House, with his mother and his father standing beside his bed.

When he woke his mind was clear again, and he saw that there was a tube going into his arm and another into his thigh, and he knew that this must be a hospital and that they were trying to repair the various kinds of damage that his long journey had inflicted on him. A younger man who said his name was Reynaldo was with him. "I am Federigo's son," he told Joseph. "If you have things to ask, you can ask me." He was about thirty, dark-haired, smooth-skinned, as handsome as an actor. Joseph had things to ask, yes, but he hardly knew where to begin. "Did the Folk conquer all of Manza?" he said, after a moment's hesitation. That seemed like as good a starting-point as any.

"Most of it, yes," Reynaldo said. "All but here." He explained that the Masters had been able to hold the line at Eivoya, that the rebel forces in the far south had not been strong enough to break through it and eventually they had abandoned the attempt and worked out an armistice acknowledging the continued sover-

eignty of the Masters over the southern tip of
Manza. The rest of the northern continent, he
said, was in Folkish hands, and he supposed that
most or all of the Great Houses had been destroyed. The fighting had ended, now. Occasional straggling survivors from the north still
made their way down here, said Reynaldo, but
they were very few and far between these days.
He said nothing about any plans to reconquer
the territory that had been lost, and Joseph did
not ask him about that.

"And Helikis?" Joseph said. "What happened
there?"

"There was no rebellion in Helikis," said Reynaldo. "Everything in Helikis is as it always has
been."

"Is that the truth, or are you just telling me that
to make me feel better?"

"You should have no reason to distrust me,"
Reynaldo said, and Joseph let the point drop,
though he realized that what Reynaldo had told
him had not exactly been a reply to what he had
asked.

He knew that he was very ill. In his struggle to
survive, going again and again to the brink of
starvation, he must have consumed most of his
body's resources. Perhaps he had been operating
on sheer force of will alone, most of the time since
he had left Eysar Haven. At his age he was still
growing; his body needed a constant rich supply
of fuel; instead it had been deprived, much of the

time, of even a basic input of nourishment. But they were kind to him here. They knew how to heal him. He was back among his own, or almost so. Joseph had never heard of House Eivoya, but that did not matter: he had never heard of most of the Houses of Manza. He was grateful for its existence and for his presence at it. He might not have been able to survive much longer on his own. It was possible to take the position that his being captured by those rebel troops was the luckiest thing that had happened to him during his journey.

Once again Joseph began to recover. He realized that the innate resilience of his body must be very great. They took out the tubes; he began to eat solid food; soon he was up, walking about, leaving his room and going out on the balcony of the building. It appeared that the hospital was at the edge of a forest, a very ancient one at that, dark, primordial, indomitable giant trees with their roots in the prehistory of Homeworld standing side by side, green networks of coiling vines embracing their mammoth trunks to create an impenetrable barrier. For a moment Joseph thought that when he left here it would be necessary for him to enter that forest and cross it somehow, to solve all the terrible riddles that it would pose, the next great challenge on his journey, and the thought both frightened and excited him. But then he reminded himself that he had reached sanctuary at last, that he would not have to wander in dark forests any longer.

"Someone is here to see you," Reynaldo told him, a day or two later.

She came to his room, a tall dark-haired young woman, slender, elegantly dressed, quite beautiful. She looked astonishingly like his mother, so much so that for one startled moment Joseph thought that she *was* his mother and that he must be having hallucinations again. But of course his mother was dead, and this woman was too young, anyway. She could not have been more than twenty and might even be younger. And only then did it occur to Joseph that she must be his sister.

"Cailin?" he asked, in a small, tentative voice.

And she, just as uncertainly: "Joseph?"

"You don't recognize me, do you?"

She smiled. "You look so good with a beard! But so different. Everything about you is so different. Oh, Joseph, Joseph, Joseph, Joseph—"

He held out his arms to her and she came quickly to him, rushing into the embrace and then drawing back a little from it as though pausing to consider that he was still very fragile, that a hug that had any fervor to it might well break him into pieces. But he clung to her and drew her in. Then he released her, and she stepped back, studying him, staring. Though she did not say it, Joseph could see that she still must be searching, perhaps almost desperately, for some sign that this gaunt bearded stranger in front of her was in fact her brother.

He too was searching for signs to recognize her by. That she was Cailin he had no doubt. But the Cailin that he remembered had been a girl, tall and a little awkward, all legs and skinny arms, just barely come into her breasts, her face still unformed. This one—a year and a half later, two years?—was a woman. Her arms, the whole upper part of her body, had become fuller. So had her face. She had cut her long, wondrous cascade of black hair so that it reached only to her shoulders. Her chin was stronger, her nose more pronounced, and both changes only enhanced her beauty.

They were little more than a year apart in age. Joseph had always been fond of her, fonder than he was of any of the others, though he had often showed his liking for her in perversely heartless ways, callous pranks, little boorish cruelties, all manner of things that he had come to regret when it was too late to do anything about them. He was glad that she, rather than Rickard or one of the House servants, had come for him. Still, he wondered why she was the one who had been chosen. Rickard would be old enough to have made the journey. Girls—and that was what she really was, still, a girl—were not often sent on such extended trips.

"Is everything all right at Keilloran? I've heard nothing—nothing—"

She glanced away, just for the merest instant, but it was a revealing glance none the less. And she paused to moisten her lips before answering. "There have been—a few problems," she said. "But we can talk about that later. It's you I want to talk about. Oh, Joseph, we were so sure you were dead!"

"The combinant was broken. I tried to get in touch, the very first night when they attacked Getfen House, but nothing would happen. Not then or later, and then I lost it. It was taken away from me, I mean. By an Indigene. He wanted it, and I had to let him have it, because I belonged to them, I was a sort of slave in their village, their doctor—"

She was staring at him in amazement. He covered his mouth with his hand. He was telling her too much too soon.

"Communications were cut off for a while," Cailin said. "Then they were restored, but not with the part of Manza where you were. They attacked Getfen House—but you got away, and then what? Where did you go? What did you do?"

"It's a complicated story," he said. "It'll take me quite a while to tell it."

"And you're all right now?"

"Oh, yes. Yes. Thinner. A few scars, maybe. Some changes here and there. It was a difficult time. —How is Rickard? Eitan? The girls?"

"Fine. Fine, all of them fine. Rickard had a difficult time too, thinking you were dead, knowing that he was going to have to be the Master of the House eventually in your place. You know what Rickard is like."

"Yes. I know what Rickard is like."

"But he's been coming around. Getting used to the idea. He's almost come to like it."

"I'm sorry to be disappointing him, then. — And Father?" Joseph said, the question he had been holding back. "How is he? How did he take it, the news that I was probably dead?"

"Poorly."

Joseph realized that he had asked two questions in one breath, and that Cailin had given him a single answer.

"But he rode with the shock, didn't he? The way he did when Mother died. The way he taught us all to do."

She nodded. But suddenly she seemed very far away.

Something is wrong, he thought. Those "problems" to which she had alluded. He was afraid to ask.

And she wanted to talk about him, anyway, where he had been, the things that had befallen him. Quickly he told her as much as he could, leaving out only the most important parts. That he had lived among a family of Folkers as a guest in their house, dependent on their mercy, not as a Master but as a weary hapless wayfarer whom they had taken in, and thus that he had discovered things about the Folk that he had never understood before. That he had accepted aid also in his wanderings from even humbler races, noctambulos, Indigenes, poriphars, and had come to see those beings in new ways too. That he had eaten insects and worms, and that he had been brought to the verge of madness more than once, even death. And that he had slept with a Folker girl. He was not ready to tell her any of that. But Joseph did describe his gaudier adventures in the forests, his perils and his escapes, and some of his hardships and injuries, and his strange new career as a tribal doctor, and his final captivity among the rebels. Cailin listened openmouthed, awed by all he had been through, amazed by it. He saw her still studying him, too, as if not yet fully convinced that the stranger behind this dense black beard was the brother she remembered.

"I must be tiring you," she said, when at last he let his voice trail off, having run through all the easy things he could tell her and not willing yet to attempt the difficult ones. "I'll let you rest now. They say you'll be ready to leave here in another two or three days."

He wanted to go sooner, and told Reynaldo that. He insisted that he was strong enough to travel again. The doctors thought so too, Reynaldo told him. But the plane on which Cailin had arrived had already gone back to Helikis, and the next one would not be getting here until the day after tomorrow, or possibly the day after that, no one was quite certain. Joseph saw from that that the lives of the Masters of Home-world must be far more circumscribed than they had been before the uprising, that even in sup-posedly untouched Helikis certain cutbacks had become necessary. Perhaps a good many of the planes that at one time had constantly gone back and forth between the continents had fallen into rebel hands and now served only the needs of the Liberation. But there was nothing to do except wait.

It turned out that the plane from Helikis did not arrive for five days. By then Joseph was able to move about as freely as he wished; he and Cailin left the building and walked across the hospital's broad gleaming lawn to the place where the lawn ended and the forest abruptly began, and stood silently, hand in hand, peering in at that dim, primordial world, wonderstruck by its self-contained forbiddingness, its almost alien strangeness. There was no way to enter it. The strangler vines that ran from tree to tree made entry impossible. A thin grayish light lit it from within. Bright-feathered birds fluttered about its perimeter. Sharp screeching noises came from the forest depths, and the occasional deep honking of some unknown creature wallowing in some muddy lake. Joseph found himself thinking that that gigantic, brooding, immemorial forest, forever untouched and untouchable by human hands, reduced all the little quarrels of the human world, Masters and Folk, Folk and Masters, to utter insignificance.

He did not take up with his sister the question of whatever it was that had happened at House Keilloran in his absence. He almost did not want to know. She volunteered nothing, and he asked nothing. Instead he told her, day by day, bit by bit, more about his journey, until at last he came to the part about Thayle, which he related quickly and without great detail, but leaving no doubt of what had actually taken place. Color came to Cailin's face, but her eyes were aglow with what seemed like unfeigned delight for him. She did not seem in any way shocked that he had yielded up his physical innocence, or that he had yielded it to a Folkish girl. She simply seemed pleased for him, and even amused. Maybe she knew that it was a common thing for Master boys to go to the girls of the Folk for the first time. He had no idea of what she might know about any of this, or of what she might have experienced herself, for that matter. It was not a subject he had ever discussed with her. He did not see how he could.

The plane from Helikis arrived. It stayed overnight for refueling, and in the morning he and Cailin boarded it for the return journey.

Joseph was carrying his pack. "What is that?" Cailin asked, and he told her that a Folkish woman had given it to him the night of his flight from Getfen House, and that he had carried it everywhere ever since, his one constant companion throughout his entire odyssey. "It smells terrible," she said, wrinkling up her nose. He nodded.

The flight south took much longer than Joseph expected. They were over the Isthmus quickly— Eivoya, Joseph saw, was in the very last broad part of Manza before the narrowing of the land began, which told him just how little of the continent remained in Master control—and then, quite soon, he found himself looking down on the great brown shoulder of northern Helikis, that parched uppermost strip that marked the beginning of the otherwise green and fertile southern continent, and although he knew a Master was not supposed to weep except, perhaps, in the face of the most terrible tragedy, he discovered that a moistness was creeping into his eyes now at this first glimpse of his native soil, the continent that he had so often supposed he might never live to see again.

But then the stops began: at Tuilieme, at Gheznara, at Kem, at Dannias. Hardly did the plane take off and reach a decent altitude but it started to enter a pattern of descent again. Passengers came and went; freight was loaded aboard below; meals were served so often that Joseph lost track of what time of day it was. The sky grew dark and Joseph dozed, and was awakened by daybreak, and another landing, and the arrival of new passengers, and yet another takeoff. But then came the announcement, just when he had begun to think that he was fated to spend the rest of his life aboard this plane, that they were approaching Toroniel Airport, the one closest to the domain of House Keilloran, and Joseph knew that the last and perhaps most difficult phase of his journey was about to commence.

Rickard was waiting at the airport with a car and one of the family drivers, a sharp-nosed man whose name Joseph did not remember. He was startled to see how much his brother had grown. He remembered Rickard as a boy of twelve, plump, pouty, soft-faced, short-legged, still a child, though an extremely intelligent child. But he had come into the first spurt of his adolescent growth in Joseph's absence. He was half a foot taller, at least, just a few inches shorter than Joseph himself, and all that childish fat had been burned away in the process of growing: Rickard was gawky, now, even spindly, the way Cailin had been before him. His face was different, also: not only leaner but with a far more serious expression about the eyes and lips, as though Joseph's absence and presumed death had sobered him into a first awareness of what life now was going to be like for him as an adult, as the future Master of House Keilloran. Joseph felt a little shiver go traveling down his back at the sight of this new, changed Rickard.

They embraced in a careful, brotherly way.

"Joseph."

"Rickard."

"I never thought to see you again."

"I never doubted I'd come back," said Joseph. "Never. Oh, Rickard, you've grown!"

"Have I? Yes, I suppose I have. You look different too, you know. It's been practically two years. That beard—"

"Do you like it?"

"No," Rickard said. He gestured toward the car. "We should get in. It's a long drive."

Yes. Joseph had forgotten just how long it was. This was not Keilloran territory here, not yet. The airport was in the domain of House Van Rhyn. They drove off toward the west, through the broad savannahs thick with purplish quivergrass that Joseph had loved to set trembling, and through the immense grove of blackleaf palms that marked the boundary between Keilloran and Van Rhyn, and past hills of pale lavender sand that marked the ancient seabed where Joseph and Cailin had sometimes gone hunting for little fossils. Then they came to the first of the cultivated fields, fallow at this time of year, a series of neat brown rectangles awaiting the winter sowing. Even now it was a good distance to the Inner Domain and the manor-house itself. Rickard asked just a few questions of Joseph during the drive, the barest basic inquiries about the rebellion, his wanderings, the current state of his health. Joseph replied in an almost perfunctory way. He sensed that Rickard did not yet want the complete narrative, and he himself was not at the moment in the mood for telling it yet again. A great deal of chatter seemed inappropriate now anyway. Once they had settled into the car there was an air of reserve, even of melancholy, about Rickard that Joseph neither understood nor liked. And about Cailin too: she scarcely spoke at all.

Now they were in the Inner Domain, now they were going past the Blue Garden and the White Garden and the Garden of Fragrance, past the gaming-courts and the stables, past the lagoon, past the statuary park and the aviary; and then the airy swoops and arabesques of Keilloran House itself lay directly before them, rising proudly on the sloping ridge that formed a pedestal for the great building. Joseph saw that the Folk of the House had come out to welcome him: they were arrayed in two lengthy parallel rows, beginning at the front porch and extending far out onto the entrance lawn, hundreds and hundreds of them, the devoted servants of the clan. How long had they been waiting like this? Had some signal been given fifteen minutes before that the car bearing Master Joseph had entered the Inner Domain, or had they lined up in this formation hours ago, waiting here with Folkish patience for him to arrive?

The car halted on the graveled coachgrounds

along the border of the lawn. Flanked by Rickard and Cailin, Joseph set out down the middle of the long lines of waiting Folk toward the house.

They were waving, grinning, cheering. Joseph, smiling, nodding, waved back at them with both hands. Some he recognized, and he let his eyes linger on their faces a moment; most of them he had forgotten or had never known, though he smiled at them also as he passed them by.

His smiles were manufactured ones, though. Within his soul he felt none of the jubilation that he had anticipated. In his fantasies in the forests of Manza, whenever he let his mind conjure up the longed-for moment of his return to Keilloran, he had imagined himself skipping down this path, singing, blowing kisses to shrubs and statues and household animals. He had never expected that he would feel so somber and withdrawn in the hour of his homecoming as in fact he was. Some of it, no doubt, was the anticlimactic effect of having achieved something for which he had yearned for so many months, and which had so often appeared to be unattainable. But there was more to it than that: there was Rickard's mood, and Cailin's, their silences on the drive, the questions that they had not answered because he had not had the courage to ask them.

His youngest brother Eitan was waiting at the door, and his other two sisters, the little ones,

Bevan and Rheena. Eitan was still only a small
boy—ten, now, Joseph supposed, still round-
faced and chubby—and he was staring at Joseph
with the same worshipful look as ever. Then
tears burst into his eyes. Joseph caught him up,
hugged him, kissed him, set him down. He
turned to the girls—virtual strangers to him in
the time before his departure for High Manza,
they had been, one of them five, the other seven,
forever busy with their dolls and their pets—and
greeted them too with hugs and kisses, though
he suspected they scarcely knew who he was.
Certainly they showed little excitement over his
return.

Where is Father? he wondered. Why is Father
not here?

Cailin and Rickard led him inside. But as the
three of them entered the house Rickard caught
him by the wrist and said in a low voice, almost
as though he did not want even Cailin to hear
what he was saying, "Joseph? Joseph, I'm so
tremendously glad that you've come back."

"Yes. You won't have to be Master here after
all, will you?"

It was a cruel thing to say, and he saw Rickard
flinch. But the boy made a quick recovery: the
hurt look went from his eyes almost as swiftly as
it had come, and something more steely replaced
it. "Yes," Rickard said. "That's true: I won't have
to. And I'm happy that I won't, although I would

have been ready to take charge, if it came to that. But that's not what I meant."

"No. I understand that. I'm sorry I said what I did."

"That's all right. We all know I never wanted it. But I missed you, Joseph. I was certain that you had been killed in the uprising, and—and—it was bad, Joseph, knowing that I'd never see you again, it was very bad, first Mother, then you—"

"Yes. Yes. I can imagine." Joseph squeezed Rickard's hand. And said then, offhandedly, "I don't see Father. Is he off on a trip somewhere right now?"

"He's inside. We're taking you to him."

Strange, the sound of that. He did not ask for an explanation. But he knew he had to have one soon.

There were more delays first, though: a plethora of key household officials waiting in the inner hall to greet him, chamberlains and stewards and bailiffs, and old Marajen, who helped his father keep the accounts, and formidable Sempira, who had come here from the household of Joseph's mother's family to supervise all domestic details and still ran the place like a tyrant, and many more. They each wanted a chance to embrace Joseph, and he knew it would take hours to do the job properly; but he summoned up a bit of the training he had had from Balbus, and smilingly moved through them without stopping, calling out names, waving, winking, showing every evidence of extreme delight at being among them all once more, but keeping in constant motion until he was beyond the last of them.

"And Father—?" Joseph said, insistently now, to Rickard and Cailin.

"Upstairs. In the Great Hall," said Rickard.

That was odd. The Great Hall was a place of high formality, his father's hall of judgment, his seat of power, virtually his throne-room, a dark place full of echoes. It was not where Joseph would expect a long-lost son to be welcomed. But his father was, after all, Martin Master Keilloran, the lord of this estate these many years past, and perhaps, Joseph thought, many years of lordship will teach one certain ways of doing things that he was in no position yet to comprehend.

Joseph and his brother and his sister went up the grand central staircase together. Joseph's mind was spilling over with thoughts: things he would ask, once he had told his father the tale of his adventures, and things he must say.

He had it in mind to resign his rights as the heir to House Keilloran. It was an idea that had been lurking at the corners of his mind for days, only half acknowledged by him; but it had burst into full power as he came down that double row of smiling, waving, cheering Folk of the House. He would abdicate, yes. He would rather go to live among the Indigenes again, or as a peasant-farmer among the cuylings of Manza, than rule here as Master of the House, rule over the Folk of Keilloran like a king who has lost all yearning to be king. By what right do we rule here? Who says we are to be the masters, other than ourselves, and by what right do we say it? Let Rickard have the task of ruling. He will not like it, of course. But Rickard does not deny that we have the right, and he claims to be ready for it: he said that with his own lips, just a few minutes before. It is his, then, whenever the time comes for it. Let him be the next Master, the successor to their father, the next in the great line that went back so many centuries, when the time came.

"In here," Rickard said.

Joseph glanced at him, and at Cailin, whose eyes were cast down, whose lips were tightly clamped.

There was a twilight dimness in the Great Hall. The heavy damask draperies were closed, here on this bright afternoon, and only a few lamps had been lit. Joseph saw his father seated at the far end of the room in his huge ornate chair, the chair of state that was almost like a throne. He sat in a strange unmoving way, as though he had become a statue of himself. Joseph went toward him. As he came close he saw that the right side of his father's face sagged strangely downward, and that his father's right arm dangled like a mannequin's arm at his side, a limp dead thing. He looked twenty years older than the man Joseph remembered: an old man, suddenly. Joseph halted, horror-stricken, stunned, twenty feet away.

"Joseph?" came the voice from the throne. His father's voice was a thick, slurred sound, barely intelligible, not the voice that Joseph remembered at all. "Joseph, is that you, finally?"

So this was the little problem that Cailin had alluded to when Joseph was in the hospital at Eivoya.

"How long has he been this way?" Joseph asked, under his breath.

"It happened a month or two after word reached here of the attack on Getfen House," Cailin whispered. "Go to him. Take him by the hand. The right hand."

Joseph approached the great seat. He took the dead hand in his. He lifted the arm. There was no strength in it. It was like something artificial that had been attached recently to his father's shoulder.

"Father—"

"Joseph—Joseph—"

That slurred sound again. It was dreadful to hear. And the look in his father's eyes: a frozen look, it was, alien, remote. But he was smiling, with the part of his mouth over which he still had control. He raised his left hand, the good one, and put it down over Joseph's, and pressed down tightly. That other arm was not weak at all.

"A beard?" his father said. He seemed to be trying to laugh. "You grew a beard, eh?" Thickly,

thickly: Joseph could barely understand the words. "So young to have a beard. Your grandfather wore a beard. But I never had one."

"I didn't mean to, not really. It just wasn't easy for me to shave, in some of the places where I was. And then I kept it. I liked the way it looked." He thinks I'm still a boy, Joseph realized. How much of his mind was left at all? Suddenly Joseph was wholly overcome with the sadness of what he saw here, and he drew his breath inward in a little gasping sound. "Oh, Father—Father, I'm so sorry—"

He felt Rickard kick him in the heel from behind. Rickard made a tiny hissing noise, and Joseph understood. Pity is not being requested here. My little brother is teaching me the proper way to handle this, he thought.

"I like it," his father said, very slowly. Again the twisted smile. He appeared not to have noticed Joseph's little outburst. "The beard. A new fashion among us. Or an old one revived." Joseph began to realize that his father's mind must still be intact, or nearly so, even if his body was no longer under its control. "You've been gone such a long time, boy. You look so different, now. You must *be* so different, eh?"

"I've been in some unusual places, Father. I've learned some strange things."

Martin nodded slowly. That seemed to be a supreme effort, that slow movement of his head. "I've been in some unusual places too, lately,

without—ever—leaving—Keilloran—House."
He seemed to be struggling to get the words out.
"And I—look—different—too," he said. "Don't
I?"

"You look fine, Father."

"No. Not true." The dark, hooded eyes drilled
into him. "Not—fine—at—all. But you are here,
finally. I can rest. You will be Master now,
Joseph."

"Yes. If that's what you wish."

"It is. You must. You are ready, aren't you?"

"I will be," Joseph said.

"You are. You are."

He knew it was so. And knew also that he could
not possibly think of abdication, not now, not after
seeing what his father had become. All thought of
it had fled. It had begun to fade from his mind the
moment he had entered this room and looked
upon his father's face; now it was gone entirely.
Now that you are back, I can rest, is what his father
was saying. That wish could not be ignored or de-
nied him. The doubts and uncertainties that had
been born in Joseph during the months of his
wanderings were still there; but still with him, too,
was that inborn sense of his obligation to his family and to the people of House Keilloran, and now,
standing before the one to whom he owed his existence, he knew that it was not in him to fling that
obligation back in the face of this stricken man.
Rickard had not been trained for this. He had
been. He was needed. He could not say no. When

his time came to be Master, though, Joseph knew he would be Master in a way that was different from his father's.

The hand that was holding his pressed down harder, very hard indeed, and Joseph saw that there was still plenty of strength in what remained of Martin Master Keilloran. Not enough, though, to perform the tasks that the Master of the House must perform, and which, he saw now, would—in a month, six months, whenever—devolve upon him.

"But we need to talk, Father. When I've been home a little while, and when you feel up to it. There are things I need to ask you. And things I need to say."

"We'll talk, yes," his father said.

Cailin nudged him. She signalled with a roll of her eyes that it was time for Joseph to go, that this was the limit of their damaged father's endurance. Joseph gave her a barely perceptible nod. To Martin he said, "I have to leave, now, Father. I've had a long journey, and I want to rest for a while. I'll come to you again this evening." He squeezed the dead right hand, lifted it and kissed it and set it carefully down again, and he and Cailin and Rickard went from the room and down the hall, and into the family wing, and to the suite of rooms that had been his before his trip to Getfen, and where everything seemed to have remained completely as he had left it.

"We'll leave you to rest," Cailin said. "Ring for us when you're ready, and we can talk."

"Yes."

"That was hard, wasn't it?"

"Yes," Joseph said quietly. "Yes, it was."

He watched his brother and sister going down the hall, and closed the door, and was alone in his own bedroom once again. He sat down on the edge of the bed, his old bed that seemed so small, now, so boyish. As he sat there, letting the facts of his return wash over him, the bed became all the places that had been bed for him as he made his way across Manza, the rough hollows in the forest floor where he slept on bundles of dry leaves, and the stack of musty furs in the Ardardin's village, and the hard cot, sharp as bone, in the prisoner compound, and the place under the bush where he had drifted into the hallucinations of starvation that he untroubledly believed heralded the end of his life, and the little bed in Eysar Haven that had taken on the fragrance of Thayle's warm breasts and soft thighs, and all the rest of them as well, all flowing into one, this bed here, the little bed of his boyhood, the boyhood that now was done with and sealed.

In the morning, Joseph thought, he would go out and walk about the estate and reacquaint himself with its land and with its people. He would pull its air deep into his lungs. He would reach down and dig his fingers into its soil. He would visit the farms and the factories and the stables. He would look at everything, and he knew that there would be much that he would be seeing as though for the first time, not just because he had been away so long but because he would be seeing it all through the eyes of a different person, one who had been to far-off places and seen far-off things. But all that was for the next day, and for the days to come. For the moment he just wanted to lie here atop his own bed in his own room and think back through all that had befallen him.

I've had a long journey, and I want to rest for a while.

A long journey, yes, a journey which had begun in thunder that had brought no rain, but only endless thunder. And now it was over, and he was home, and some new sort of journey was just beginning. He was not who he had been before, and he was not certain of exactly what he had become, and he was not at all sure who he was going to be. He was full of questions, and some of those questions might never have answers, though he wanted to think he would go on asking them, over and over, nevertheless. Well, time would tell, or maybe not. He was home, at any rate. He had come by the longest possible route, a journey that had taken him deep into the interior of himself and brought him out in some strange new place. He knew that it would take time for him to discover the nature of that place. But there was no hurry about any of that. And at least he was home. Home. Home.

A.U.C. 1203: Prologue

The historian Lentulus Aufidius, whose goal it was to write the definitive biography of the great Emperor Titus Gallius, was now in his third year of research in the Imperial archives at the Palatine Library. Every morning, six days a week, Aufidius would trudge up the hill from his lodgings near the Forum, present his identification card to the Keeper of the Archives, and set about his daily exploration of the great cabinets in which the scrolls pertaining to the reign of Titus Gallius were stored.

It was a formidable task. Titus Gallius, who had come to the throne upon the death of the madman Caracalla, had ruled over Roma from 970 to 994 and in that time had completely reorganized the government that his predecessor had left in such disheveled condition. Provinces had been merged, others had been broken up, the system of taxation had undergone reform, the army had been ripped apart and reconstructed from top to bottom to meet the growing menace of the northern barbarians, and so on and so on. Lentulus Aufidius suspected that he had two or three more years of study ahead of him before he could at last begin writing his text.

Today would be devoted, as each previous day of the past two weeks had been, to an inspection of Cabinet 42, which contained the documents concerning Titus Gallius's religious policies. Titus Gallius had been much troubled by the way mystical Oriental cults were spreading through the Empire—the worship of Mithras the bull-slayer, of the mother-goddess Cybele, of Osiris of Aegyptus, and many others. The Emperor feared that these alien religions, if allowed to become deeply established, would weaken the fabric of the state; and so he had done what he could to suppress them without at the same time losing the loyalty of the common folk who adhered to them. That was a delicate task, and it had been only partly accomplished in Titus Gallius's time. It remained for Titus Gallius's nephew and successor, the Emperor Gaius Martius, to finish the work by founding the cult of Jupiter Imperator, which was intended to replace all the foreign religions.

Someone else was already at work at Cabinet 42 when Aufidius reached it. After a moment he recognized the man as an old friend and colleague, Hermogenes Celer, a native of Tripolis in Phoenicia who was, perhaps, the Empire's lead-

ing scholar of Eastern religions. Aufidius, though
he had corresponded occasionally with Celer, had
not seen him in many years, nor had he known
that Celer was planning a visit to the capital. The
two men embraced warmly and—to the annoyance of the librarians—began at once to discuss
their current projects.

"Titus Gallius?" Celer said. "Ah, yes, a fascinating story."

"And you?"

"The Hebrews of Aegyptus," said Celer. "A remarkable group of people. Descendants of a nomadic desert tribe, they are."

"I know next to nothing about them," Aufidius
said.

"Ah, you should, you should!" said Celer. "If
things had gone differently for them, who can say
what path our history would have taken?"

"*Please*, gentlemen, *please*," one of the librarians
said. "Scholars are at work in here. If you must
have a conversation, there is a hall available outside."

"We must talk later," Aufidius said. And they
agreed to meet for lunch.

Celer, as it turned out, was overflowing with
tales of his Hebrews, and spoke of little else while
they ate. In particular he told of their passionate
belief in a single lofty god, remote and stern, who
had decreed for them an intricate set of laws that
controlled everything from how they should
speak of him (it was forbidden to utter his name)

to what foods they could eat on which days of the week.

Because they were such a stubborn and difficult tribe, he said, they were often in trouble with their neighbors. Having conquered a large portion of Syria Palaestina, these Hebrews—who also called themselves Israelites—founded a kingdom there, but eventually were subjugated by the Aegyptians and forced into slavery in the land of the Pharaohs. This period lasted hundreds of years. But Celer declared that he had identified a critical moment in Hebrew history, some seventeen centuries in the past, when a charismatic chieftain named Mosaeus—*Moshe*, in their language—had attempted to lead his people on a great exodus out of Aegyptus and back to their former homeland in Palaestina, which they believed had been promised to them as an eternal homeland by their god.

"And then what happened?" said Aufidius politely, although he found none of this very interesting.

"Well," said Celer, "this grand exodus of theirs was a terrible failure. Mosaeus and most of the other leaders were killed and the surviving Hebrews wound up back in slavery in Aegyptus."

"I fail to see—"

"Ah, but I do!" cried Celer, and his plump, pasty face lit up with scholarly fire. "Think of the possibilities, dear Aufidius! Let's say the Hebrews *do* reach Syria Palaestina. They settle themselves permanently, this time, in that hotbed of mystical fertility and harvest cults. Then, many centuries later, someone combines the ferocious religious zeal of the Hebrews with some native Palaestinian belief in rebirth and resurrection derived from the old Aegyptian business about Osiris, and a new religion under an invincible new prophet is born, not in distant Aegyptus but in a province of the Roman Empire much more closely connected with the center of things. And, precisely because Syria Palaestina by this time is a province of the Roman Empire and Roman citizens move freely about from district to district, this cult spreads to Roma itself, as other Eastern cults have done."

"And?" said Aufidius, mystified.

"And it conquers everything, as Cybele and Mithras and Osiris have never been able to do. Its prophets preach a message of universal love, and universal sharing of all wealth—*especially* the sharing of wealth. All property is to be held in common. The poor people of the Empire flock to the churches of this cult in huge droves. Everything is turned upside down. The Emperor himself is forced to recognize it—to convert to it himself, perhaps, for political reasons—this religion comes to dominate everything, and the basic structure of Roman society is weakened by superstition, until the Empire, consumed by the new philosophy, is toppled by the barbarians who forever lurk at its borders—"

"The very thing that Titus Gallius fought to prevent."

"Yes. Therefore in my new book I have postulated a world in which this Hebrew Exodus *did* happen, in which this new religion eventually was born, in which it spread uncontrollably throughout the Empire—"

"Well," said Aufidius, suppressing a yawn, "all that is sheer fantasy, you know. None of that happened, after all. And—admit it, Celer—it never *could* have happened."

"Perhaps yes, perhaps no. I find speculating about such possibilities very stimulating."

"Yes," Aufidius said. "I have no doubt that you do. But as for me, I prefer to deal with matters as they really are. No such cult ever infiltrated our beloved Roma, and the Empire is sturdy and sound, and for that, Celer, let us give thanks to nonexistent Jupiter, or to whichever other deity you pretend to believe in. And now, if you will, I'd like to share with you a few discoveries of my own concerning the tax reforms of the Emperor Titus Gallius—"

A.U.C. 1282: With Caesar in the Underworld

The newly arrived ambassador from the Eastern Emperor was rather younger than Faustus had expected him to be: a smallish sort, finely built, quite handsome in what was almost a girlish kind

of way, though obviously very capable and sharp,
a man who would bear close watching. There was
something a bit frightening about him, though
not at first glance. He gleamed with the impervi-
ousness of fine armor. His air of sophisticated and
fastidious languor coupled with hidden strength
made Faustus, a tall, robust, florid-faced man
going thick through the waist and thin about the
scalp, feel positively plebeian and coarse despite
his own lofty and significant ancestry.

That morning Faustus, whose task as an official
of the Chancellery it was to greet all such important visitors to the capital city, had gone out to
Ostia to meet him at the Imperial pier—the Greek
envoy, coming west by way of Sicilia, had sailed
up the coast from Neapolis in the south—and had
escorted him to the rooms in the old Severan
Palace where the occasional ambassadors from
the Eastern half of Empire were housed. Now it
was the time to begin establishing a little rap-
port. They faced each other across an onyx-slab
table in the Lesser Hall of Columns, which several reigns ago had been transformed into a somewhat oversized sitting-room. A certain amount of
preliminary social chatter was required at this
point. Faustus called for some wine, one of the
big, elegant wines from the great vineyards of
Gallia Transalpina.

After they had had a chance to savor it for a little while he said, wanting to get the ticklish part
of the situation out in the open right away, "The

prince Heraclius himself, unfortunately, has been called without warning to the northern frontier. Therefore tonight's dinner has been canceled. This will be a free evening for you, then, an evening for resting after your long journey. I trust that that'll be acceptable to you."

"Ah," said the Greek, and his lips tightened for an instant. Plainly he was a little bewildered at being left on his own like this, his first evening in Roma. He studied his perfectly manicured fingers. When he glanced up again, there was a gleam of concern in the dark eyes. "I won't be seeing the Emperor either, then?"

"The Emperor is in very poor health. He will not be able to see you tonight and perhaps not for several days. The prince Heraclius has taken over many of his responsibilities. But in the prince's unexpected and unavoidable absence your host and companion for your first few days in Roma will be his younger brother Maximilianus. You will, I know, find him amusing and very charming, my lord Menandros."

"Unlike his brother, I gather," said the Greek ambassador coolly.

Only too true, Faustus thought. But it was a remarkably blunt thing to say. Faustus searched for the motive behind the little man's words. Menandros had come here, after all, to negotiate a marriage between his royal master's sister and the very prince of whom he had just spoken so slightingly. When a diplomat as polished as this finely

oiled Greek says something as egregiously
undiplomatic as that, there was usually a good
reason for it. Perhaps, Faustus supposed, Menandros was simply showing annoyance at the fact
that Prince Heraclius had tactlessly managed not
to be on hand to welcome him upon his entry into
Roma.

Faustus was not going to let himself be drawn
any deeper into comparisons, though. He allowed himself only an oblique smile, that faint
sidewise smile he had learned from his young
friend the Caesar Maximilianus. "The two brothers are quite different in personality, that I do
concede. —Will you have more wine, your excel-
lence?"

That brought yet another shift of tone. "Ah, no
formalities, no formalities, I pray you. Let us be
friends, you and I." And then, leaning forward
cozily and shifting from the formal to the intimate
form of speech: "You must call me Menandros. I
will call you Faustus. Eh, my friend? —And yes,
more wine, by all means. What excellent stuff! We
have nothing that can match it in Constantinopolis. What sort is it, actually?"

Faustus flicked a glance at one of the waiting
servitors, who quickly refilled the bowls. "A wine
from Gallia," he said. "I forget the name." A swift
flash of unmistakable displeasure, quickly concealed but not quickly enough, crossed the Greek's
face. To be caught praising a provincial wine so
highly must have embarrassed him. But embar-

rassing him had not been Faustus's intention. There was nothing to be gained by creating discomfort for so powerful and potentially valuable a personage as the lord of the East's ambassador to the Western court.

This was all getting worse and worse. Hastily Faustus set about smoothing the awkwardness over. "The heart of our production lies in Gallia, now. The Emperor's cellars contain scarcely any Italian wines at all, they tell me. Scarcely any! These Gallian reds are His Imperial Majesty's preference by far, I assure you."

"While I am here I must acquire some, then, for the cellars of His Majesty Justinianus," said Menandros.

They drank a moment in silence. Faustus felt as though he were dancing on swords.

"This is, I understand, your first visit to Urbs Roma?" Faustus asked, when the silence had gone on just a trifle too long. He took care to use the familiar form too, now that Menandros had started it.

"My first, yes. Most of my career has been spent in Aegyptus and Syria."

Faustus wondered how extensive that career could have been. This Menandros seemed to be no more than twenty-five or so, thirty at the utmost. Of course, all these smooth-skinned dark-eyed Greeks, buffed and oiled and pomaded in their Oriental fashion, tended to look younger than they really were. And now that Faustus had

passed fifty, he was finding it harder and harder
to make distinctions of age in any precise way:
everybody around him at the court seemed terribly young to him now, a congregation of mere
boys and girls. Of those who had ruled the Empire when Faustus himself was young, there was
no one left except the weary, lonely old Emperor
himself, and hardly anyone had laid eyes on the
Emperor in recent times. Of Faustus's own generation of courtiers, some had died off, the others
had gone into cozy retirement far away. Faustus
was a dozen years older than his own superior
minister in the Chancellery.

His closest friend here now was Maximilianus
Caesar, who was considerably less than half his
age. From the beginning Faustus had always regarded himself as a relic of some earlier era, because that was, in truth, what he was, considering
that he was a member of a family that had held the
throne three dynasties ago; but the phrase had
taken on a harsh new meaning for him in these lat-
ter days, now that he had survived not just his
family's greatness but even his own contempo-
raries.

It was a little disconcerting that Justinianus
had sent so youthful and apparently inexperienced an ambassador on so delicate a mission.
But Faustus suspected it would be a mistake to
underestimate this man; and at least Menandros's lack of familiarity with the capital city
would provide him with a convenient way to

glide past whatever difficulties Prince Heraclius's untimely absence might cause in the next
few days.

Stagily Faustus clapped his hands. "How I
envy you, friend Menandros! To see Urbs Roma
in all its splendor for the first time! What an overwhelming experience it will be for you! We who
were born here, who take it all for granted, can
never appreciate it as you will. The grandeur. The
magnificence." Yes, yes, he thought, let Maximilianus march him from one end of the city to the
other until Heraclius gets back. We will dazzle
him with our wonders and after a time he'll forget how discourteously Heraclius has treated
him. "While you're waiting for the Caesar to return, we'll arrange the most extensive tours for
you. All the great temples—the amphitheater—
the baths—the Forum—the Capitol—the palaces—
the wonderful gardens—"

"The grottos of Titus Gallius," Menandros said,
unexpectedly. "The underground temples and
shrines. The marketplace of the sorcerers. The cat-
acomb of the holy Chaldean prostitutes. The pool
of the Baptai. The labyrinth of the Maenads. The
caverns of the witches."

"Ah? So you know of those places too?"

"Who doesn't know about the Underworld of
Urbs Roma? It's the talk of the whole Empire." In
an instant that bright metallic facade of his
seemed to melt away, and all his menacing poise.
Something quite different was visible in Menan-

dros's eyes now, a wholly uncalculated eager-
ness, an undisguised boyish enthusiasm. And a
certain roguishness, too, a hint of rough, coarse
appetites that belied his urbane gloss. In a soft,
confiding tone he said, "May I confess something, Faustus? Magnificence bores me. I've got a
bit of a taste for the low life. All that dodgy stuff
that Roma's so famous for, the dark, seamy un-
derbelly of the city, the whores and the magi-
cians, the freak shows and the orgies and the
thieves' markets, the strange shrines of your
weird cults—do I shock you, Faustus? Is this
dreadfully undiplomatic of me to admit? I don't
need a tour of the temples. But as long as we
have a few days before I have to get down to serious business, it's the other side of Roma I want
to see, the mysterious side, the dark side. We
have temples and palaces enough in Constantinopolis, and baths, and all the rest of that. Miles
and miles of glorious shining marble, until you
want to cry out for mercy. But the true subterranean mysteries, the earthy, dirty, smelly, underground things, ah, no, Faustus, those are
what really interest me. We've rooted all that
stuff out, at Constantinopolis. It's considered
dangerous decadent nonsense."

"It is here, too," said Faustus quietly.

"Yes, but you permit it! You revel in it, even! Or
so I'm told, on pretty good authority. You heard
me say I was formerly stationed in Aegyptus and
Syria. The ancient East, that is to say, thousands

of years older than Roma or Constantinopolis. Most of the strange cults originated there, you know. That was where I developed my interest in them. And the things I've seen and heard and done in places like Damascus and Alexandria and Antioch, well—but nowadays Urbs Roma is the center of everything of that sort, is it not, the capital of marvels! And I tell you, Faustus, what I truly crave experiencing is—"

He halted in midsentence, looking flushed and a little stunned.

"This wine," he said, with a little shake of his head. "I've been drinking it too quickly. It must be stronger than I thought."

Faustus reached across the table and laid his hand gently on the younger man's wrist. "Have no fear, my friend. These revelations of yours cause me no dismay. I am no stranger to the Underworld, nor is the prince Maximilianus. And while we await the return of Prince Heraclius he and I will show you everything you desire." He rose, stepping back a couple of paces so that he would not seem, in his bulky way, to be looming in an intimidating manner over the reclining ambassador. After a bad start he had regained some advantage; he didn't want to push it too far. "I'll leave you now. You've had a lengthy journey, and you'll want your rest. I'll send in your servants. In addition to those who accompanied you from Constantinopolis, these men and women—" he indicated the slaves who

stood arrayed in the shadows around the room—
"are at your command day and night. They are
yours. Ask them for anything. *Anything*, my lord
Menandros."

STEPHEN R. LAWHEAD

THE CELTIC CRUSADES

A story rich in history and imagination,
here is the magnificent saga of a
Scottish noble family and its divine quest
during the age of the Great Crusades

THE IRON LANCE
◄ BOOK I ►
0-06-105109-8 • $7.99 US • $10.99 Can

THE BLACK ROOD
◄ BOOK II ►
0-06-105110-1 • $7.50 US • $9.99 Can

THE MYSTIC ROSE
◄ BOOK III ►
0-380-82018-8 • $7.99 US • $10.99 Can

(((((**Listen to**)))))

NEW YORK TIMES BESTSELLING AUTHOR

RAYMOND E. FEIST

Krondor
◇ Tear ◇
of the Gods

BOOK THREE OF THE RIFTWAR LEGACY

ISBN: 0-694-52470-0
$25.95 / $38.95 Can.
6 hours / 4 cassettes

Performed by
Sam Tsoutsouvas

Available wherever books are sold
or call 1-800-331-3761 to order.

 HarperAudio

RFA 0602